Henry Onderdonk

A History of Maryland Upon the Basis of M'Sherry, From its Settlement, to 1867

Anatiposi

Henry Onderdonk

A History of Maryland Upon the Basis of M'Sherry, From its Settlement, to 1867

Reprint of the original, first published in 1872.

1st Edition 2023 | ISBN: 978-3-38212-889-0

Anatiposi Verlag is an imprint of Outlook Verlagsgesellschaft mbH.

Verlag (Publisher): Outlook Verlag GmbH, Zeilweg 44, 60439 Frankfurt, Deutschland
Vertretungsberechtigt (Authorized to represent): E. Roepke, Zeilweg 44, 60439 Frankfurt, Deutschland
Druck (Print): Books on Demand GmbH, In de Tarpen 42, 22848 Norderstedt, Deutschland

A HISTORY OF MARYLAND

UPON THE BASIS OF M'SHERRY,

FROM ITS SETTLEMENT, TO 1867,

With Illustrations,

And an Appendix Containing the Constitution of the State,

FOR THE USE OF SCHOOLS.

BY HENRY ONDERDONK, A.M.
Head Master of College of St. James, and Late President of the Maryland Agricultural College.

Second Revised

Enlarged Edition.

BALTIMORE:
PUBLISHED BY JOHN MURPHY & CO.
PUBLISHERS, BOOKSELLERS AND PRINTERS,
182 BALTIMORE STREET.
1872.

LANDING OF THE PILGRIMS OF MARYLAND.

PREFACE.

The first edition of this History having met with such favor from the public that a second edition is demanded, opportunity has been given to correct some typographical errors, and to adapt it more thoroughly to the uses of the class-room. A portion has been entirely re-written. That which relates to the period of the civil war has been made quite full. The facts have been obtained as far as possible from official sources, or from parties personally connected with the events narrated. In other instances, they are drawn from sources regarded as authorities, at least by those who were in sympathy with the power controlling at that time.

The History of the Proprietary government, under which Maryland was established and grew, is also full, for it is in that government that we find the germs of those principles of popular liberty that resulted in the Revolution; and it is in the free institutions founded under it that we recognize the school in which our fathers learned both the true objects of government, and their own rights as individuals.

There is perhaps no stimulus to worthy deeds, or at least to the preservation of self-respect, equal to that which is furnished in the legacy of a good name. That our youth should know how rich the History of Maryland is in all that can inspire noble emulation, is not only desirable in itself, but is the surest pledge that they will be animated to deeds worthy of their sires, and that, by "imitating the virtue, the valor, and the liberality of their forefathers," they will hand down the State to posterity with untarnished lustre.

In the former editions, the hope was expressed that this little book might be instrumental in promoting this knowledge among the rising generation of the State. The adoption of the book as a text-book by the Public Schools of the City of Baltimore, and the subsequent adoption by the State Board of Education, and their recommendation of its use by all the Schools of the State, both justify the hope expressed, and give assurance that this history supplies a want so long felt.

With a view of meeting the requirements of the School Law of 1872, the Constitution of the State has been added in an Appendix.

College of St. James,
September, 1872.

HENRY ONDERDONK.

CONTENTS.

PART I.

PART II.

History of Maryland.

Part I.

CHAPTER I.

INTRODUCTORY.

Motives for coming to this Country—Religion thought to be a part of the business of Government—Intolerance, the Spirit of the Age—Maryland an exception—Why Colonists left England—Different kinds of Colonial Governments.

1. The general history of the discovery and settlement of North America is presumed to be so familiar to the students of this History, as not to require any recapitulation here.

2. Many motives induced the people of the Old World, as Europe was called, after the discovery of America, to come to this country. Some came to seek for gold; some, for adventure and the improvement of their worldly affairs; and some, to seek an asylum where they could worship God according to the dictates of their own consciences,

Questions.—2. What were some of the motives that led emigrants to come to this country?

without disobeying the laws of the land, or coming in conflict with those in power.

3. In that age, it was thought a part of the business of the government to legislate about religious matters. No one, then, objected to the principle that the government had this right. They objected to the right being enforced against themselves. We see this from the history of the Puritans, who, however they resisted, or fled from, laws against the exercise of their own religion, did not hesitate to pass very severe enactments against those who conscientiously differed from themselves.

4. The case is very different now. None but the most misguided partizans claim that "government is based upon the religious ideas of those who carry it on, and, that they have the right to control the religion." But at the time of the settlement of the colonies, it was thought "that in a well governed and Christian community, matters concerning religion and the honor of God, ought, in the first place, to be taken into earnest consideration and endeavored to be settled;" in other words, that the law should determine each man's belief.

5. We are not, then, to blame any particular body of Christians for its intolerant spirit, for it was exercised by all denominations alike,—if we

---

Questions.—3. What was thought to be a part of the business of the government? What is said of the Puritans? 4. What is the case now? What was thought at the time of the settlement of the colonies? 5. Are we to blame any particular body of Christians for intolerance? Why?

exclude the Quakers, or Friends. It was the spirit of the age.

6. The toleration, and freedom of conscience that characterized the Colony of Maryland, have placed it in advance of its age, and made its history the proudest of that of any of the colonies. For here, in the language of Bancroft, "religious liberty obtained a home, its only home in the wide world. Every other country in the world had persecuting laws; but through the benign administration of the government of Maryland, no person professing to believe in Jesus Christ was permitted to be molested on account of religion."

7. In England the laws bore very hard on all who did not conform to the established religion. These Non-Conformists consisted chiefly of the Puritans and the Roman Catholics. The Puritans left the country in great numbers, and settled chiefly in New England. A colony under a Roman Catholic proprietary, and governor, and consisting mostly of Roman Catholic gentlemen, came to Maryland.

8. North America having been discovered by English subjects, belonged by right of discovery to the crown. Hence, when colonies were formed to settle any part of the newly acquired territory,

---

Questions.—6. What characterized the Colony of Maryland? What does Bancroft say? Who could not be molested? 7. What is said of the laws in England? Who were the Non-Conformists? What of the Puritans? Who formed the Maryland colony? 8. Who gave the colonies their land, and by what right?

the crown gave them tracts of land, together with rights and privileges, at the same time imposing certain conditions which the colonists were to fulfil.

9. The deed or document by which all this was done was called the *Grant* or *Charter*. These charters were given by the King to individuals, to companies, or to the colonists themselves. Hence there arose among the colonists three kinds of governments, viz: The *proprietary government, the charter government*, and the *royal government.*

10. The royal governments were under the immediate rule of the crown. The charter governments were those in which the administration of their affairs was in their own hands. The proprietary governments were those in which the charter granting territory, conferred upon the person or persons to whom it was made, the right of governing the people who settled within the limits of their charter.

11. The charter of Maryland exhibits to us the form of a proprietary government. The proprietary was not a company, but a single person, and at his death his heir succeeded to his rights and privileges.

Questions.—9. What is meant by the *Charter?* To whom were they given? 10. What were the royal governments? What, the charter? What, the proprietary? 11. What kind of government had Maryland?

CHAPTER II.

LORD BALTIMORE—*The Founder of Maryland—Early Schemes—Newfoundland—Sails for Virginia—Chesapeake Bay—Return to England—Death—Cecil Calvert—Opposition of Virginia Colony—Claiborne.*

GEORGE CALVERT.

1. The founder of Maryland, Sir George Calvert, afterwards Lord Baltimore, was an English gentleman of finished education. He was one of the principal Secretaries of State, and was subsequently a member of the House of Commons. He always maintained the rights of the king, and protected his interests. The king did not fail to prove his grateful recollection of Calvert's loyalty.

2. Sir George had early engaged in the schemes of colonization of that period, and very important trusts had been committed to him. His devotion

---

Questions.—1. The founder of Maryland? Who was Lord Baltimore? What is said of him? 2. Why did he resign his office?

to the duties of his office earned for him the esteem and confidence of the king. But in 1624, he resigned, either because his oath of office was incompatible with his religious belief as a Roman Catholic, or lest it might become his duty as Secretary, to execute the penal laws against the members of that church.

3. As was mentioned in the previous chapter, the spirit of intolerance pervaded England, in fact, the whole world. Although Sir George felt assured of the protection of the king, he determined to seek another land, and to found a new state, where, what hitherto was unknown, conscience should be free, and every man might worship God according to his heart, in peace and perfect security.

4. At first, he fixed his eyes on Newfoundland, in the settlement of which he had before been interested. But finding the climate and soil unsuitable, he determined to seek a more genial country in the south. Accordingly, in 1628, he sailed to Virginia, with the intention of settling within the limits of that colony, or, more probably, to explore the uninhabited country on its border, in order to secure a grant of it from the king.

5. Being unwilling to subscribe to the oath of allegiance that was tendered him by the colony,

---

Questions.—3. What did he determine to do? 4. Where did he first think of settling? Why did he abandon that intention? When did he set sail and for what place? What was his design? 5. Why did he leave Virginia?

he left their borders and explored the Chesapeake above the settlements.

6. He was pleased with the beautiful and well-wooded country, which surrounded the noble inlets and indentations of the great bay, and determined there to found his colony. He felt satisfied that he had selected a territory possessing all the elements of future prosperity, fertile in soil, traversed by majestic rivers, and enjoying a climate unsurpassed elsewhere upon the continent.

7. Lord Baltimore returned to England, it is supposed, in 1629. In 1632, without any difficulty, he procured from his Majesty, Charles I, son of his former patron, the promise of a grant. The patent was prepared by Lord Baltimore himself, but before it was executed, he died, on April 15th 1632.

8. His eldest son, Cecil, having inherited his father's title and estate, received from the king the Charter promised to the father. The date of the Charter is the 20th of June, in the eighth year of the reign of Charles I, or 1632. The country granted by this charter was named Maryland, in honor of Queen Henrietta Maria, instead of Crescentia, which was to have been the original name

---

Questions.—6. Where did he determine to found his colony? 7. When did he return to England? When, and from whom did he obtain his charter? Who prepared it? When did he die? 8. Who received the charter? What was its date? What was the country called?

9. The Virginia colony opposed the scheme of Lord Baltimore, claiming that the grant transferred to others, territory belonging to it. William Claiborne had, under virtue of powers granted him by the Virginia colony, established a trading post on Kent Island, a part of the Maryland grant.

10. But as the charters of Virginia had been dissolved, the king and his ministers considered that the right was vested in the crown, of re-granting such parts of the territory of Virginia formerly included within the lines of these charters, as had not before been given to particular individuals. As will be seen, this was a source of future trouble in the colony of Maryland.

Questions.—9. Who opposed the scheme of Baltimore? Why? 10. How did the king and his ministers regard this claim?

CHAPTER III.

THE CHARTER—*Powers granted by the Charter—Land and Churches—"Hitherto uncultivated" lands—Application of the term—Claiborne—Swedes and Dutch—Boundary lines by the Charter.*

CECIL CALVERT.

1. By this charter, Cecil, now Lord Baltimore, and his heirs, were created absolute Proprietaries of Maryland. The Proprietary had full, free and absolute power to enact laws, with the advice, assent, and approbation of the freemen of the Province. But another clause of the charter seems to grant this power to the Proprietary without the necessity of calling the Assembly, "provided these ordinances be consonant to reason, and be not repugnant nor contrary, but (so far as may be conveniently done) agreeable to the laws, statutes or rights of the kingdom of England," and further these ordinances must not

---

Questions.—1. What were the powers of the proprietary? What is said of another clause in the charter?

interfere with the persons or property of any one. This afterwards led to some disagreement between the Proprietary and the Assembly.

2. The Proprietary had full power to grant to his colonists such tracts of land as they might purchase. He was also granted the "license and faculty of erecting and founding churches, chapels and places of worship in convenient and suitable places, and of causing the same to be dedicated according to the laws of our kingdom of England."

3. In the second section of the charter,—in that part which is technically called the recital—it is said that Calvert "being animated with a laudable and pious zeal for extending the *Christian religion*, and the territories of our empire, besought leave to transport a numerous colony of the English nation to a certain region afterwards to be described, in a country *hitherto uncultivated and partly occupied by savages.*"

4. The opponents to this charter claimed that these words *hitherto uncultivated* rendered the grant void, because, within the limits marked out by the charter, there were already settlements, namely, one on Kent Island, established by William Claiborne, and one by the Swedes and Dutch.

5. Whether there is any validity in these objections or not, there is some doubt whether these

---

Questions.—2. What is said of granting lands? Of building churches? 3. What is said in the second section of the charter? 4. What did the opponents to the charter claim? 5. What is said of this objection?

settlements existed at the time Lord Baltimore visited the Chesapeake, and there can be none that he was perfectly honest in describing the country as "hitherto uncultivated." It seems that these words in the recital, or preamble to the charter itself, were very general in their application, and, in this sense, the region marked out by the charter, was uncultivated. The trading station on Kent Island could, with no show of reason, be claimed as rendering a country cultivated.

6. The Dutch settlements were afterwards included in the colony of Delaware, and gave no trouble. They were, however, made the plea upon which William Penn deprived the Maryland colony of a large and fertile territory. But Claiborne, basing his claim upon the words, *hitherto uncultivated*, asserted his independence of Calvert's grant.

7. The territories described by the charter, extended from Watkins's Point, opposite the mouth of the Potomac river, northward to the fortieth degree of north latitude, and from the Atlantic ocean and Delaware bay on the East, to the Potomac river on the West. By examining a map it will be seen that this included a part of what is now Pennsylvania and the whole of Delaware.

Questions.—5. What of Kent Island? 6. What, of the Dutch settlements? Of Claiborne? 7. What were the boundaries of the province, by the charter?

CHAPTER IV.

EARLY SETTLEMENT OF MARYLAND — *Preparations — Leonard Calvert — Embarkation — The "Ark" and "Dove," and the "Mayflower"—Arrival—Landing—Explorations — Interview with Indians — Treaty with them—Treatment of them—Advantages enjoyed by other colonies—The striking features of this colony.*

LEONARD CALVERT.

1. As soon as the grant was obtained, Cecil Calvert commenced his preparations for the establisment of a colony. It was originally his intention to accompany it, but deeming that the interest of the enterprise demanded his remaining in England, he confided his colony to his brother, Leonard Calvert, whom he constituted lieutenant general, or governor.

2. The colony was soon prepared for embarkation, and on the 22d of November, 1633, it de-

---

Questions.—1. Did Cecil Calvert accompany his colony? Whom did he send? 2. Date and place of embarkation?

parted from the Isle of Wight. The company consisted of about two hundred persons, who embarked in two vessels, THE ARK, and THE DOVE.

3. These names are not so familiar to the people of the country, or even of Maryland, as those of the *Mayflower* and *Speedwell*. Most of our school histories having emanated from that part of the country settled by the emigrants of these vessels, perhaps an undue prominence is given to the Pilgrims of Plymouth Rock over those of St. Mary's. Whatever can be claimed for the Puritan colony, as commanding our admiration, the Maryland colony can claim with greater justice. Their motive for leaving their homes, their friends and relatives, was not only the selfish one of enjoying their own freedom of conscience, it was that and something more; it was to open an asylum, where *others* could enjoy the privileges they claimed for themselves.

4. Though they have had neither poet nor painter to celebrate from sea to sea their heroic motive, their pious devotion of themselves to the care of Him who rules the raging of the sea, their no less pious thanksgiving on their landing, theirs was none the less a mighty undertaking, standing out in history as an era in the progress of mankind.

Questions.—2. Names of the vessels? 3. What is said of these names? How does their departure compare with that of the Mayflower and Speedwell? 4. What further is said?

5. After many difficulties and some dangers, these two vessels, though separated by storms on the ocean, arrived safely off Point Comfort, in Virginia, on the 24th of February, 1634. Having remained in Virginia a few days, they set sail for the banks of the Potomac, where they found mighty forests, a soil rich and fertile; the air sweet and balmy; and they returned thanks to God for the beautiful land which he had given them—for this was MARYLAND.

6. Although they beheld groups of armed savages prepared to prevent their landing, and making other demonstrations of hostility, they succeeded in establishing confidence in the breasts of the natives. Having satisfied them of their peaceful intentions, they, at length, purchased from them the territory they required. Maryland was almost the only State whose early settlement was not stained with the blood of the natives

7. They landed on the 25th of March on an island, to which they gave the name of St. Clement's (now Blackiston's.) The colonists took solemn possession of Maryland, with religious services, conducted according to the usages of the Roman Catholic church, and erected a cross as an emblem of Christianity and Civilization,

---

Questions.—5. When did they arrive at Point Comfort? What further is said? 6. What did they see on the shores? How did they obtain the land? 7. When did they land? What did they, on landing?

both of which they were about to plant on those shores.

8. In order to make further discoveries, Governor Leonard Calvert proceeded further up the Potomac, near to the place now called New Marlboro', where there was an Indian village governed by Archihu, uncle to the king, or Wero-wance, who was still an infant.

9. When the governor asked the Indian chief if he were willing that his people should settle in his country, he replied, "I will not bid you go, neither will I bid you stay, but you may use your own discretion." Using this discretion the governor concluded it was not safe to settle so high up the river. He, therefore, returned down the Potomac to St. Clement's Island, and thence to a small river on the north side of the Potomac, which he called St. George.

10. He explored the St. George about twelve miles upwards, and anchored at the village of the Yo-a-comico Indians. The Governor explained to the chief, or Wero-wance, his object in coming to his country.

11. The Wero-wance, after the custom of the Indians, made but little answer to the proposition of Governor Calvert; but, nevertheless, hospitably

---

Questions.—8. Where did the governor then go? 9. What did the governor ask, and what did the chief reply? What did the governor do? 10. What river did he explore? 11. How did the chief receive him?

entertained him and his companions, giving up his own rude bed for the accommodation of the governor.

12. Having carefully examined the surrounding country, and finding it possessed of many advantages which rendered it an eligible site, Calvert determined to commence, at this place, his first settlement. The ship and pinnace which he had left at St. Clement's, were ordered to join him at Yo-a-comico.

13. To prepare the way for a peaceable admission into the country, he presented the Werowance and principal men with clothes, axes, hoes and knives, in return for which they granted him about thirty miles of territory, which he called Augusta Carolina, afterwards the county of St. Mary's.

14. The character of these presents to the Werowance indicates the desire of the colonists, namely, to introduce among the savages the first rudiments, as it were, of civilization—the implements of agriculture.

15. The Indians further agreed to give up to the settlers, for their immediate accommodation, one-half of their village, and corn grounds which they had already commenced to plant, reserving

---

Questions.—12. What did he determine upon? 13. What presents did he make? 14. What did these presents indicate? 15. What agreement did the Indians make?

the other part for their own use, until the harvest should be gathered, when the whole of the purchased territory was to be surrendered to the colonists. Upon the 27th day of March, 1634, the governor took possession of the place, and named the town ST. MARY'S.

16. Most of the principal men, if not all, were Roman Catholics, and their object in colonizing was to enjoy, without molestation, liberty of conscience, and to secure religious toleration on the American continent. The American historian, Bancroft, in speaking of Calvert, says that "he deserves to be ranked among the most wise and benevolent lawgivers of all ages. He was the first in the history of the Christian world to seek for religious security and peace by the practice of justice and not by the exercise of power."

17. While they lived in company with the natives at St. Mary's, the greatest harmony prevailed. The natives hunted with the English for deer and turkeys, and received from them in return knives, beads, and such other trifles as they desired. The women and children became domesticated in the English families. In the treatment of the savages of Maryland, the colony was always governed by the most exalted principles of Christianity and philanthropy.

Questions.—15. When did the governor take possession? What did he call the place? 16. What does Bancroft say of Calvert? 17. Describe the life of the colonists with the natives?

18. The right of the natives to their own land, and other property, was scrupulously respected, and earnest and persistent efforts were made to teach them religious truth and the arts of civilized life. Their lands were not taken from them by force and without their consent, but by honorable negotiation and purchase. The colonist purchased the rights of the aborigines for a consideration which gave them satisfaction. They offered no reward for Indian scalps, and their history is not stained with a King Philip's war. They extended to the Indians words and *acts* of love and mercy.

19. Fair and beautiful then was the origin of the State. No wrong or injustice towards the native stained the hands of its founders; no persecuting domination or exclusive franchise was reared upon its shores, but around the rough-hewn cross on the island of St. Clement's, gathered Catholic and Protestant, hand in hand, friends and brothers, equal in rights and secure alike in the free and full enjoyment of either creed. It was a day that should make the Maryland heart bound with pride and pleasure.

20. The descendants of other colonies have not only had the happiness of having historians, but also of making literature a business and a trade,

---

Questions.—18. What is said of the rights of the natives? What did the colonists try to teach them? How were the lands obtained from them? 19. What is said in this section? 20. What happiness have other colonsts enjoyed?

and have supplied the whole country with histories of their own making. Hence, at least, in school histories of our country one section has appropriated a very large share, and the other sections have been treated of in a very few chapters. To such an extent is this true, that these histories of the United States are very much like a Chinese map of the world, the Celestial Empire occupying all but the small corner that is left for the rest of mankind. In this way, the claim that Maryland has to be regarded as the pioneer of Civil and Religious liberty have been made less prominent than those of other colonies, who have, almost with the consent of her own citizens, snatched from her the honor that is justly her own.

21. The first altar to religious liberty on this Continent was erected in MARYLAND; and the "Freedom of Conscience" that characterized the pilgrims of St. Mary's was not, as in other parts of the country, such as stained the annals of its history with the whipping of naked women, or the boring of the tongue with a red hot iron for being a Quaker.

22. For the first time in the history of the colonies, the savages were treated with *justice* and *mercy* in *Maryland*. Their land was bought from them, and their condition was improved. There is

---

Questions.—21. Where was the first altar to religious liberty raised? What kind of freedom of conscience was in Maryland? 22. What is said in this section?

no national historical painting to perpetuate the memory of this treaty of amity and good will, but, assuredly, when on this first altar of religious liberty, the fires ascended to heaven amid the blessings of the savage, the memory of such a people "should not pass away from their descendants as an idle dream."

CHAPTER V.

1634-1638 — CLAIBORNE'S REBELLION — *Claiborne, the Evil Genius of the Colony—His Claim—Excites the Indians—Resorts to Violence—Flees to Virginia—Sent to England—First Legislative Assembly—Division of Land.*

1. The friendly relations which subsisted between the natives and the English were first disturbed by the improper insinuations circulated by Claiborne, called by historians the Evil Genius of the colony.

2. Before the charter had been issued, but probably after Lord Baltimore's visit to the Chesapeake, Claiborne had established a trading post on Kent Island. This he had done in virtue of a license to traffic with the natives, and thereupon, claimed a

---

Questions.—1. What first disturbed the friendly relations of the natives? 2. Where had Claiborne established trading posts?

right to the property of the soil, not only of this island, but also of another settlement at the mouth of the Susquehanna.

3. He obtained his license to trade from Charles I, and afterwards from the Governor of Virginia. He was, therefore, subordinate to that colony, and dependent upon it. But when this island was included in the grant to Calvert, he was notified that if he remained he would be deemed subject to Maryland. He applied to the council of Virginia for instruction how to act.

4. This colony being opposed to that of Lord Baltimore, and not being unwilling to thwart it, the council replied they saw no reason why he should give up any territory he had held of them. Lord Baltimore had ordered his arrest should he refuse to submit to his authority. He, however, was not taken, and being enraged that Baltimore had obtained a grant including the places where he had been accustomed to trade, sought every means in his power to defeat the success of the colony at St. Mary's.

5. As a means to this end he excited the fears and jealousies of the Indians, by persuading them that the new comers were not English, but Spaniards, the enemies of the English. The simple

---

Questions.—3. From whom had he received his license? To whom was he subordinate? What did he do when his post was included in the Maryland colonies? 4. What did the council reply? What had Lord Baltimore ordered? 5. What did he do?

natives believed him, and suddenly withdrew from St. Mary's.

6. To meet any hostile attack that they might be stimulated to, the settlers postponed the building of their own houses and erected a block house, or fortification. At the same time, they regulated their conduct towards the savages so as to re-awaken the old feelings of confidence and intimacy. The natives became convinced of the falsehood of the insinuations against the settlers, and again resorted to the colony.

7. Having failed in these efforts to rouse the jealousies of the savages, Claiborne resorted to more violent measures to support his pretensions. These pretensions were based upon the authority of Virginia. But, as has previously been mentioned, the Virginia charter had been annulled; notwithstanding, he determined to uphold his claim, and, if possible, drive the colony from the province.

8. To accomplish this he fitted out an armed vessel, under one lieutenant Warren, with orders to seize and capture any of the government or colony of St. Mary's. The second in command was Thomas Smith. The colonists promptly met this hostile demonstration by fitting out two armed boats under command of Thomas Cornwallis.

Questions.—6. What did the settlers do? 7. What did Claiborne now resort to? Upon what did he base his pretensions? What did he determine to do? 8. What did he fit out? With what orders? Who was second in command? Who commanded the boats of the colonists?

9. In a battle between the hostile boats, commenced by Claiborne's men firing first upon those of Cornwallis, Claiborne's vessel was captured. He was thus deprived of his last resource, and his only safety was in flight. He sought security in Virginia, but was followed by commissioners sent by Calvert, to demand his surrender. Governor Harvey, of Virginia, however, sent him with the witnesses to England for trial. This was early in the year 1635.

10. During this year it appears that the first legislative assembly met. The records having been lost or destroyed, little is known of their proceedings. The laws which they passed, whether "wholesome" or otherwise, were dissented to by the Lord Proprietary, it is supposed, because, under the charter, he claimed the right of *initiating* or proposing the laws. He immediately, however, set about to frame a code for their acceptance. By referring to the beginning of Chapter III, the reader will see the clauses in the charter, which refer to this matter.

11. In accordance with the instructions of the Proprietary, the land was divided among the settlers. Under the circumstances of danger, both from the savages and their own countrymen, the colonists were not disposed to extend their settle-

---

Questions.—9. What was the result? Where did he go? What did Calvert do, and what, Governor Harvey? What year was this? 10. When did the first legislative assembly meet? What is said of the laws they passed? 11. How was the land divided?

ments beyond the limits of St. Mary's; within the city, lots of five and ten acres were granted to all who might apply for them. And, in the interior, tracts ranging from one hundred to three thousand acres, were granted, in proportion to the number of settlers, whom the applicant introduced into the colony. A quit rent of twenty shillings for every thousand acres was reserved for the Proprietary.

12. These liberal terms were well calculated to induce men of wealth, who were able to bear the expense of transporting servants and dependents, to emigrate to this province, and contribute to the growth and prosperity of the colony.

CHAPTER VI.

1638–1642—THE SECOND GENERAL ASSEMBLY—*Missionaries—Kent Island—New Hundred—New Code of Laws—Trial of Smith—Claiborne's efforts in England—Returns to Virginia—Missionaries—Conversion and Baptism of Tayac—Father White—Privileges of the Governor extended.*

1. Prior to 1638, the inhabitants of Kent Island had, to a certain extent, submitted to the government of Maryland, and courts were established there, in the name of the province, for the trial

---

Questions.—12. What was the effect of these liberal terms? 1. What is said of the inhabitants of Kent Island?

of civil and criminal cases. The factious followers of Claiborne, still looking forward to the success of their leader resisted the processes and warrants of the civil courts. A visit from the governor himself with a military force was necessary to bring it to complete subjection to his authority.

2. In the settlement at St. Mary's, the plantations had already extended to the west side of St. George's river, and there being large accessions from the northern country, a new hundred—a division similar to our election district—was erected.

3. Lord Baltimore now caused the code which he had prepared, to be presented. But the people thinking that the power of making the laws was vested in them, and that the Proprietary had only a veto power, immediately rejected the laws sent by Baltimore, and set about framing such as they thought proper.

4. After a short time, however, the controversy was concluded by the Proprietary abandoning his claim. Preferring the welfare of the colony to his own individual privileges, and satisfied that the veto power was sufficient to protect his authority, he gave to his brother, the Governor, the right to assent to any law, "which he might think good for

---

Questions.—1. What was necessary? 2. Where was a New Hundred erected? 3. What dispute between Lord Baltimore and the people? 4. How was the controversy concluded? What right did he give the Governor?

the government of the province, and not contrary to the laws of England." The Assembly met in 1639, and passed a Code of laws. Among these laws was one interesting to farmers, as it legalized a custom still existing in this State. It was in reference to the measurement of a barrel of corn. "A barrel of new corn, at or before the fifteenth day of October in any year, shall be twice shaked in the barrel, and afterwards heaped as long as it shall lie on; and at or before the Feast of Nativity (Christmas), shall be twice shaked and filled to the edge of the barrel, or else not shaked and heaped as before; and after the said feast it shall not be shaken at all, but delivered by strike."

5. Thomas Smith, who had been captured in the expedition sent out by Claiborne, was tried for murder. He was found guilty, and sentenced to death, though it is not ascertained that he was executed. A bill of attainder was passed against Claiborne by which his property was confiscated to the Proprietary.

6. Claiborne was still in England endeavoring to accomplish his object through the known avarice and unscrupulousness of the royal court. He boldly laid claim to the Isle of Kent and its dependencies, and charged the Proprietary's officers with having attacked and slaughtered his men.—

Questions.—4. When did the Assembly pass laws? 5. What was done with Smith? 6. Where was Claiborne, and what was he doing? What did he charge upon the colonists?

In the trial of Smith, however, it was proved that the first fire was from Claiborne's boat. In a petition to the king, he offered to pay the crown two hundred pounds sterling for a grant of the Isle of Kent and other valuable possessions.

7. The whole matter having been referred to a proper committee, they reported, after a full investigation, that the lands in question belonged absolutely to Lord Baltimore, and that no trade with the Indians could be carried on without his consent.

8. Claiborne, thus baffled, returned to Virginia to carry on his old schemes of annoyance. The legislature, however, interfered and compelled him to desist. Then he dispatched an agent to Maryland praying the restoration of his property which had been confiscated to the government. His prayer was rejected, and, for a while, he abandoned his efforts.

9. During the earlier years of the colony, the settlement was circumscribed within narrow limits, and the presence of the two missionaries who had accompanied the colony was required in the settlements. For these reasons their efforts at converting Indians, were confined to those who were in friendly relationship with the settlers. But as the

---

Questions.—6. What was proved on the trial of Smith? What did Claiborne offer the king? 7. What was the report of the committee? 8. What did Claiborne do? 9. How many missionaries accompanied the colonists? Why did they not go abroad among the Indians? Did they teach the Indians in the settlement?

colony increased, new missionaries arrived from England.

10. These zealous men immediately began to penetrate into the interior, and visit every tribe and village. The Indians at Patuxent received them very kindly, and bestowed upon them a plantation called St. Mattapany, on the Patuxent, where a missionary station and a store house were immediately erected. The missionaries travelled in a boat, subsisted by hunting, and at night slept under cover of a slight tent. Confiding themselves to the protection of God, they slept as soundly as if surrounded by the luxuries of a palace.

11. In five years they had extended their stations throughout a large portion of the province; they had visited many tribes, and made many converts; they possessed four permanent stations, the most distant of which was one hundred and twenty miles from St. Mary's. They went in every direction preaching Christianity to the savages, and by their gentle influence they maintained the peace and quiet of the settlements more firmly and securely than could have been done by all the militia of the province.

12. The conversion and baptism of Clitomachen, the Tayac, was a remarkable event. The Tayac was the chief officer of the Piscataways, the most

---

Questions.—9. When did more arrive? 10. What did they do? How did the Indians receive them? How did they travel? 11. What was the result of their labor? 12. Describe the baptism of the Tayac?

extensive and powerful tribe in Maryland. Shortly after the arrival of Father White, the missionary, the Tayac was taken sick, and forty medicine men tried all the arts of conjuring within their power, to cure him. The missionary gained permission to treat the sick chief, and by his treatment shortly restored him to perfect health. After having been properly prepared for the reception of the holy rite, the Tayac and his household were baptized.

13. The Tayac after this abandoned the habits and dress of the savage, adopted those of the English, and learned their language. In a conversation with the governor on the advantages of trading with the settlers, he is reported to have said: "I consider these as trifling, when compared with this one benefit, that, by their aid, I have arrived at the true knowledge of the *one* God, the most important of all knowledge."

14. Thus surrounded by Christian Indians, the colony suffered but little from the hostilities of the natives, nothing that rose to the dignity of an Indian war. What troubles they had were caused by the Susquehannas, the Wycomeses and Nanticokes, who were too far from the settlements to be brought under the good influences of the whites. The promptness and energy, however, of the governor, prevented any serious disaster to the colony,

---

Questions.—13. What is said of the Tayac, after his baptism? What remarkable language is attributed to him? 14. What Indians were troublesome?

and in a short time a truce was concluded with the Nanticokes.

15. The colony had gone on improving, strengthening their settlements, and extending their legislation, and, although by act of the Assembly which met in 1639, the privileges of the Governor had been greatly extended—privileges that might have been of dangerous consequences—the wise and virtuous administration of Leonard Calvert, fully justified the confidence which the people placed in his honor and integrity.

CHAPTER VII.

1643-1647.—CLAIBORNE AND INGLE'S REBELLION—*Troubles in England—Insubordination of Claiborne—Calvert Visits England—Indian Troubles—Ingle—Gov. Brent—Calvert's Return—Endeavors to obtain Possession of Kent Island—Calvert compelled to Flee—Conduct of the Insurgents—Success of Parliamentary Party—Calvert Regains Possession—Death of Calvert.*

1. The contest which had broken out in England, between the King and Parliament, materially affected the good order of the Maryland colony. The government was a royal grant, and the Proprietary was an adherent of the king. As the

Questions.—15. What is said of Leonard Calvert's administration? 1. What is said of the contest in England? To which side did the Proprietary belong?

cause of the king at home declined, the friends and adherents of Claiborne, and the advocates of the Parliament considered this a favorable moment to throw off the authority of the Proprietary.

2. Uncertain what course to pursue, and anxious to view in person the tendency of affairs in the mother country, Governor Calvert determined to visit England and consult his brother, Lord Baltimore. He set sail in the early part of the year 1643. During his absence the spirit of disaffection increased, and at length broke out in Claiborne and Ingle's rebellion.

3. The Indians, either urged by the malcontents, or perceiving the internal divisions of the settlers, again began to be troublesome. The Susquehannas were particularly so, having, contrary to the laws of nations, been furnished with fire-arms by the Swedes and Dutch.

4. Whilst the Indians were threatening the colony on the north, Captain Richard Ingle, an associate of Claiborne, a pirate and a rebel, was hovering about the settlement with an armed ship, holding communication with the disaffected, and endeavoring to strengthen their numbers. Governor Brent, who was acting in the absence of

---

Questions.—1. What did the advocates of Parliament think? 2. Why did Calvert return to England? What happened during his absence? 3. What is said of the Indians? Who furnished them with arms? 4. Who was Ingle, and what was he doing? Who acted in the absence of Calvert?

Gov. Calvert, issued a proclamation ordering his arrest and the seizure of his ship. Ingle was taken, but soon effected his escape, to join Claiborne and concoct new trouble for the colony.

5. On his return in 1644, Calvert found the province in great disorder, the public officers at variance, the Indians encroaching, the pirate Ingle at large, his enemy, Claiborne, in arms, and once more in possession of Kent Island.

6. Calvert endeavored to obtain possession of Kent Island, but his efforts failed; and the rebels, emboldened by success, and certain of assistance from their friends, invaded the Western shore, and, after a short struggle, obtained complete possession of the province. Governor Calvert was compelled to fly to Virginia.

7. The conquerors immediately commenced a system of outrage and oppression upon those who had adhered to his fortunes, and had supported the laws of the colony. Many were robbed of all their possessions, and banished from the province. Even the missionaries, among whom was Father White, called the apostle of Maryland, were seized and sent in chains to England. The provincial records were mutilated and destroyed, so that it is almost impossible to get accurate accounts of their

---

Questions.—1. What proclamation did he issue? 5. Describe the condition of the colony on the return of Calvert? 6. What did Calvert endeavor to do? What, the rebels? 7. How insurgents act? Whom did they seize?

proceedings, or of the struggle which followed their success.

8. The parliamentary party being now completely in the ascendant, and having the king in their hands, Claiborne and Ingle acted in the name of parliament. Their success seemed a death-blow to the supremacy of Lord Baltimore in the province. He felt this, and accordingly, in 1646, directed his brother, the governor, to collect and take charge of his private property, and save what he could from the wreck of his fortunes, apparently abandoning the hope of recovering his rights.

9. Leonard Calvert was not willing to yield.—The people of Virginia were loyal to their sovereign, and he believed that the majority of the people of Maryland were attached to the mild and parental sway of the Calverts. In Virginia he found not only a safe refuge, but also the means for a final effort to subdue the rebels. The outrage, oppression and misrule of the usurpers in Maryland, soon prepared the people to sustain him in the attempt.

10. Having completed his arrangements, at the close of the year 1646, he crossed the Potomac with a military force, surprised the enemy, entered St. Mary's in triumph, and once more took possession of the government.

Questions.—8. In whose name did Claiborne act? What did Lord Baltimore direct? 9. Why did not Calvert yield? What did he find in Virginia? 10. When did he return, and with what success?

11. Kent Island, the stronghold of the malcontents, did not submit so easily as the rest of the province. It was found necessary to declare martial law; to cut off all communications from without, and send an expedition under the governor himself, into the island before the rebels could be reduced once more under the authority of the Proprietary. The governor having secured the tranquillity of the island, granted an amnesty to most of the offenders and returned to St. Mary's.

12. Just as order was once more restored to the colony, and renewed prosperity began to dawn upon the settlers, they met with a heavy blow in the death of their governor. Governor Calvert died, surrounded by his family and friends, on the 9th of June, 1647, having named Thomas Green his successor.

13. During the space of fourteen years he had guided the colony through the storms which had darkened around its infancy—he had devoted his whole life and energies to its permanent establishment — with a disinterested self-devotion, he had striven in the wilderness for its glory and its prosperity: and it seemed as if, through a special providence of heaven, to reward his labors, a beam of sunshine had broken over the province as he was about to die, at peace with all, triumphant

---

Questions.—11. What did he do on Kent Island? 12. What misfortune befel the Colony? 13. What had been the character of Calvert's administration?

over the enemies of Maryland, full of honor, and enriched with the prayers and blessings of a rescued people. His character, public and private, was without stain, his abilities were undoubted, his government, kind and parental, and his memory was long cherished by the colonists with grateful recollection. He was indeed a great and good man.

CHAPTER VIII.

LIBERTY OF CONSCIENCE—*New guards to Liberty of Conscience—Oath of Office—Acts of Assembly—Protection to Feelings—Who formed the Assembly.*

1. Lord Baltimore now perceived, that, while some concessions to the disaffected might be necessary to maintain his provinces, new guards were necessary to prevent the growing feeling of intolerance manifested by the insurgents, and which was tending to destroy the sanctuary he had erected at the cost of so much care and treasure.

2. Therefore, in 1648, he appointed William Stone, governor of the province, and prescribed the famous oath of office, as a further guaranty for the continuance of liberty of conscience, and full

---

Questions.—1. What did Lord Baltimore now perceive? 2. Whom did he appoint governor? What oath did he prescribe to the governor?

toleration to all persons who believed in Jesus Christ.

3. The assembly that met on the 2d of April, 1649, after enacting severe penalties for the crime of blasphemy, and providing that certain penalties shall be inflicted upon any one who shall call another a sectarian name of reproach—such as "heretic," "idolater," "schismatic," "round-head," &c.—declared that "no person or persons professing to believe in Jesus Christ, shall from henceforth be any ways troubled, or molested, or discountenanced for, or in respect of his or her religion, nor in the free exercise thereof, nor any way compelled to the belief or exercise of any religion against his or her consent."

4. The passage of this act, when compared with the intolerant laws existing in other colonies, is one of the proud boasts of Maryland. Whoever was oppressed and suffered for conscience, might here find refuge, protection and repose.

5. It is said that some of these legislators could neither read nor write. "Two of them at least were in the habit of making their signet mark. But did they not leave a mark also upon the country, and upon the world? In depth and earnestness, in real dignity and propriety, in profound

---

Questions.—3. Against what penalties did the assembly make enactments? 4. How does this act compare with laws in other colonies? 5. What is said of the learning of some of these legislators?

views of human nature, and in true legislative wisdom, they were not behind those earlier law givers who bore the appellation of 'The Wise.'"* Their want of culture, though sometimes made the subject of ridicule, adds to the numerous examples in history, that progress is not so much dependent upon mental culture as upon force of character. This is the motive power in the progress of events.

6. No person was allowed to stigmatize his fellow-man by any term of reproach on account of his religious belief, or the sect to which he belonged. The law protected not only the property and persons of the citizens, but also their feelings. It also made it penal to deny the Saviour, and to blaspheme. It has been objected, therefore, that the "freedom of conscience" was not entire. But freedom to deny and blaspheme God and his worship is not, in any sense, freedom of conscience, for conscience never yet required any man to deny or blaspheme his Maker. There is no conscience where God is denied, for conscience is man's recognition of what the law of God commands.

7. This act, passed by an assembly made up of men of many different creeds, introduced no new principle in the colony, but, in its best provisions,

*Davis.

Questions.—6. What was disallowed? What were protected? What was made a penal offence? What is said of this? 7. Who composed this assembly?

was merely affirming and recording the law which had hitherto governed the province. This liberality, as we shall see in subsequent chapters, was the cause of greatest misfortune to the province.

CHAPTER IX.

1649-1664—PURITAN SETTLEMENTS—*The Liberal Policy attracts Settlers—Richard Bennett and his Puritans—Chivalric Conduct of Marylanders—Influx of Puritans—Reduction of Virginia—Claiborne and Bennett's Descent upon Maryland—The Proprietaryship Abolished—Indian Troubles—Claiborne and Bennett's Invasion.*

1. The liberal policy of Maryland could not fail to attract the attention of the colonies. The Puritans, on the James river, in Virginia, having been ordered to leave that colony, soon found an asylum here. Under the leadership of Richard Bennett, they founded settlements on the Severn. They called the place New Providence. It was near the present City of Annapolis.

2. These settlers governed themselves entirely independently of any connection with the colony, which received and protected them. They did not even obtain grants for the land they occupied.

Questions.—1. Who were ordered to leave Virginia? Where did they go? 2. What is said of this settlement?

3. At this time an event happened that showed the generous and chivalric character that has ever marked the sons of Maryland. Charles I, by a tribunal constituted for the purpose, had been put to death, and the parliament had passed a decree declaring it to be treason for any one to acknowledge his son Charles, as king He was immediately proclaimed sovereign by the authority of Maryland. This daring act of loyalty aroused the adherents of parliament, and finally led to the reduction of the province.

4. The Puritans, attracted by the liberal policy of the province, were settling in it, in considerable numbers. Besides those who came from Virginia, a colony came from England, under the patronage, it is supposed, of Governor Stone; another, on South river, and also a Protestant settlement, twenty miles from the mouth of the Patuxent, under Richard Brooke. When the assembly was called, it was found that the partizans of Cromwell, who had usurped the power in England, were in the majority.

5. Parliament had passed an ordinance for the reduction of Virginia. The armed force that was sent out to effect this, was joined by Claiborne and Bennett, the Puritan, who had been appointed commissioners. The governor of Virginia made

---

Questions.—3. What happened at this time? What was the effect of this daring act? 4. What other Puritans came to the colony? 5. What decree had Parliament passed? Who joined the armed force? What did Virginia do?

his submission and received favorable terms. Although his duties as commissioner had now been performed, Claiborne could not forego the favorable opportunity he enjoyed of gratifying his ancient hostility to the colony of Maryland. The Puritan Bennett, who had lately been so kindly received in the province, when exiled from Virginia, eagerly joined in the schemes of Claiborne.

6. Having come to St. Mary's, towards the close of March, 1652, they demanded that the colony should submit to the Commonwealth, which was the name given to the government; they insisted that the name of the Proprietary should be erased from all writs and processes; they removed the governor from his office, and entirely abolished the authority of Lord Baltimore, in the province.—Stone was subsequently reinstated, but with modified powers.

7. Simultaneously with the ascendancy of the Puritans, the Indians began to be troublesome. The Nanticokes broke in upon the Eastern Shore settlers, burning, killing and ravaging. Great efforts were made to raise a force and protect their frontiers. The Puritans of Anne Arundel, however, refused to make their levies, and the expedition had to be abandoned.

Questions.—5. What did Claiborne then do? Who united with him? 6. What did they require? 7. When did the Indians begin to be troublesome? Who refused aid?

8. Lord Baltimore did not rest quietly under the wrong that had been done him. He immediately took steps to call the commissioners to account for their unlawful proceedings, and directed Governor Stone to require all persons to take the oath of fidelity, and to re-establish the Proprietary government, which was accordingly done in 1664.

9. Claiborne and Bennett immediately invaded Maryland with a considerable force, and Stone, either from timidity or disaffection, submitted.—Bennett and his party having seized the government, disfranchised the very men who had received them into the province when flying from persecution abroad. An assembly was called, but no Roman Catholic or adherent to the royal cause was allowed to vote for delegates to it, or sit therein as a member. This body representing a minority of the people, immediately passed a law excluding Roman Catholics and members of the Church of England from the protection of the government. This act, disgraceful as it was, can hardly be called a stain upon the fair fame of Maryland. It was the act not of Marylanders, but of those whom they had received in their midst, and those, who, protected by the arms of

---

Questions.—8. What did Lord Baltimore do? 9. Who invaded Maryland? Who were disfranchised? Who were excluded from the assembly? Can this be called an act of Marylanders?

the usurping government at home, usurped the government of Maryland, of those who, like the serpent in the fable, stung to death the benefactor that had warmed them into life.

CHAPTER X.

RESTORATION OF THE PROPRIETARY — *Rebuke to Governor Stone—Recovery of the Records—Unsuccessful Expedition to Providence—Barbarity of the Puritans—Appeal to Cromwell—Decision of the Board of Trade—Bennett Makes Terms—Fendall—The Last of Claiborne.*

1. When Lord Baltimore was apprised of the proceedings, he dispatched William Eltonhead to the colony, with a severe rebuke to Governor Stone, for thus yielding up his authority without a blow, and with instructions to resume it immediately. In 1655, Stone began to make levies among the people of St. Mary's, who had always remained faithful to the Proprietary.

2. He dispatched Eltonhead with a force of twenty men, to recover the provincial records, which the commissioners had seized, and to capture a magazine of arms, which the Puritans had gathered.

Questions.—1. Who was sent to the colony and for what purpose? 2. Where did the governor send Eltonhead?

3. Being successful in this, he pressed into his service ten or twelve vessels lying in the harbor. Embarking his force upon these, Governor Stone set out against the people of Providence.

4. By the aid of an armed merchantman lying in the harbor, the Puritans were successful. The fight that took place was well sustained, but the undisciplined levies of St. Mary's were no match to the Puritans, many of whom doubtless were used to battle under the victorious banner of Cromwell.

5. This victory of the Puritans was stained by an act, as cruel and bloody as it was unnecessary. The governor and his council, and others, to the number of ten, were condemned to death, although they had surrendered themselves upon the pledge of quarter. Four of them were shot in cold blood. The rest escaped at the stern intercession of the soldiers themselves.

6. The governor and his council were detained prisoners for a long time. They were prohibited from communicating with their friends; and Stone was not allowed even to write to his wife, at St. Mary's, without submitting his letter to the inspection of his keepers. She was subsequently allowed to nurse him during the recovery of his wounds.

Questions.—3. What second expedition did he undertake? 4. What prevented its success? 5. What barbarity were the Puritans guilty of? 6. What was their treatment of the governor and council?

7. Both parties now appealed to Cromwell.—After some delay the controversy was referred to the "commissioners of trade" in England. They reported entirely in favor of the Lord Proprietary. Capt. Josias Fendall was appointed governor, and directed by Baltimore to see that the act for freedom of conscience was duly observed in Maryland. He was also ordered to reward with grants of land all who had been active in his behalf, and to take especial care of the widows of those who had fallen.

8. To give aid and countenance to his governor, Lord Baltimore appointed his brother, Philip Calvert, secretary of the province. The governor and secretary obtained possession of the capital without difficulty, but beyond the faithful county of St. Mary's, their success did not immediately extend.

9. The Puritans being determined to consider their authority as undisputed, summoned an assembly, which convened on 24th of September, 1657. They levied a tax to pay the public expenses, and appointed commissioners to collect the fines imposed upon the adherents of the Proprietary. But their domination was at an end.

Questions.—7. To whom did both parties appeal? To whom did he refer the matter? Their decision? Who was now appointed governor? What instructions did he receive? 8. Who was appointed secretary to the province? They obtained possession of what place? 9. What did the Puritans do?

10. The negotiations of Lord Baltimore with Cromwell, began to be successful. The Puritan Bennett, perceiving the turn affairs were taking, and despairing of retaining the supremacy of his party, hastened to come to terms with the Proprietary. Fendall was acknowledged Governor; and Maryland was once more restored to the government of the Proprietary, after nearly six years of rebellion.

11. But no sooner had Fendall overthrown the power of the Puritans, than he set about undermining that of the Lord Proprietary. At the session of 1659, the house of delegates demanded that the governor and council should no longer sit as an upper house. For a time, Fendall made a show of resistance, but at length yielded and took his seat in the lower house.

12. The upper house was then declared dissolved. Fendall resigned his commission from the Lord Proprietary, into the hands of the assembly, and accepted a new one from that body in their own name and by their own authority.

13. The power of this new rebel was of short duration. The people were tired of intestine commotions, and, remembering the mild government of Leonard Calvert, joyfully submitted to Philip Calvert, who was appointed governor upon intelli-

---

Questions.—10. What is said in this section? 11. What did Fendall do? 12. What further? 13. What is said of the people of the colony?

gence of Fendall's rebellion. Fendall gave himself up, and was respited. He abused this clemency to excite new trouble in after days.

14. Claiborne, "the evil genius of Maryland," the arch-disturber of its peace, returned into Virginia, where he still continued a man of some distinction. He met his death in battle with the Indians, and was buried in the field. His life and death were those of an heroic adventurer.

CHAPTER XI.

1660–1689 — PEACE AND PROSPERITY — *Calm — Charles Calvert — Increase of Population — Planters — Maryland Domestic Life — Slavery — Servants — Quakers — Fox — Land of the Sanctuary — Death of the Proprietary — Fendall's Attempt at Rebellion — End of the Period of Repose.*

1. After these storms a calm of thirty years succeeded. The colony, again under a brother of its founder, having proclaimed Charles II, king, set about to remedy the consequences of the late troubles.

2. In 1662, Philip Calvert was superseded by Hon. Charles Calvert, son of the Lord Proprietary.

Questions.—13. What of Fendall? 14. What became of Claiborne? 1. What is said in this section? 2. Who superseded Philip Calvert?

When Philip Calvert assumed the government of the colony, in 1660, the number of inhabitants was twelve thousand; in five years, it had increased to fifteen thousand, and in 1671, to twenty thousand.

3. The number of counties was increased. But as yet there were few towns. St. Mary's contained little more than sixty houses. The people were planters and farmers. There were no influences to draw people together in towns, and the people, free from the excitement, turmoil and ambition of commercial communities, laid the foundation of that peculiar domestic life, which has always been the characteristic and charm of Maryland.

4. The first evidence of slavery in Maryland, is to be found in the laws relating to masters and slaves, passed during this period of repose.—Slavery was probably introduced from Virginia.*

5. There was another species of servant in the colony, of whom mention is frequently made. They were white emigrants, who wanting the means to emigrate, apprenticed their time, for a certain period, to those who would bear that expense.

*As the Puritans of New England were the first to engage in the traffic of slaves, after the trade was re-opened in South Carolina, and the very last to abandon it, it is not impossible that Maryland is indebted for the existence of slavery in her borders to the Puritans she received from Virginia.

Questions.—3. What was the number of inhabitants? What is said of domestic life? 4. First evidence of slavery? 5. What other species of servant was there?

This was made a matter of trade. The captain of a ship would bring out a party of emigrants, taking in lieu of passage money an indenture, whereby the emigrant agreed to serve for a given time.

6. On the arrival of such emigrants, their unexpired time was sold to the highest bidder. The price was paid in tobacco, which was the currency of the province.

7. The Quakers or Friends here found peace and refuge. In Massachusetts, the law had proscribed them as a "*cursed sect.*" They were to be imprisoned "without bail," and "sentenced to banishment upon pain of death." They were to be maimed, whipped, and, "man or woman, to have their tongues bored through with a red hot iron."

8. In Maryland, on the contrary, George Fox, their zealous leader, tarried and preached. Indian chiefs and their subjects, the legislature and the council, persons of quality, justices of the peace, and the heir of the Proprietary himself, came to listen to his preaching. To the Friends indeed was Maryland THE LAND OF THE SANCTUARY.— Whatever difficulty they had with the government, it arose from their refusal to perform military duty, and their rejection of oaths, but even of these requirements they were subsequently relieved.

Questions.—7. What is said of the Quakers? How were they treated in Massachusetts? 8. What is said of the preaching of Fox?

9. Charles Calvert continued to act as governor until the death of his father, November 30th, 1675, by which event he became himself the Lord Proprietary. Having revised and reformed the laws, and believing his presence no longer necessary in the province, he appointed Thomas Notely to act as deputy governor in the name of his infant son, Cecil Calvert, and returned to England.

10. While in Europe, he met and refuted the charges that had been made against his colony. He then, in 1680, returned to his province and assumed the government.

11. In the following year, Fendall, in conjunction with a restless spirit, named Coode, attempted to excite a rebellion among the people; they failed and were arrested, tried and convicted, but escaped with their lives again to disturb the peace of the province.

12. After governing the colony for four years, the Proprietary, thinking it necessary for him to return to England, appointed a council to direct the affairs of the colony, and departed from the province, never to return.

13. Events in Maryland were bringing to a close the long period of repose and toleration enjoyed under the mild administration of the second

---

Questions.—9. How long did Charles Calvert govern the colony? What did he do upon the death of his father? 10. What did he in England? 11. What is said of Fendall? 12. How long did Charles Calvert govern in person after he was proprietary? 13. What is said in this section?

Lord Proprietary. Dissensions, excited by the troubles in the mother country, and nourished by a sympathising spirit of intolerance in the colony, at length broke out in open revolution.

CHAPTER XII.

STATE OF SOCIETY, to 1689—*Friendship of the Natives—Kind of Government—Trade—Coin—Luxuries—Fruit—The Baltimore Bird—Tobacco—Travelling.*

1. Up to this time, the aborigines and the colonists were living side by side upon terms of the greatest friendship. The Chesapeakes had disappeared from Maryland, and the remnant of their tribe was seated on the banks of the Elizabeth river, in Virginia, under the dominion of the Powhatans.

2. The Yo-a-comicos lived upon the St. Mary's, and, as has been mentioned, were almost domesticated with the settlers.

3. The Susquehannocks, at the head of the Chesapeake bay, were at some distance from the early settlers, and less under the influence of the whites than the Yo-a-comicos, and were less

---

Questions.—1. What is said of the Indians? 2. Of Yo-a-comicos? 3. Of the Susquehannocks?

friendly to them. They were also hostile to the Yo-a-comicos, and were, therefore, sometimes troublesome.

4. The government was essentially a monarchy. But no powers were ever exercised with more entire reference to the interest and welfare of the governed than this power was by the Proprietary.

5. Trade was conducted through the midium of barter, or the exchange of one commodity for another. There was, however, a silver coin issued by the Proprietary, of various denominations, having Lord Baltimore's arms on one side, with the motto, *Crescite et multiplicamini* on the other. Probably very little of this coin was used, tobacco being the most common currency of the province, one pound of it, in 1650, being about three-pence English money; in 1732 it was made a legal tender at one penny a pound.

6. The luxuries of the present day were unknown. Our forefathers sat upon stools and forms, and dined without forks; but they paid especial attention to the furniture of their bed chamber. Tea and coffee were scarcely used, but cider and sack were freely drunk.

7. Great attention was paid to fruit. The waters of the bay furnished the greatest of delicacies—oysters and canvas-back duck. The oriole was

---

Questions.—4. Of what kind was the government? 5. How was trade conducted? What coin was issued? 6. What is said of luxuries? 7. Fruit? Chesapeake bay? Baltimore Bird?

common, and the settlers were so pleased with its plumage—black and yellow—corresponding with those upon the arms of the Calverts, that they called it the Baltimore Bird.

8. Tobacco was the greatest product of the province. It is said, "that a hundred sail of ships" traded in this article. Indian corn and the sweet potato were also cultivated at an early period. The words *potato, pone* and *homony* are derived from the Indians.

9. There was no regular post. Travelling was performed on horseback by land, and in canoes or other small boats by water. Letters were sent by private hand.

CHAPTER XIII.

REVOLUTION OF 1689—*James II Banished—William and Mary—Delay of Instructions—Protestant Association—John Coode—First Royal Governor—Acts of Assembly—Lord Baltimore Appeals to the King—Removal of the Capital—Second Royal Governor—Improvements—Efforts of the Royal Administration.*

1. In England, James II, who had succeeded Charles II, had been banished, and was succeeded by William and Mary.

2. Upon their accession, the Lord Proprietary immediately gave in his adherence, and sent in-

---

Questions.—8. Tobacco, &c.? 9. Travelling? 1. By whom was James II succeeded? 2. What did the proprietary do?

structions to have them proclaimed in the province. Unfortunately, these instructions did not arrive in due time, and, even after the new sovereigns had been acknowledged by the neighboring colonies, the authorities hesitated to act until they should receive instructions from the Proprietary.

3. The ill-will of the people had been excited against the deputies, and every measure they adopted was looked upon with suspicion. The public arms were collected, in fear of a general outbreak. At length the unfortunate delay to proclaim William and Mary brought affairs to a crisis.

4. In April, 1689, "*An association in arms for the defence of the Protestant religion, and for asserting the rights of King William and Queen Mary to the province of Maryland and all the English Dominions*" was formed. John Coode, who had already been once guilty of treason and rebellion, was at the head of this association.

5. The character of this man may, perhaps, cast a light upon the professions of religion and of loyalty made by the association. He was a man of loose morals and desperate habits. Assuming to be in holy orders, he was yet so depraved that he was presented by the grand jury for atheism and blasphemy. To escape trial he fled to Virginia, whence he would frequently come back, declaring

---

Questions.—2. Why did not the authorities act? 3. What is said in this section? 4. What association was formed? Who was at the head of it? 5. What was the character of this man?

as he had overthrown one government he would pull down another.

6. The king sustained the acts of a revolution, which was, in fact, only a continuation of that which placed him on the throne, and, in 1691, appointed Sir Lionel Copley, first royal governor of the province.

7. Early in 1692, Governor Copley summoned a General Assembly, which met at St. Mary's.—Their first act was the recognition of William and Mary; their next, the overthrow of equal toleration, and the establishment of the Church of England as the State Church of Maryland.

8. The legislature proceeded to pass oppressive acts against all who differed from the creed of the dominant party. These laws, in time, were modified or repealed, though some of the obnoxious restrictions continued until the revolution of 1776, when religious liberty was the acknowledged right of all.

9. They next endeavored to deprive the Proprietary of his personal rights in the province. Lord Baltimore appealed to the king, who issued a royal letter authorizing him to collect his revenues. The convention refused to submit, and threw his agents into prison. The king and council, however, having expressly decided in favor of Lord

---

Questions.—6. What is said of the king? 7. What was the first act of the Assembly? 8. What further acts did the legislature pass? 9. What did they attempt? What did Lord Baltimore do? and what the convention?

Baltimore, the assembly at length yielded, as far as port and tonnage duties were concerned.

10. From the Proprietary the assembly turned to old St. Mary's. In that part of the province his firmest supporters dwelt, and the assembly determined to punish them by removing the seat of government from their capital. Another weighty reason was that the colony had now so extended that St. Mary's was inconveniently situated for those who had business before the legislature and the courts.

11. As the very existence of the town depended upon its being the seat of government, it is natural that its inhabitants prayed and protested against this change. Their prayers and protests were in vain. The seat of government was removed to New Providence, which thenceforth was called Annapolis.

12. Sir Lionel Copley was succeeded by Francis Nicholson, who was principally active in securing the success of the established Church, and promoting the cause of Education. He was commissioned in 1691, but did not enter upon his duties until 1694, the government being administered by Sir Edmond Andros, after the death of Copley, till the arrival of his successor.

13. During the administration of Nicholson, several beneficial improvements were effected. In

---

Questions.—10. What was the next step of the assembly? 11. Why did the town of St. Mary's protest? Where was the capital removed to? 12. By whom was Copley succeeded? 13. What took place during the administration of Nicholson?

1695, a public post was established; the route extended from the Potomac, through Annapolis, to Philadelphia. The system, in some of its features, was well suited to the condition of the province.

14. Under the royal government, the population did not increase as rapidly as formerly. Three principal causes operated to check immigration, namely, universal toleration had ceased; lands were no longer given as a bounty to the immigrants; and, the fluctuations in the tobacco trade. To add to these misfortunes, a destructive disease made its appearance among the stock of the farmers and planters; and, two years later, a violent and raging mortality made its appearance among the people of Charles county.

15. During the administration of the royal governors, the hand of the crown seemed to weigh like an incubus upon the prosperity of Maryland. For a quarter of a century the limits of the settlements were but little advanced; the population but feebly increased, and the foreign and domestic resources, at best, remained stationary. Religious liberty had taken flight, and with the overthrow of equal toleration, and the establishment of a church, was destroyed that true civil freedom which cannot exist for the body while the spirit is enchained.

Questions.—14. What is said of the population under the royal government? What were the causes? 15. What is said of the prosperity under the royal governors?

CHAPTER XIV.

1714-1751—THE RESTORATION OF THE PROVINCE—*Death of Charles, Lord Baltimore—Province restored to his Son—Undisturbed Tranquillity—Policy towards Indians—Establishment of Baltimore—Fell's Point—Commercial Advantages—Elk Ridge Landing—Annapolis—Maryland Gazette—Frederick—Georgetown—Death of Proprietary—State of the Colony.*

SEAL OF BALTIMORE.

1. Charles, Lord Baltimore, expired on the 20th of February, 1714, at the age of eighty-four years. His title and his province descended to his son, Benedict Leonard Calvert, who, having abandoned the faith of his father, and become a Protestant, secured the favor of the king, and had the government of the province restored to him. He only lived long enough, however, to be acknowledged Lord Proprietary.

2. By his death in 1715, the province fell to his infant son, Charles, who was educated in the Pro-

---

Questions.—1. Who succeeded Charles, Lord Baltimore? What is said of him? 2. How long did he live, and who succeeded him?

testant religion. Governor Hart, the last royal governor, was continued in office as representative of the Proprietary. The restoration produced but little change in the province. The Roman Catholics were still disfranchised.

3. For a period of forty years the colony enjoyed almost undisturbed tranquillity. It had no greater troubles than contests between the governor and council, who formed the upper house, and the delegates of the people, in the lower house. These struggles were the germ of that mighty contest in which the liberties of the people were finally secured.

4. From the earliest period, the government of the colony had pursued a peaceful and just policy towards the Indians. In 1698, an act was passed to assure to the Nanticokes, the possession of their lands in Dorchester county.

5. Thus even the warlike Nanticokes had yielded to the mild influence of the colonial government, and became peaceful dwellers under its protection. But the red man cannot long remain in the vicinity of the white, and by degrees they began to remove.

6. In 1729, Baltimore, the great emporium of the State, was first laid out on the lands of Charles Carroll, in sixty lots of one acre each, by commis-

---

Questions.—3. What was the condition of the colony? What is said of these struggles? 4. What act had been passed in 1698? 5. What is said of the Indians? 6. When was Baltimore founded? On whose land?

sioners appointed by the legislature. The northwestern corner lot was that whereon St. Paul's church now stands. In 1732, it was increased by an addition of ten acres east of the falls, commencing where the Gay street bridge now stands. In 1763, Edward Fell laid off a further portion called Fell's Point, which, in the year 1773, was added to Baltimore Town. In 1781, he laid off "the addition to Fell's Point," which was annexed to Baltimore, by act of assembly of that year.

7. The commercial advantages possessed by Baltimore Town soon drew population, and the town grew and flourished. For a time, the town of Elk Ridge Landing contended with it for the commerce of the northern part of the colony, and was a great tobacco market. But the superior advantages of Baltimore soon enabled it to surpass its rival.*

* The original lines of Baltimore were as follows: From near the corner of Pratt and Light streets to McClellan's alley, from that point to the corner of St. Paul and Saratoga streets, thence east to about 165 feet from Gay street, including Fish street; thence south to near where Water street is, and following the line of that crooked street—which was the line of the low lands—back to the beginning. Old Town was so-called from an early settlement made by Coles, or Gorsuch, or Jones.

It was not originally a part of Baltimore Town, but was called Jones' Town. It consisted of ten acres, and was laid

---

Questions.—6. When increased and by what addition? 7. What is said of the advantages of its position? What rival had it?

8. At Elk Ridge Landing, where now there is a meadow and a marsh, rather than the channel of a river, vessels came for their cargoes of tobacco The greater part of this tobacco was still housed upon the plantations on which it was raised, awaiting notice of shipment.

9. When this notice arrived, there was great stir and activity. The huge and stout hogsheads were fitted up with rough shafts, fastened to cleats, in which revolved the strong axle-like pins inserted in either end. A single horse was attached, and the driver, walking by the side, began to "roll" his tobacco to the little port. Some of the roads near Baltimore, leading to Elk Ridge Landing are still known as "Rolling roads."

10. Annapolis, which had been erected into a port of entry in 1683, continued to increase after it had been made the seat of government. In 1745, the earliest, and, for a long time, the only newspaper in the colony was issued. It was called the "Maryland Gazette," and was continued, by the descendants of the founder, until 1839. The early wealth of Annapolis is still shewn in the

off in twenty lots in the year 1732. It was bounded by Pitt, now East Fayette street, by Jones' Falls and by French street. It was connected with Baltimore by the Gay street bridge in 1732, but was not made part of Baltimore until 1745.

Questions.—8. Describe Elk Ridge Landing? 9. The Rolling of tobacco? 10. What is said of Annapolis?

ancient buildings, many of them displaying by their decorations the taste and resources of the original owners.

11. Frederick, for a long time the second city of the State, was laid out in 1745. It was made county town in 1748, at which time Frederick county was formed, having been carved out of Prince George's.

12. Georgetown was laid out in 1751. Falling within the limits of the "ten miles square" that were ceded to the United States by the States of Maryland and Virginia, it has ever since formed a part of the District of Columbia.

13. In 1751, Charles, Lord Baltimore, died, having ruled his province, in person or by his governors, for the space of thirty-six years. This period was marked by general peace and increasing prosperity; it was also full of evidences of the unyielding spirit of the people in defending their rights, and in the acquisition of new ones.

14. New counties were added; the population had increased, and the internal resources of the province were developed by the establishment of factories, mills and furnaces. Domestic wine was manufactured as early as 1748.

Questions.—11. When was Frederick laid out? When made county town? 12. What is said of Georgetown? 13. When did the proprietary die, and how long did he govern? 14. What further is said?

CHAPTER XV.

BOUNDARY DISPUTES—*Watkins' Point—Disputes with Penn—Penn's Grant—The Proprietary will not be Robbed—Penn attacks the Charter—Baltimore out of favor at Court—The King is Patron to Penn—His Expulsion—Settlement Postponed—Mason and Dixon's Line—Shrewdness of Penn—Virginia Boundary.*

1. Notwithstanding the clearness with which the boundaries of the province were laid down in the charter, it was nevertheless subjected to great difficulties about the limits.

2. The first contest was with Virginia about the position of Watkins' Point, on the Chesapeake Bay, this being the starting point of the line of Southern boundary. After some difficulties between the two colonies, the dispute was finally adjusted on the 25th of June, 1668; and the line was distinctly indicated and exists as the present boundary of the two States.

3. The most serious difficulty, however, was that respecting the Northern boundary. The Swedes and Dutch, in 1629, had made a settlement within the limits of the present State of Delaware, which was included in Baltimore's grant. In 1681, William Penn received a grant of territory comprising

---

Questions.—2. What was the first contest about? 3. With whom was the most serious difficulty? What is said of Penn's grant?

twenty-six millions of acres. The Southern boundaries of this tract encroached upon the grant to Lord Baltimore.

4. To further his plans, Penn found it necessary to procure a grant of that part of the present State of Delaware which was excluded from the original grant, namely, the town of New Castle and all the territory for twelve miles around it. This grant, as well as a release of his rights in Pennsylvania, was obtained from the Duke of York, to whom had been previously granted, by his brother King Charles II, all the territory from the mouth of the Connecticut to the shores of the Delaware River.

5. Penn produced this grant and a letter from Charles II, directing the Proprietary of Maryland to assent to an adjustment of his Northern boundary by measuring two degrees from his Southern boundary, at the rate of sixty miles to the degree. The Proprietary, resting firmly upon the terms of his charter, namely, the 40th degree, declined to submit to be robbed of territory which Penn had no right to take, and the Duke of York, no right to give.

6. To shake Baltimore's confidence in his charter, he attacked it by objecting that the Delaware settlements had been planted by the Dutch, before that charter was granted. The Proprietary at

---

Questions.—4. What did Penn find necessary? From whom was it obtained? 5. What did Penn produce? Did the proprietary submit? 6. How did Penn attack the charter?

that time was under the displeasure of the crown, and upon the king's referring the matter to the board of trade, it was decided that Lord Baltimore's grant included only "lands uncultivated" and inhabited by savages, and that the territory along the Delaware had been settled by Christians antecedently to his grant, and was not therefore included in it.

7. At the time of this decision, 1685, Lord Baltimore was not in a condition to resist it. Through the avarice of the crown, he was threatened with a total loss of his whole grant. Where power was on one side, and only right on the other, resistance would have hastened and ensured his loss of the province.

8. But James II, the patron of Penn and the author of the grant, who was now king, was about to experience in his own person, how little rights are respected when they come in conflict with power. He was expelled from the throne, and the final settlement of the boundary question was postponed until 1732, when an agreement was entered into by the Proprietary, to adopt the border fixed by the decree of 1685.

9. The matter being subject to further dispute, it was not until 1766, that Messrs. Charles Mason

---

Questions.—6. What was the decision of the board of trade? 7. What was the condition of Lord Baltimore at this time? 8. What advantages had Penn? Why was the settlement postponed? When was the agreement entered into? 9. Who marked the line agreed upon?

and Jeremiah Dixon, astronomers of celebrity, in England, chosen by the respective Proprietaries for the purpose, completed the division line between the two provinces. This line is known as "Mason and Dixon's," and was marked by setting at the end of every mile a stone with the letter P and the arms of the Penns, on the north, and the letter M, with the escutcheon of Lord Baltimore, on the south side.

10. Thus, after a struggle of more than a century, by the shrewdness of Penn, in availing himself of a mere quibble, a large and fertile territory was lost to Maryland.

11. The last of the boundary disputes has never been settled. The charter of Maryland defined the western boundary by the meridian passing through the first fountain of the Potomac. The question arose whether the north or south branch of the Potomac was the main head. A glance at the map will show that the decision involved a large tract of land. Several attempts had been made to adjust the line prior to the revolution, and in 1766, Virginia recognized the rights of the territory contained within the charter, but it yet holds the disputed district.

Questions.—9. How? 10. How was a large and fertile territory lost to Maryland? 11. What was the dispute with Virginia?

CHAPTER XVI.

1751-1755—FREDERICK, LAST LORD BALTIMORE—*English and French War—Claims of each—Bold design of the Governor of Canada—Maryland stands aloof—Opposition to Arbitrary Demands—Dinwiddie's Perplexities—Maryland takes a part—Fort Cumberland—Acts of Assembly.*

1. 1751, Frederick, last of the Lords Baltimore, became Proprietary of Maryland.

2. A contest was now approaching in which Maryland was deeply interested. It was the last war between the English and French, for dominion in the New World.

3. Immense regions in America were claimed by both nations, and each was eager to forestall the other by getting possession of them. The most desirable of these regions lay west of the Alleghany mountains.

4. The French claimed all this country by right of discovery, because in 1673, Father Marquette, and Joilet, of Quebec, French subjects, had passed down the Mississippi in a canoe, as far as Arkansas.

5. The English claimed all land west of the Alleghany mountains to the Mississippi. This claim was based upon a purchase that had been

---

Questions.—1. Who was the last Lord Baltimore? 2. What contest was now approaching? 3. What were the grounds of this contest? 4. What was the French claim? 5. What was the English?

made by commissioners from Pennsylvania, Maryland and Virginia, and the Six Nations. The Indians had a tradition that this land had been conquered by their forefathers.

6. Such were the foundations of claims which plunged two nations into a series of wars ending in a loss to England of a great part of her American possessions, and, to France of the whole.

7. In furtherance of the French claim, the governor of Canada conceived the bold design of constructing a chain of forts along the Mississippi and Ohio rivers, where the English had already established trading posts.

8. Virginia was chiefly interested in the controversy. Maryland became involved simply in self-defence. The legislature of Maryland stood aloof, in spite of the commands of the crown, the remonstrances of the governor, and the entreaties of Virginia. They declared, however, their determination to resist foreign invasion, and contribute to the assistance of the neighboring colonies when they conceived their necessity required it.

9. Even in Virginia, which was so deeply interested in the controversy, the growing spirit of Republicanism led to an opposition to the arbitrary demands of the governor for means to carry

---

Questions.—7. What design did the governor of Canada conceive? 8. Who was chiefly interested in this controversy? How was Maryland drawn in? Why did she stand aloof at first? What did she declare? 9. What trouble was there in Virginia?

on the war against the French, when all efforts at a peaceful settlement had failed.

10. Governor Dinwiddie, of that colony, was sorely perplexed, and exclaimed, "There appears to me an infatuation in all the assemblies in this part of the world." He urged the home government to tax the colonies for the benefit of the common cause, *independently of assemblies.*

11. But the time was come when Maryland was compelled to take part in the war. The Virginia troops under Colonel Washington had been captured by the French and Indians, who, from Fort Duquesne, erected on the present site of Pittsburgh, poured their savage and plundering bands on the unprotected frontiers of Pennsylvania, Maryland and Virginia.

12. The Assembly at Annapolis, in 1754, voted supplies and assistance to the Virginians in their efforts to reduce this fort. Many of the people of the province had, before this, organized companies of rangers and frontier guards for the protection of the border settlements. A fort had been erected at Cumberland, far beyond the settlements, which served as a resting point in the expeditions undertaken against the French on the Ohio. In these expeditions the people of Maryland bore a

---

Questions.—10. What did Dinwiddie exclaim? What did he urge? 11. Why was Maryland now compelled to take a part? 12. What did the assembly vote? What had the people already done? Where had a fort been erected?

part. Governor Sharpe, of Maryland, was, by a royal commission, commander-in-chief of all the forces engaged against the French, on the Ohio.

13. On the 24th of December, 1754, the General Assembly of Maryland was again convened, and passed a law for the levying of troops for the ensuing campaign. In the session of February, 1755, they passed other laws providing for the energetic prosecution of the expedition which ended so disastrously for the whole country, known as *Braddock's Defeat.*

CHAPTER XVII.

1755–1758—BRADDOCK'S DEFEAT—*Braddock's Arrival—Council at Alexandria—Braddock at Frederick—Arrival of Franklin —Franklin's Suggestions—Braddock's Confidence—Franklin's Proposition— March over the Mountains—Baggage—Mutual Disgust—Braddock rejects the Indians and Backwoodsmen—Slow Movements —The Contest—The Defeat.*

1. Although the expedition which resulted in Braddock's defeat belongs more properly to the history of Virginia, yet as the disaster involved

---

Questions.—12. Who was commander-in-chief of all the forces? 13. When did the assembly meet? What act did they pass?

serious consequences to Maryland, and the story is one of peculiar interest, it calls for more than a passing notice.

2. Early in the year, Gen. Braddock, at the head of a strong body of troops, embarked for the colonies. On his arrival at Alexandria, a council of colonial governors was summoned to meet him at Annapolis, on the 3d of April. Gen. Braddock, Gov. Dinwiddie, and Commodore Keppel, arrived at Annapolis, where they were shortly after joined by the governors of Massachusetts, New York and Pennsylvania.

3. The place of meeting having been changed, these gentlemen, together with Gov. Sharpe, of Maryland, proceeded to the General's head-quarters at Alexandria.

4. In the council three expeditions were determined on: the first, against Fort Duquesne, under Braddock himself, reinforced by the Maryland and Virginia levies; the second, against Niagara and Fort Frontignac; and the third, against Crown Point.

5. Gov. Sharpe immediately proceeded to Frederick, where a portion of the army was already quartered. He was joined here by Gen. Braddock, who had left Alexandria, on the 20th of April. Braddock intended to remain at Frederick, until

---

Questions.—2. When did Braddock embark for the colonies? What council was held? 3. Where did they adjourn to? 4. What expeditions were determined upon? 5. What delayed Braddock?

his stores should be forwarded to Fort Cumberland. The Virginia contractors having failed to fulfil their engagements, his stay at Frederick, very much to his chagrin, was protracted beyond his expectation or his patience. He was compelled to send round the country to buy food and cattle for the subsistence of his troops.

6. While Braddock was venting his spleen against army contractors, Benjamin Franklin arrived at Frederick. He came ostensibly in the character of Post Master General, to arrange for the transmission of dispatches, but in reality was sent by the Assembly of Pennsylvania to conciliate Braddock, who, they understood, was incensed against them.

7. Notwithstanding the entire confidence Braddock had in himself and his regulars, Franklin, relying upon his better knowledge of the difficulties of the country, and the peculiarities of Indian warfare, modestly observed to the general, that if he arrived before Fort Duquesne, with his troops and artillery, the fort could probably make but a short resistance, but that he himself feared the ambuscades of the Indians.

8. Braddock smiled at what he thought Franklin's ignorance, and replied: "These savages may indeed

---

Questions.—5. What was he compelled to do? 6. Who joined Braddock at Frederick? For what purpose had he been sent? 7. What suggestions did Franklin make? 8. How did Braddock receive the suggestions? What did he reply?

be a formidable enemy to raw American militia, but upon the king's regular and disciplined troops, sir, it is impossible for them to make any impression."

9. During his stay at Frederick, he was joined by George Washington, then Colonel, whom he had invited to join him as aid-de-camp. It was to the skill and courage of Washington, that the remnant of the army owed its preservation.

10. As the whole delay of the army was caused by the want of wagons and teams, the few in the neighborhood of Frederick having been all impressed, and found insufficient, Franklin, one day, expressed his regret to the general that he had not landed in Pennsylvania, where almost every farmer owned a wagon.

11. Braddock immediately commissioned Franklin to contract for one hundred and fifty wagons, and a proper supply of draught and saddle horses. The reluctant Pennsylvania farmers, however, would not yield their property without the further security of Franklin's personal responsibility.

12. On the 10th of June, Braddock set off from Fort Cumberland. The march over the mountains proved a tremendous affair. Owing to the difficulties of the way, the line of wagons and troops often

---

Questions.—9. Who joined him at Frederick? What is said of Washington? 10. What caused the delay? What did Franklin say? 11. For how many wagons did he order him to contract? What did the farmers require? 12. When did Braddock start from Cumberland? What of the march?

extended for three or four miles. Washington was outraged at the number of wagons required for the baggage and luxuries of the officers,—backwood's campaigning admitting only what could be carried in a portmanteau. He thought that men who required so much for their comfort, could hardly be efficient in the field. On the other hand, the British officers were disgusted at the "languid, spiritless, unsoldier-like appearance" of the colonial levies, "which gave little hope of future good behavior." The sequel proved how much deceived both parties were in their estimate of each other.

13. Braddock, in his blind confidence in his regulars, rejected the aid of Indians and backwoodsmen, acquainted with Indian warfare, saying, he had "experienced troops on whom he could rely for all purposes."

14. The military education of Braddock was in his way. He could not adapt himself to the nature of circumstances in which he was placed.—Hence his march was exceedingly slow, sometimes not advancing more than twelve miles in four days. Although a stranger to fear, he was charged at home "*with not marching as if at all impatient to be scalped.*"

Questions.—12. What Were Washington's feelings? At what were the British disgusted? 13. What is said of this section? 14. What was in Braddock's way? What was the result?

15. In this march Washington saw enough of British regulars to have his confidence in them shaken, when it should come to wild bush-fighting. He ventured to suggest that the Virginia rangers, being accustomed to the country and Indian warfare, might be thrown in advance. The veteran, indignant that a young provincial should presume to make a suggestion to him, gave him only an angry reply.

16. On July 9th, the army was in the neighborhood of the fort, marching "as if in a review in St James' Park," without having sent out scouts or rangers in advance, when suddenly was heard a quick and heavy firing in front. The van of the advance had been taken by surprise; a murderous fire broke out from among trees and a ravine on the right, and the woods resounded with unearthly whoops and yellings.

17. A perfect panic seized the troops, all orders were unheeded; in their fright they shot at random, killing their own troops. In a short time most of the officers and many of the men of the advance were killed or wounded. The advance fell back upon the working party, which was equally dismayed, and which, together with the advanced party, fell back upon the reinforcement sent up, and all was now confusion.

Questions.—15. What did Washington suggest? How was it received? 16. What is said in this section? 17. Describe the panic?

18 When the general came upon the ground, he tried to rally the men. "They would fight," they said, "if they could see their enemy; it was useless to fire at trees and bushes, and they could not stand to be shot down by an invisible foe."

19. The Virginia troops scattered themselves, and took post behind trees. In this way they, in some degree, protected the regulars. Braddock would not consent to depart from the system he had been trained in, and, instead of adopting the same plan, insisted upon forming his troops in platoons. The result was they were cut down as fast as they could advance.

20. The bravery of the officers was now seen. Their courage seemed to kindle with the thickening horrors. In the vain hope of inspiriting their men, they would dash forward singly or in groups. They were invariably shot down.

21. Washington was the only aid left alive. He was sent to the main body to bring the artillery into action. The men who served the guns were paralysed. Had they raked the ravine with grape shot the day might have been saved. But the men could not be kept to the guns.

22. Braddock was undaunted; five horses had been killed under him, still he kept his ground,

---

Questions.—18. What did the general try to do? What did the men reply? 19. What did the Virginia troops do? What Braddock? 20. What is said of the bravery of the officers? 21. What is said of Washington? What of the men? 22. What of Braddock?

vainly endeavoring to check the flight of his men. At length a bullet passed through his right arm, and lodged itself in his lungs, inflicting a mortal wound.

23. The rout now became complete. Out of eighty-six officers, twenty-six had been killed, and thirty-six wounded. The rank and file lost upwards of seven hundred. The Virginia corps suffered most, one company had been almost annihilated—another had lost all its officers, even to the corporal.

24. The victorious force of the enemy consisted only of thirty Frenchmen and three or four hundred Indians, of whom seven Indians and four Frenchmen were killed.

CHAPTER XVIII.

1755–1758—FRENCH AND INDIAN WAR CONTINUED—*Terror and Desolation—Plantations laid Waste—Panic—Expedition against Fort Duquesne—Grant's Bravado and Defeat—Gallantry of Marylanders—Abandonment of the Fort by the French.*

1. A period of terror and desolation ensued—the settlements were attacked and broken up. The

---

Questions.—23. Describe the rout? 24. What did the victorious force consist of? 1. What is said in this section?

outposts were driven in, and some of the smaller posts captured, and their garrisons massacred.—The panic spread even to the bay shore. Many of the inhabitants from the interior fled to Baltimore. Preparations were made by the citizens of that town to embark their women and children on board of vessels, preparatory to a flight to Virginia; while some of the Virginians even believed there was no safety short of England itself.

2. As soon as the disastrous intelligence of Braddock's destruction reached Annapolis, Governor Sharpe set out for Frederick; the militia were called out, and volunteers were raised.

3. In this disastrous year, more than twenty plantations were laid waste, and their occupants massacred or carried into captivity. In November, it was reported that a body of French and Indians were within thirty miles of Baltimore, and immediately two thousand men assembled to meet their advance.

4. Even the people of Annapolis, far removed as they were from the frontiers, caught the infection, and began to fortify their town. The excitement was allayed by the return of several volunteers from the West, who reported affairs as in a better condition.

Questions.—1. How far did the panic extend? 2. Gov. Sharpe's movements? 3. What is said of the ravages of the Indians? 4. What of Annapolis?

5. Fort Cumberland being so far from the frontier, was found to afford no protection. Governor Sharpe, therefore, selected a site for a new fort, near the present town of Hancock, to be called Fort Frederick, which was ready for the reception of troops by the middle of August, 1756.

RUINS OF FORT FREDERICK.

6. Provision having thus been made, the confidence of the people to the westward was somewhat restored. But the petty warfare of posts and defensive expeditions, while it exhausted the force of the colony, could produce no permanent results.

7. The neighboring colonies of Virginia and Pennsylvania, at length, with that of Maryland, became convinced that the only way to protect

Questions.—5. What new site for a fort was selected? 6. What is said in this section? 7. Of what were the colonies now convinced?

their frontiers was by expelling the enemy from their stronghold.

8. It was hoped by the colonies that active and energetic measures would now be taken. Virginia, which was most interested, had one regiment in the field. The forces of Maryland amounted to five hundred men, aided by Indian allies, under Col. Dagworthy.

9. In September, 1758, an advanced body having proceeded about ten miles beyond Laurel Hill, Major Grant, with a body of more than eight hundred men, consisting of three hundred and thirty Highlanders, one hundred royal Americans, one hundred and seventy-six Virginians, ninety-five Maryland, one hundred and twelve Pennsylvania, and thirteen Carolina troops was detached to reconnoitre.

10. In the night, unobserved by the French, Grant took a post upon a hill about eighty rods from Fort Duquesne, and in the morning, by way of bravado, beat the reveille, and sounded the bagpipes in several places.

11. As soon as the English were discovered, the Indians sallied out from the fort, and having reached a height that overlooked Grant's position, surrounded him and commenced the attack.

Questions.—8. What forces were now in the field? 9. What is said of Grant? 10. What further? 11. What did the Indians do?

12. The Highlanders, suffering from the deadly fire, at length gave way. The Maryland troops, joined by the Carolinians, took cover in bushes and behind trees, and keeping the enemy at bay, sustained the action. The Virginians were two miles behind guarding the baggage; as soon as the action began they hastened up to the assistance of Grant, but were unable to maintain their ground. The English were defeated with a loss of two hundred and seventy-three killed, and forty-two wounded.

13. The Marylanders behaved with great gallantry, and, although they suffered severely, succeeded in covering the retreat of the remainder of the troops. Out of ninety-five men, their loss was twenty-three privates and one officer.

14. The main body was still toiling on its way, and did not reach the scene of the conflict until a month after the battle. It was determined to defer any attack until the next campaign. But the enemy were not so slow The troops from the fort, with the Indians, to the number of one thousand men, attacked the English on the 12th of October. After a hard fight, they were repulsed. Lieut. Prather, of Maryland, was killed.

Questions.—12. What the Highlanders? Who kept the enemy at bay? What about the Virginians? 13. How did the Marylanders behave? 14. What about the main body? Who attacked it? Result?

15. After this battle, several skirmishes ensued. In one of these, Capt. Evan Shelby, of Frederick county, killed, with his own hand, one of the leading chiefs of the enemy.

16. The Indians now abandoned their allies, and left the fort, saying it was an easy matter to deal with the regulars, but impossible to withstand the provincials. On the 22d of November, after a painful march, the English succeeded in reaching Fort Duquesne, which they found had been abandoned and burnt by the French. A new fort was built, named Fort Pitt.

17. Gov. Sharpe, in sympathy with the joy that filled the colony, appointed a day of public thanksgiving and praise. The Assembly appropriated money to be divided among the brave men who had served in their forces.

18. From this time, Maryland had little concern in the war, and the principal features of its history are of a pacific and legislative character. Yet that legislative history is full of interest, for it is the history of that continuous struggle for the rights of the people, that led eventually to the war of the Revolution.

Questions.—15. Who was killed? 16. What did the Indians do? When did the English reach the fort? What did they find? 17. What is said in this section? 18. And what in this?

CHAPTER XIX.

THE DAYS BEFORE THE REVOLUTION—*The Democratic and the Aristocratic Elements—Claims of the Two Houses—Peace—Debt—Condition of Maryland—Influence of the French War—The Old Controversy Revived—Preparatory Steps to the Stamp Act.*

1. The Charter of Maryland contained the germs of two contending principles—the aristocratic and the democratic. From the earliest period of its history, there had been contests between the parties representing these principles.

2. The result of the contest, in every stage, was in favor of the democratic element. The spirit of the people, and the necessities of the times, contributed to its vigorous growth. The contest was now verging to its final issue.

3. The representatives of the people, who sat in the lower house, insisted upon the right to frame and amend bills for raising money. The upper house, consisting of the governor and his council, claimed for themselves a share in the imposition of taxes.

4. As long as danger was threatening the existence of the colony, the commons did not insist upon

---

Questions.—1. What is said of the charter? 2. What was the result of every contest? 3. Upper and lower houses? 4. What was the claim of the commons?

their claim, but when the war was over, they planted themselves firmly upon their old position—"that the people could only be taxed by their own consent."

5. Peace was declared in 1763, and the French colonies were ceded to England. But to counterbalance this acquisition, she found herself laboring under a heavy war debt. To aid her in managing this, she turned her eyes towards the colonies, all of whom, excepting Maryland alone, which had resisted, had been compelled to furnish requisitions.

6. The condition of Maryland was prosperous. In 1761, its population amounted to 164,000 persons. The greatness of its resources was undisputed. Its people were frugal and industrious, and had spread themselves almost to the utmost limits of the province. Its physical features made it peculiarly fitted for commerce and navigation; its soil was rich, and exuberantly productive to the labor of the husbandman and planter. This condition of prosperity being shared by the other colonies, England determined to avail herself of their increasing wealth to replenish her own exhausted coffers.

7. Disastrous as the French war apparently was to the colonies, it was not without great advantage to them. The spirit of independence and

---

Questions.—5. When was peace declared? What was the condition of England? 6. Condition of Maryland? Character of her people? What further is said? 7. Influence of French war?

self-reliance had had time to grow, and opportunities to develop itself. With an active and watchful enemy ready to seize upon the colonies, England was too dependent upon them to offend them.—She, therefore, in a measure, closed her eyes to the growing spirit of independence, while the colonies learned their power to maintain that spirit.

8. Now that the war was over, England on the one hand was determined to make the colonies feel her authority, and the colonies, on the other, resolved to re-assert their old rights. It was a contest for supremacy on one side, and for freedom on the other.

9. In 1763, the English government began to take preparatory steps. The Prime Minister gave notice to the colonies that, at the ensuing session of Parliament, he intended to propose a duty on stamps for the purpose of raising a revenue from the provinces to defray the expenses of the war. The colonies had always insisted that they should not be taxed without their own consent. The Minister hoped they would propose a compromise, and thus commit themselves to an abandonment of their principle by negotiating instead of resisting.

10. In the session of Parliament which followed, a resolution to the same effect was adopted, but not yet executed. The trade of the colonies was

---

Questions.—7. Effect upon mother country? 8. What controversy now arose? 9. What steps did the English government take? 10. What is said in this section?

interfered with and injured. But all this, instead of arousing the spirit of compromise, had the contrary effect. The indignation of the people was aroused. They saw the design was to deprive them of their liberties and make them the mere subjects of the British Parliament.

CHAPTER XX.

STAMP ACT—*Stamp Act Imposed—Maryland Assembly Prorogued—No Stamps in Maryland—Protest of Assembly—Treatment of Hood—Acts of Assembly—Frederick County Court—"Sons of Liberty"—Repeal of Stamp Act.*

1. On the 22d of March, 1765, the Stamp Act was finally passed. The interval between its first proposal and final passage had enabled the people to gather their energies for universal resistance.

2. In open manifestation Massachusetts and Virginia took the lead, but the silence of Maryland was not the result of lukewarmness. Her assembly was disabled from declaring its hostility to the measure, as its meeting was prevented by prorogation.

Questions.—1. When was the stamp act imposed? 2. Why could not Maryland declare her hostility?

3. It is the proud boast of Maryland that her soil was never polluted by the obnoxious stamps. In unanimity, firmness and success, she exceeded all the other colonies. The Assembly could not speak until September, 1765, when it solemnly protested against the measure, and indignantly complained that they had for two years been deprived of the power of publicly declaring their lasting opposition.

4. The people of the colony, however, had previously taken the matter in their own hands.—Hood, a native of Maryland, was appointed stamp distributor for the province. On his arrival at Annapolis with the stamps, there was a great excitement. The people would not suffer him to land; the vessel was compelled to draw off, and land Hood secretly, at another time and place. The country people gathered into the city, prepared to show their detestation of the man who could consent to become the instrument in enslaving his own country.

5. The people not only refused to buy his goods, which he offered at reduced prices, to secure favor, but they even destroyed the house in which he was to place them, lest it should also be a depository for the hated stamps. Having insulted him in various ways, they at length threatened personal

---

Questions.—3. What is the boast of Maryland? When did the assembly protest? 4. How had the colony shown its hostility? 5. What was Hood compelled to do?

violence. He fled for refuge to the governor, who could not protect him from popular fury. He then escaped to New York, but was followed even there by a number of daring spirits, who compelled him to renounce and abjure forever, under oath, his office and the exercise of its functions.

6. When the Assembly met, it made a solemn declaration of their rights, which the people had vindicated, by measures in which the principal men in the province had borne a part. The Assembly appointed representatives to the "Congress of Deputies," and instructed them to see that whatever petition was presented to the English government, it should contain an assertion of the right of the colonies to be free from taxation "save by their own consent, or that of their representatives, freely chosen and appointed."

7. The law had made stamps necessary in many business transactions; for a time, therefore, there was a cessation of business. The Frederick county court had the high honor of first deciding, in a legal manner, the unconstitutionality of the stamp act. In the public offices at Annapolis, however, business still continued to be interrupted. The officers hesitated to treat the law as a nullity, and feared to attempt its enforcement.

8. To meet this difficulty the inhabitants of Baltimore and the adjoining country formed themselves

---

Questions.—6. What did the assembly do? 7. What court made the first decision? 8. What did the people of Baltimore and the country do?

into an association, called "The Sons of Liberty," and adjourned to meet at Annapolis. They came together in great strength and compelled the courts and public offices to be kept open, without the stamps. Business was again renewed, and the stamp act, though still unrepealed, was a dead letter in Maryland.

9. In 1766, the obnoxious act, long since dead in all the colonies, and never enforced in Maryland, was repealed. The House of Delegates did not fail to express their sense of gratitude to those who had, in the British Parliament, proved themselves the friends of the colonies. They decreed a statue of marble to Chatham, and a portrait by some eminent hand to Lord Camden, but through the action of the upper house, the decree was never carried into effect.

CHAPTER XXI.

THE DUTY ON TEA—*Tax on Tea, &c.—Massachusetts' Circular—Non-Importation—The "Good Intent"—Alarm of the British Ministry—Defection of other Colonies.*

1. The English government still clung to the idea of raising a revenue from the colonies. But

---

Questions.—9. When was the stamp act repealed? How did the House of Delegates show their gratitude to the friends of the colonies? 1. How did the English government now proceed?

they determined to proceed in a more cautious manner. A tax, under the specious pretence of regulating commerce, was laid on tea, paints, glass and paper, imported into the colonies.

2. The old spirit of resistance broke out; the press teemed with appeals to the public; and the colonists were soon prepared to meet it, as they had met the stamp tax. The Legislature did not assemble until the 24th of May, 1768, but public opinion had already settled its course. Instructions had been received by the various governors to dissolve the assemblies of their provinces, if they manifested any disposition to unite in measures of opposition.

3. But the Assembly of Maryland was too wary to be thus circumvented. It prepared its measures in advance. Massachusetts had issued a circular advising the sister colonies to frame petitions to the crown. The Assembly took into consideration the Massachusetts circular, and appointed a committee to draft a petition to the king.

4. The governor warned them that they would be prorogued if they persisted. Without reply or delay, they instantly adopted the petition, passed a series of resolutions, which they had already framed; and, having taken every step the occasion demanded, drew up a sharp reply to the gov-

---

Questions.—2. What is said of the press? Instructions to governors? 3. What had the Assembly of Maryland done? 4. What further took place?

ernor, stating their readiness to be prorogued.—They were accordingly dissolved.

5. The colonists were not yet prepared for an appeal to arms. Having tried petition and remonstrances, they determined to resort once more to "non-importation" which had been introduced in the days of the stamp act.

6. At an early period of the struggle, county associations had been formed in Maryland. For the purpose of united action, it was now deemed expedient to embody them together. On the 20th of June, 1769, the people assembled at Annapolis, and entered into articles of non-importation of British superfluities, for promoting frugality, economy and the use of American manufacture.

7. In the beginning of the ensuing year, the spirit of the associators was put to the test. "The Good Intent," a British bark, arrived in the harbor of Annapolis, with a cargo of obnoxious articles. It was resolved that the goods should not be landed, and the bark was compelled to return to London with her whole cargo.

8. Long before the destruction of tea in Boston harbor by disguised men, the patriots of Maryland, calmly, openly and in the presence of the governor and the provincial officers, discussed and set at

---

Questions.—5. To what did the colonies now resort? 6. What is said of county associations? Of the meeting at Annapolis? 7. What test of their determinations did they now have? 8. What is said in this section?

defiance this obnoxious act, and more effectually, though more peacefully, prevented its execution.

9. The British merchants sent no more prohibited goods to Maryland; and the ministry, alarmed at the opposition, promised the repeal of the duty on all articles except tea. While Maryland stood firm, the other colonies began to give way. New York deserted the association; Philadelphia followed. Several merchants of Baltimore requested the associators to consider the matter. Delegates from all the counties met at Annapolis, but so far from yielding their consent, they denounced both the proposition and its authors. At last, Boston gave up the system. Maryland never abandoned its pledge.

CHAPTER XXII.

THE PROCLAMATION AND THE VESTRY ACT—*Pay of Public Officers—Tithes—Expiration of the Law—Proclamation—Party Spirit—Dulany and Carroll.*

1. The public officers did not receive regular salaries, but were paid by fees given for each service performed. The profits of some officers became enormous, and the people became restless under these exactions.

Questions.—9. What did the ministry promise? What is said of Maryland? Did Boston yield? Did Maryland? 1. What is said of the pay of public officers?

2. There was also another burden. The clergy of the Church of England, which had been established by law, were supported by tithes, or taxes. The rate was, at first, forty pounds of tobacco a head, afterwards, thirty pounds. As the population increased, the income of the parishes became enormous.

3. In the spirit of opposition to unjust burdens, these too did not escape. The legislature endeavored to diminish the amount of the fees, and obtain other reforms. The House of Delegates, having ordered the arrest of a clerk for taking illegal fees, was prorogued by the governor.

4. The law that gave the clergy thirty pounds of tobacco a head, instead of forty, having expired, they claimed that the old law was in force, and the governor issued a proclamation fixing the old rates of fees.

5. The intolerant spirit which had cheerfully sustained the tax for the support of the clergy, as a weapon of offence against non-conformists, was now passing away. The clergy moreover being appointed by the governor, the sympathies, therefore, as well as the interests of that body, were likely to be with the governor and his party, who were the representatives of arbitrary power.

Questions.—2. What other burden? 3. What did the legislature endeavor to do? 4. What law expired? What did the clergy claim? What proclamation? 5. What is said in this section?

6. The people, therefore, were generally opposed to the clergy, and as they never would submit to the exercise of arbitrary power, the proclamation at once roused up all the fire of "The Sons of Liberty."

7. Parties were immediately formed. The governor, officials, and their adherents, formed one party; the body of the people, headed by the lawyers, the other. Great excitement prevailed; public opinion was appealed to in every mode.

8. Prominent among the disputants were the leaders of the two parties. That of the party of privilege, was Daniel Dulany, at that time the most eminent lawyer in the province, who also had done the people good service in the days of the stamp act, but who now formed an exception to his class, which was all with the people. He held the most lucrative office, and resisted every attempt to infringe upon the profits of place. The leader of the popular party was a young man, spirited, wealthy, and highly educated, one of the brightest in the galaxy of bright names that have shed lustre upon the history of Maryland—Charles Carroll of Carrollton.

Questions.—6. What was the effect of the proclamation? 7. What parties were formed? 8. Who were the leaders?

CHAPTER XXIII.

CHARLES CARROLL OF CARROLLTON—*Birth and Education—Return to Maryland—First entrance into Public Life—"First Citizen"—Dulany—Triumph of Carroll.*

CHARLES CARROLL, *of Carrollton.*

1. This eminent man, and intrepid champion of liberty, was descended from a family which had settled in the province before the revolution of 1689. He was born at Annapolis in 1737, and at eight years of age was sent to France to be educated.

2. At the age of twenty he commenced the study of law in London. He returned to Maryland in 1764, just in time to enter into the strife which his countrymen were waging against tyranny. As he was a Roman Catholic, he was numbered among the disfranchised. But this personal injustice, while it excluded him from the councils, did not prevent him from sympathising in the wrongs of his people.

Questions.—1. Birth and education? 2. Why disfranchised?

3. His first entrance into the conflict was his opposition to the stamp act, and the taxation of commerce. But now he had to deal with a powerful and skilful adversary. Mr. Dulany was his equal in education, his superior in age, experience and reputation; in fine, with all the odds in his favor.

4. Trusting, however, in the justice of his cause and the integrity of his purpose, Carroll did not hesitate to enter into the contest. The dispute was carried on under the names of "*First Citizen*" and "*Antilore*," Carroll adopting the first name.

5. The way by which he came to adopt this singular title was as follows: Dulany had written a dialogue, as if held by two citizens, and, instead of giving them names, he called them "First Citizen" and "Second Citizen." He so managed this supposed discussion that the "First Citizen," who was meant to represent the party opposed to the proclamation, was defeated in the argument. Carroll assumed the name of the "First Citizen," and carried on the dialogue with more justice to the side represented by that character.

6. Dulany found a foeman worthy of his steel, and the man of straw which he had made proved a

---

Questions.—3. What was his first entrance into the conflict? Who was his opponent? 4. What name did he adopt? 5. How came he to adopt it? 6. Who was his opponent?

giant in his path. Though attacked with invective, and taunted with that, which if not his glory was their shame — "that he was a disfranchised man, and could not even vote at an election,"— Carroll calmly fought the fight of liberty, and triumphed.

7. He triumphed with the people; he lived to see them free, and great, and prosperous. He was the last survivor of the noble band of patriots who signed the Declaration of Independence, and when he died, in the ninety-sixth year of his age, the tears not only of Maryland, but of the American people flowed for him.

8. The election that took place in the midst of all this excitement, resulted in the complete success of the popular party. The people acknowledged their gratitude to their able champion. They could not select him as their delegate, for though the champion of their liberty, he was himself enthralled. But, in accordance with instructions given by the people in public meetings held in Frederick, Baltimore and Annapolis, the delegates presented the thanks of the people to "The First Citizen."

Questions.—7. What is said of his triumph? 8. What party succeeded at the election? How did the people shew their gratitude to Carroll?

CHAPTER XXIV.

1773-4—REVIVAL OF THE TAX ON TEA—*Tax, the Badge of Servitude—The right to Tax, not the Amount, the matter of Dispute—Convention—Aid to Boston—Burning of the Tea at Annapolis—Characteristics of this Act.*

STATE HOUSE, *Annapolis.*

1. During all these excitements, the colony had been free from the difficulties with the mother country, which so agitated the Northern colonies. From the nature of the Proprietary government, the crown could not exercise any control over the affairs of the province; it was therefore free from many of the dissensions arising under the royal governments.

2. But Maryland was not less ready to contend, when a principle was at stake. The tax on tea had not yet been repealed, but the hatred to it, for it was the badge of servitude, kept the people

Questions.—1. From what had the colony been free? Why? 2. What is said of the tax on tea?

faithful to their pledge that they would not use the article.

3. Great quantities of tea, therefore, accumulated in the store-houses of the East India Company, and their business was interferred with. The English goverment offered the company to pay them back the duty on all tea which they exported to the colonies. This would enable the company to sell the tea as cheap in the colonies, with the tax added, as they sold it in England; and at the same time the government would not be giving up their right to impose the tax.

4. But it was about the right to impose the tax, and not the price of tea, that colonists were contending, and they were too shrewd to be deceived. The duty on tea was the badge of English supremacy, and they never consented to wear it; they knew too, that the most successful resistance is that which is prompt, and they acted accordingly.

5. Public meetings were held, and resolutions adopted to prevent the landing of the tea. In Charleston, it was landed, but never exposed for sale; the vessels containing it, that arrived in New York and Philadelphia, were compelled to return. In Boston, the tea was thrown overboard by persons disguised as Indians.

Questions.—3. What did the English government propose? 4. Why did not the colonies accede? 5. What was done to the tea in different places?

6. The people of Maryland called for a convention. This body proposed an absolute cessation of all intercourse with the mother country, and directed subscriptions to be made for the relief of the Bostonians, who were suffering the vengeance of the thwarted and enraged government. This was the second time Massachusetts had experienced the generosity of Maryland. The first, was on the occasion of a disastrous fire in Boston, when the governor of Maryland ordered collections to be made in all the churches, for the relief of the sufferers. And it was done.

7. In August, 1774, the brigantine "Mary and Jane," arrived in the St. Mary's river, with tea on board for merchants in Georgetown and Bladensburg. The committee of Charles county summoned the master, and one of the consignees to appear before them. But as the tax had not been paid, they were discharged upon their pledge that the tea should not be landed, but sent back to England. The committee of Frederick county pursued a similar course with the consignees at Georgetown.

8. Every child is familiar with what is called "the tea party of Boston," but an affair equalling it in every respect was transacted at Annapolis, namely, the tea-burning—open and *undisguised*, shewing the high toned and manly trait that has

---

Questions.—6. What did the people of Maryland do? What assistance did they render Massachusetts? 7. What vessel arrived with tea? What was done? 8. What is said in this section?

always characterized a true Marylander—a willingness to assume the responsibility for all he does, and to abide the consequences.

9. On the 14th of October, the brig Peggy Stewart, arrived at Annapolis, having in its cargo a few packages of tea. The duty was paid by the owner of the vessel. The people were outraged at the attempt to fix upon them the badge of servitude, by the payment of the tax.

10. A meeting was held, at which it was determined that the tea should not be landed. The owner, fearing further trouble proposed to destroy the tea. But that was not sufficient punishment. The offence was a grave one, for had this attempt succeeded, it would have been followed by others more aggressive, and thus the very principle which was contended for, would have been overthrown in the end. It was the head of the ugly beast that was thrust in the door, and it must not only be *put* out, but *driven* out by blows, lest growing bold it should push its whole body in

11. After much discussion, it was proposed to burn the vessel. The meeting did not consent to this, but many expressed their determination to raise a force to accomplish the brig's destruction.

Questions.—9. What other vessel arrived? What had the owner done? Feelings of the people? What was the payment of the tax regarded as? 10. What was determined? What did the owner propose? 11. What was proposed at the meeting?

12. Acting under the advice of Mr. Carroll of Carrollton, the owner seeing that the loss of his property was certain, and willing to repair his good name, even by that loss, proposed to destroy the vessel with his own hands. In the presence of the assembled multitude, he set fire to it with the tea on board—expiating his offence by the destruction of his property.

BURNING THE TEA, *Annapolis Harbor.*

13. The striking features of this transaction, were not only the boldness with which it was executed, but the deliberation and utter carelessness of concealment in all the measures leading to its accomplishment

Questions.—12. What did the owner now propose? 13. What were the striking features of this act?

CHAPTER XXV.

THE LAST PROPRIETARY—*First Continental Congress—Attachment of Maryland to the family of Baltimore—Extinction of the Family—Henry Harford—Condition of the Colony.*

1. The First Continental Congress met at Philadelphia, on 5th of September, 1774. It issued a manifesto setting forth the rights and grievances of the colonies, and proposing the scheme of non-importation of British goods.

2. On its adjournment, the Maryland Convention again assembled, and approved of the proceedings of the Congress; with the organization of this convention closed the power and dominion of the last Proprietary of Maryland.

3. The people of Maryland had always loved and revered the family of the founder of the province. Under the government of his descendants, they had enjoyed a large liberty, and a constantly increasing prosperity. They ever bore testimony to the kind and paternal rule of the Proprietaries.

4. It seemed as if Providence, when the great struggle for independence was approaching, severed the link, which might have so held them to their old allegiance, that they would have been less ardent in the common cause.

Questions.—1. Meeting of Congress? What did it issue? 2. Meeting of the Maryland Convention? 3. What had been the feelings toward the family of the founder of the colony?

5. In 1758, Frederick, last of the lords of Baltimore, became a widower. He had no children by his wife, and he never married again. He was in the same year charged with a criminal offence, of which he was acquitted, but it is known that he led a dissolute and degraded life. He died at the age of forty, in Italy, in 1771.

6. He devised the province to his illegitimate son, Henry Harford, Esq. The title of Lord Baltimore could not descend to him, and thus the name of the founders of the colony passed from their descendants just as the rule over it was about to cease. The people of Maryland cared nothing for the man who was an alien in name, and of illegitimate birth. A Proprietary of this kind could only increase the discontent.

7. Henry Harford was the last Proprietary, and Robert Eden was the last English Governor of Maryland. After the close of the war of the Revolution, the late proprietary and his governor returned together into the State. Eden died shortly after, near the City of Annapolis.

8. A period of one hundred and forty years had passed since two hundred pilgrims, under Leonard Calvert, landed at the southern extremity of the province. Their descendants had extended themselves to its northern boundary, covered its eastern

---

Questions.—5. What is said of Frederick, last lord of Baltimore? 6. Who was his heir? 7. Who was the last proprietary? Who the last English governor?

shore with wealth and civilization, crossed the Blue Ridge, filling its valleys with a bold and hardy population. Commerce was filling its bays and rivers with fleets; the forge and the furnace were already at work; in short, though hampered by the restrictive laws of England, the germs of her future prosperity were budding forth and giving promise of the greatness which this day sees realized.

9. Thus stood the colony in the crisis which was approaching, with a people liberal in their sentiments, proud of their liberties, prepared to extend them, and ready to maintain them with their blood.

THE LORDS PROPRIETARY OF MARYLAND.

1632—CECILIUS CALVERT..................*Second Lord Baltimore.*
1675—CHARLES CALVERT..................*Third Lord Baltimore.*
1715—BENEDICT LEONARD CALVERT...*Fourth Lord Baltimore.*
1715—CHARLES CALVERT..................*Fifth Lord Baltimore.*
1751—FREDERICK CALVERT....*Sixth and last Lord Baltimore.*
1771-1776—HENRY HARFORD, Esq.....*Last Proprietary.*

THE COLONIAL GOVERNORS.

Proprietary Governors.

1633—LEONARD CALVERT.
1647—THOMAS GREEN.
1649—WILLIAM STONE.
1654—COMMISSIONERS UNDER PARLIAMENT.
1658—JOSIAH FENDALL.
1661—PHILIP CALVERT.
1662—CHARLES CALVERT.
1667—CHARLES, LORD BALTIMORE.
1678—THOMAS NOTELY.
1681—CHARLES, LORD BALTIMORE.
1685—WILLIAM JOSEPH, *Pres. of Deputies.*
1689—CONVENTION OF PROTESTANT ASSOCIATION.

Royal Governors.

1691—SIR LIONEL COPLEY.
1693—SIR EDMOND ANDROS.
1694—FRANCIS NICHOLSON.
1699—NATHANIEL BLACKISTONE.
1703--THOMAS TENCH, *Pres.*
1704—JOHN LEYMOUR.
1709—EDWARD LLOYD, *Pres.*
1714—JOHN HART.

Proprietary Governors.

1715—JOHN HART.
1720—CHARLES CALVERT.
1727—BENEDICT LEONARD CALVERT.
1732—SAMUEL OGLE.
1733—CHARLES, LORD BALTIMORE.
1735—SAMUEL OGLE.
1742—THOMAS BLADEN.
1747—SAMUEL OGLE.
1752—BENJAMIN TASKER, *Pres.*
1753—HORATIO SHARPE.
1769—ROBERT EDEN.

COLONIAL POPULATION OF MARYLAND.

Year	Population	Year	Population
1634	about 200	1715	50,200
1660	12,000	1748	130,000
1665	16,000	1756	154,188
1671	20,000	1776	about 200,000
1701	30,000		

FORMATION OF COUNTIES UNDER COLONIAL GOVERNMENT.

1633—ST. MARY'S.
—KENT.
1650—ANNE ARUNDEL.
1654—CALVERT.
1658—CHARLES.
1659—BALTIMORE.
1661—TALBOT.
1666—SOMERSET.
1669—DORCHESTER.
1674—CECIL.
1695—PRINCE GEORGE'S.
1706—QUEEN ANNE'S.
1742—WORCESTER.
1748—FREDERICK.
1773—CAROLINE.
1773—HARFORD.
1776—WASHINGTON.
1776—MONTGOMERY.

PART II.

CHAPTER I.

THE REVOLUTION—*Convention—Power of Public Sentiment—Resolution of Maryland to stand by Massachusetts—New York and Maryland—Washington appointed Commander-in-Chief—Formation of Maryland Line—Riflemen—Want of Supplies.*

1. The convention called upon the people of Maryland to bury all private animosities, all religious disputes, all memory of past persecution, and "in the name of God, their country, and posterity, to unite in defence of the common rights and liberties."

2. On the 8th of December, 1774, the convention again assembled to make preparations for an armed resistance to the power of England. The old government still retained the form and machinery of power; the new, without these, possessed an irresistible authority throughout the colony. The source of its power was not its legal form, but public sentiment. Resting on this it

---

Questions.—1. What did the convention call upon all to do? 2. When did the convention again meet? For what purpose? What was the source of the power of the convention?

needed not penalties and judicial tribunals, for the dominion that has public sentiment for its throne is irresistible.

3. All who refused to submit to the decrees of the convention were denounced by that body, and from that moment the offenders became the object of the withering scorn and contempt of their countrymen. And this has more terrors than the stake.

4. Having provided for the exercise of their authority, the convention resolved that if the crown attempted to carry out by force the measures against Massachusetts, Maryland would assist her to the last extremity. They then ordered all males from sixteen to fifty years of age, to be enrolled and organized into companies; to be armed, equipped, and drilled, ready for instant service.

5. These resolves were immediately carried out; old and young enrolled with the greatest enthusiasm. Maryland was girding herself for the struggle in which she won so glorious a name. The convention was to meet again on the 24th of April, 1775; on the 19th the struggle broke out into open conflict, and the first blood shed in the revolutionary war was at Lexington. The blow was struck and the American people sprung to arms for the defence of their liberties.

Questions.—3. What was done to those who refused to submit? 4. What did the convention resolve to do? 5. When was the convention to meet again? What took place on the 19th.

6. Elsewhere, it was suggested by the timid that submission would ensure reconciliation. The city of New York was cold, but in Maryland, the people were long since prepared for the resort to arms. The Connecticut troops had to be placed within a short distance of New York, to overawe the tory tendencies of many of the people. But subsequently, the Connecticut troops themselves were charged by Washington with deserting the cause of their country at the most critical moment. Their ill-timed yearning for home was bad enough; but they not only took themselves off, but the ammunition also, leaving none for the Maryland troops, whose fondness for home never overcame their sense of honor.

7. After the battle of Bunker Hill, there was no more hesitation. Congress determined, not only to defend the rights of the people, but to drive out the British troops. Boston was ordered to be invested. Thos. Johnson, of Maryland, had the honor of nominating Gen. Washington, as Commander-in-Chief of the American forces. The election was by ballot, and was unanimous. Washington's modesty in accepting this important trust, was equalled only by the confidence the country reposed in his abilities, and was the surest evidence of his fitness.

Questions.—6. What did the timid suggest? What is said of New York, and of Maryland? 7. What was the result of the battle of Bunker Hill? What did Congress determine? Who nominated Gen. Washington as commander-in-chief?

8 Although Johnson, of Maryland, nominated Washington, Adams, of Massachusetts, claimed the honor of first bringing him forward as the proper person for the emergency. Hancock, of Massachusetts, who was presiding, shewed evident marks of disapprobation and resentment at Adams' honorable allusions to "a gentleman from Virginia," for he did not mention Washington by name. New England was desirious of having one of their own men made commander-in-chief.

9 On the 26th of July, the convention of Maryland again met, and their first step was to adopt the famous "Association of Freemen of Maryland." This became the written constitution of the province until the new system was framed in 1776.

10. They also set about the formation of a regular force, to be composed of a battalion, of which Colonel Smallwood received the command, and of seven independent companies, numbering in all 1444 men, besides two companies of artillery, and one of marines.

11. By a resolution of Congress, two companies of riflemen were called for, from Maryland. These companies were soon filled with the hardy pioneers of Western Maryland. Capt. Cresap's company numbered one hundred and thirty men, who were

---

Questions.—8. What is said of Hancock? What did New England desire? 9. When did the convention again meet, and what was their first step? 10 What did they set about? 11. What is said of riflemen?

armed with tomahawks and rifles, were painted like Indians, and were dressed in hunting shirts and moccasins. These men were ordered to march to the camp around Boston, being joined by like companies from Virginia and Pennsylvania.

12. The arrival of these stalwart fellows, such as Washington had known in his early campaigns —many of them upwards of six feet high, and of vigorous frame—in their fringed frocks and round hats, excited great wonder among the rustic visitors of the camp. Their dash, their skill—they could hit a mark while advancing at quick step, at the distance of two hundred and fifty yards—their striking costume, caused them to be looked upon with some jealousy by the plainer troops about them, who seemed to think that all valor, as well as virtue, was enclosed in the round jacket and trowsers of Marblehead; and it was well for the gaily clad sons of the South, that their behavior in battle was always equal to the expectation they excited. In the sharpest conflicts of the war, it was they "who stemmed the current of the heady fight."

13. The officers of these were Michael Cresap, Thomas Warren, Joseph Cresap, Jr., Richard Davis, Thomas Price, Otho H. Williams and John Ross Key.

14. Many were too impatient to endure the delay of organizing these troops, and hastened to

---

Questions.—12. What is said of their appearance in camp? What is said of their skill? 13. Who were their officers? 14. What did many do?

join the camp before Boston, at their own expense. Among these was James Wilkinson, afterwards a Major-General in the Uuited States service.

15. The great difficulty to be contended against was the want of supplies. The arsenal at Annapolis, was almost empty. To overcome these difficulties, the convention offered bounties and encouragement for the manufacture of such articles as were most needed—such as saltpetre, materials for clothes, and munitions of war. Powder mills were erected, and Mr. Hughes, of Frederick county, agreed to furnish the province with cannon.

CHAPTER II.

LORD DUNMORE—*Plans of Lord Dunmore—Attempt to inflict a Servile War—Discovery of his Plans—Aid to Eastern Shore of Virginia—Batteries Erected near Baltimore—"The Otter"—"The Defence"—State Navy—Gov. Eden—Civil Authority and Military Power—Eden Sent to England—Militia Sent to the Coast—Flying Camp.*

1. As yet Maryland had not even been threatened with hostilities. But a period of real danger was approaching. This arose from the attempts

---

Questions.—15. What was the great difficulty to be contended against? How did the convention overcome these difficulties? 1. What danger now threatened Maryland?

of Lord Dunmore, the late royal governor of Virginia. It was his plan to raise an army in the western parts, and cut off all communication between the northern and southern provinces. The tories and Indians were to be enrolled, an army to be formed with artillery gathered up from the line of fortresses on the north and west, and this army was to cut its way to Alexandria, where Dunmore would join it, bringing with him servants and negroes, and others belonging to rebels—in the words of Washington Irving—to inflict upon Virginia, the horrors of a servile war.

2. His plans, however, were discovered by the arrest of one of his agents, in Frederick county. While endeavoring to organize a force in the west, Dunmore was actively engaged in scattering the seeds of disaffection on the Eastern Shore of Maryland. He succeeded in raising several companies of men pledged to support the royal cause, if arms and ammunition should be furnished them. But this conspiracy was crushed out by the committee of safety of the Eastern Shore.

3. Two companies of militia from Kent and Queen Anne's, under Captains Kent and Henry, marched to Northampton county, on the Eastern Shore of Virginia, to repel the invasion of that

---

Questions.—1. What was Dunmore's plan? 2. How were his plans discovered? What was Dunmore doing on the Eastern Shore? What success had he? 3. How was the Eastern Shore of Virginia protected?

section. They remained there long after their term had expired, rather than leave their neighbors unprotected.

4. To prevent the harbors of Maryland from being bombarded by Dunmore, batteries were erected near Baltimore and Annapolis, and several merchant vessels were manned and armed as vessels of war. The basin at Baltimore was also obstructed by three heavy chains of wrought iron stretched across its mouth, and by vessels sunk in the channel. The public records were removed from Annapolis to Upper Marlborough.

5. Early in March, 1776, the Otter, a British sloop of war, with two tenders, captured several small vessels in the Chesapeake bay. She anchored a few miles below Baltimore, with the intention of destroying the State Ship Defence, then nearly completed, in that harbor. Captain Nicholson, who commanded the Defence, hastily prepared his vessel, with the intention of recapturing the prizes. Accompanied by several smaller vessels, on a hazy morning, he bore down upon the Otter. The British were completely surprised; the tenders escaped with difficulty, and all the prizes were retaken.

6. The Otter bore away for Annapolis, but finding this place fortified, she dropped down the bay

---

Questions.—4. What was done to the harbors in the bay? What at Baltimore? At Annapolis? 5. What British vessel threatened Baltimore? What was her design? What did Capt. Nicholson do? 6. Where did the Otter now go?

without having won either booty or success. The militia followed her down the bay shores as fast as possible, and succeeded in preventing her from capturing a prize that was almost within her grasp.

7. On the 5th of June, the gallant Nicholson received a commission in the new Continental Navy, and took command of the frigate Virginia. Many other Marylanders entered into the service, among whom none were more distinguished than Captain William Halleck and Joshua Barney.

8. Mr. Eden, the last English governor, still remained in the province, although the real supremacy was in the hands of the convention. His politic course, his want of power to hurt, and his personal popularity preserved him from the exile, which had been the fate of other provincial governors. But letters to him from the English ministry, commanding him to hold himself ready to assist the crown, having been intercepted, it was no longer deemed prudent to permit him to remain.

9. He was arrested by the military. The committee of safety of Maryland, who were the civil authority, immediately resented this usurpation of their prerogative; they summoned the officer, reprimanded him, and ordered him to return to his post. The people of Maryland were not disposed

---

Questions.—6. What did the militia do? 7. What is said of Nicholson, and other officers? 8. What is said of Mr. Eden? Why was it thought prudent that he should not remain? 9. By whom was he arrested? What did the civil authority do?

to submit to the military dogma *inter arma leges silent.** Military men, whose business is violence, are apt to confound physical power with legal and moral right. For that reason a republican people are always jealous of military rule, and keep it subordinate to civil authority. The military is the servant of the civil power, and when the master yields to the servant, liberty is gone, and tyranny is the result.

10. The committee of safety, however, considered the presence of Eden dangerous, and gave him notice to depart, which he did, on board the "Fowey," dispatched by Lord Dunmore to receive him.

11. Dunmore was threatening Maryland with his vengeance, and the militia was ordered to the coast to cut off his communication with the disaffected. At the same time the convention set about organizing the flying camp, called for by congress. The quota to be furnished was three thousand four hundred and five men.

*In the din of arms, the laws are silent.

Questions.—9. What is said of military men? What is the office of the military? 10. What was done with Eden? 11. What was Dunmore threatening? Where were the militia ordered? What camp did the convention organize?

CHAPTER III.

DECLARATION OF INDEPENDENCE—*Vain Hopes of Settlement—Rebels or Freemen—Order issued by the Convention of Maryland—Charles Carroll of Carrollton—State Government—Disposition of Troops.*

1. For a long time the people of America hoped and thought they could obtain their rights without severing their allegiance to the mother country. But the course of England in pouring troops into the country to conquer, rather than conciliate, aroused the spirit of hostility, and taught them that they had not only to resist encroachments upon their rights, but that they must advance to the position of independence. They must be either subdued rebels or triumphant freemen. Their victories during the last year convinced them that they had a reasonable hope for the latter. Maryland was in full sympathy with these feelings.

2. On the 28th of June, 1776, the convention of Maryland unanimously withdrew the instructions previously given to her delegates in Congress, "to disavow all design of independence," and ordered that they should unite on behalf of the province in declaring the colonies free and independent, reserving to the State, however, complete internal sovereignty.

Questions.—1. What did the people for a long time hope? What raised the spirit of hostility? What did they learn? 2. What did the Maryland Convention order?

3. Charles Carroll was chiefly instrumental in obtaining the passage of this act. He had been on a mission to Canada with Chase and Franklin, to induce that province to form a union with the United Colonies, for their mutual interest and common destiny. On his return, he found the Maryland delegates hampered with the "instructions" mentioned above. The loss of a single hour might deprive his beloved State of a share in the glorious act then about to be performed. In these circumstances he and his friends brought all their energies, eloquence and arguments to bear upon the Convention in favor of the immediate repeal of the old instructions, and in favor of the new.—The new instructions were received on the 2d of July. On the 4th of July, together with Matthew Tilghman, Thomas Johnson, Jr., William Paca, Samuel Chase, Thomas Stone, and Robert Alexander, he was chosen delegate to Congress.

4. On the 2d of July, the Declaration of Independence had been prepared, and was introduced. On the 4th, it was adopted, but was not signed until the second of August. Carroll, having been chosen delegate after its passage, might have avoided the signature which would have been the evidence of his treason, had America failed. As it was said there were several Charles Carrolls, and

---

Questions.—3. Who was chiefly instrumental in this? When was he chosen delegate to congress? Who else were chosen? 4. On what day was the Declaration of Independence adopted?

that he could not be identified, he immediately added "of Carrolton," the name of his estate, remarking as he did so, "They cannot mistake me now." From this circumstance he ever afterwards bore the surname "of Carrolton."

5. The declaration of independence having been made, it was necessary to frame a permanent government for the new State. The convention ordered an election of delegates to assemble and form a constitution. Then having confided the supreme power in the hands of the committee of safety, it adjourned. One of its last acts was to place the State troops at the disposal of congress. The battalion under Col. Smallwood, and the independent companies in the counties, attached to his command, were ordered to Philadelphia, to be marshalled at once into the national service.

CHAPTER IV.

THE MARYLAND TROOPS AT THE BATTLE OF LONG ISLAND—*Condition of the American Army—Landing of the British—The Macaronis—The Battle—Terrible charge of the Marylanders—Loss of Marylanders.*

1. It was at a dark hour that the Maryland line was destined to enter the field. The British gene-

---

Questions.—4. What took place when Carroll signed it? 5. What steps were taken to form a new state government? What did the convention do about the state troops? Where were they ordered? 1. What was the number of troops of the British?

ral's forces amounted to 30,000 men, while the American were only 17,000, and nearly one-fifth of these were sick and unfit for duty.

2. On the 10th of July, six companies under Smallwood himself, from Annapolis, and three from Baltimore, embarked for the head of Elk river, whence they marched to New York, and were incorporated in Lord Sterling's brigade.— They were well appointed and organized, composed of young and spirited men, who had already acquired the skill and precision of drilled soldiers. "There was none by whom an unofficer-like appearance and deportment could be tolerated less than by a Marylander, who, at this time, was distinguished by the most fashionable cut coat, the most *Macaroni* cocked hat, and hottest blood in the Union."

3. Arriving at a time when the army was lamentably deficient in discipline, they immediately won the confidence of the commander-in-chief; and, from the moment of their arrival, were thrown upon the advanced posts, and disposed as covering parties.

4. The four independent companies remaining in Maryland, were ordered to join Col. Smallwood, as was also the flying camp, now rapidly organizing.

Questions.—1. Of the Americans? 2. What is said of Smallwood's battalion? What of their appearance? 3. What of their arrival? 4. What is said of the independent companies?

5. From the 21st of August to the 27th, the British were landing their troops on Long Island. On the 20th, the Maryland troops were ordered over to the scene of the approaching conflict. Putnam, who was in command of the American forces, having been out-manœuvred by the British general, ordered Sterling, with two regiments, to hold the enemy in check. One of these regiments was Smallwood's battalion — the *Macaronis* in scarlet and buff. They turned out with great alacrity, and placed themselves along a ridge, having Col. Atlee with Pennsylvania troops in ambush in advance.

6. As the British came up, the Pennsylvanians gave them two or three volleys and then retreated, and formed on Sterling's left. For several hours a severe cannonading was kept up on both sides, but no general engagement was sought by either party. Sterling's object was to keep the enemy in check. The instructions of the British general, Grant, were, not to press an attack until aware that Sir Henry Clinton was on the left flank of the Americans.

7. At length the left wing of the Americans having been turned by Clinton, and the centre broken, the situation of Sterling became danger-

Questions.—5. When did the British land their troops? What did Putnam order? What is said of Smallwood's battalion? 6. What did the Pennsylvanians do? What was Sterling's object? What were the British General's instructions? 7. What is said of the situation of Sterling?

ous in the extreme. Washington, who had come on the field during the battle, saw the danger to which the brave fellows under Sterling were exposed, though they themselves could not. He saw the enemy's reserve under Cornwallis, marching down by a cross road to get in the rear, and thus place them between two fires; and with breathless anxiety he watched the result.

8. The sound of Clinton's cannon apprised Sterling that the enemy was between him and the lines. Grant, too, who had held back all the morning, was closing up. In the rear lay an extensive marsh, traversed by a deep and dangerous creek, eighty yards wide at its mouth.

9. Leaving part of his men to face Grant, he selected four hundred of the Maryland battalion, and, ordering the rest of the troops to make the best of their way to the creek, marched to meet Cornwallis' brigade. Washington and others, who watched every movement, had supposed that Sterling and his troops would surrender in a body, but as the Marylanders, with fixed bayonet rushed to the charge upon the overwhelming force opposed to them, Washington wrung his hands, exclaiming: "Good God! what brave fellows I must this day lose."

Questions.—7. What did Washington see? 8. What first apprised Sterling of his danger? 9. How did he meet the danger? What did Washington suppose? What did he exclaim?

10. It was indeed a desperate fight. And now Smallwood's *Macaronis* showed their game spirit. Five times this little band charged upon the powerful forces of Cornwallis; five times they were driven back to gather new energies for a fiercer assault. Under the sixth, the heavy column of the British reeled and began to give way.

11. At the moment victory was in their grasp, Grant's brigade assailed them in the rear, and the Hessians came to the aid of Cornwallis in front. Already outnumbered more than ten to one, with their ranks thinned by the terrific slaughter, and worn down by long fighting, these devoted men could no longer make head against their foes.

12. Three companies cut their way through the crowded ranks of the enemy and maintained their order until they reached the marsh, where, from the nature of the ground, they broke and escaped as quickly as possible to the creek. This desperate conflict gave time to the remainder to make good their retreat across the marsh. They swam the water, bringing with them twenty-eight prisoners, and their tattered standard.

13. The loss of the Maryland troops in this deadly struggle was murderous. From sunrise, until the last gun was in the field, they were hotly

---

Questions.—10. What is said in this section? 11. What prevented the victory? 12. Did they surrender? What was the effect of this desperate fight? 13. What is said of the loss of the Maryland troops?

engaged, and when the rest of the army had been routed, or had fled, maintained the battle unaided, against two brigades of the enemy. Nearly half of their force was annihilated. Their loss in killed and wounded was 256, officers and men. To this day, the people of Long Island point out to strangers the spot where half of the Maryland battalion stemmed the advance of the whole left wing of the British army, when no other troops were left upon the field, and where the best blood of the State was poured out like water.

Questions.—13. How long were they engaged? What do the people of Long Island still do?

CHAPTER V.

MARYLAND TROOPS IN THE RETREAT—*Maryland Troops in the Advance Posts—Crossing the Ferry—Attempt to Surround the Americans—Disgraceful Retreat of the Connecticut Militia—Maryland Line Cover the Retreat —Battle at Harlem—Battle at White Plains—Attack on Fort Washington — Destruction of the Enemy's Troops by the Maryland and Virginia Rifles.*

GEN. SMALLWOOD.

1. It having been found necessary to retreat from Long Island, it was determined to do so before the ferry should be occupied by the enemy. This masterly movement was effected on the 29th of August.

2. Although the Maryland troops had enjoyed but one day's rest since their bloody conflict, they were ordered on duty at the advanced post of Fort Putnam, within two hundred and fifty yards of the

---

Questions.—1. Why was it necessary to be prompt in the retreat? When was the retreat effected? 2. Where were the Maryland troops ordered?

enemy's line, and, with two Pennsylvania regiments on the left, were to protect the retreat of the army.

3. Under cover of a foggy night and morning, the movement was happily effected, in spite of the disorder of the eastern troops; and it was not discovered by the enemy until the last detachment of Marylanders and Pennsylvanians was half way across the river and out of reach.

4. The British now attempted to surround the Americans on New York Island, and, it being found impossible to defend the city, in the disorganized condition of the troops, Washington resolved that the army should be withdrawn into the lines below Fort Washington. On the 15th of September, the enemy effected a landing without opposition, in the face of two brigades of Connecticut militia, who fled disgracefully at the fire from sixty of the British infantry.

5. Disgusted with such cowardice, General Washington immediately sent an express for the Maryland regiment, drew it from its brigade, and ordered it down towards New York, to cover the retreat of the army. He knew well he could rely upon its maintaining its position against all odds.

6. Smallwood posted his regiment, and they remained under arms the best part of the day until

---

Questions.—3. How was the retreat effected? 4. What did the British now attempt? What did Washington resolve? When did the enemy effect a landing? What is said of the Connecticut militia? 5. What did Washington do? 6. What did Smallwood do?

the last troops had passed. Having maintained his position as long as it was necessary, and having received notice to retreat, he retired in good order, and reached the lines about dusk.

7. On the next day, a body of three hundred British appeared in the plains below the American position. Having been attacked, and receiving a reinforcement of seven hundred men, Gen. Washington ordered up Major Price, with three of the Maryland independent companies, and Colonels Richardson's and Griffith's regiments of the Maryland flying camp. These troops attacked the enemy with the bayonet and drove them from their position.

8. In the battle at White Plains, the militia having taken to flight, and the artillery having retired in confusion, Smallwood's Maryland regiment was immediately advanced to meet the enemy. A long and severe conflict ensued; but, overpowered by superior numbers, it was compelled to give ground.

9. The Maryland regiment suffered severely; Col. Smallwood was himself among the wounded. The regulars of that gallant corps, worn down by the hard service they had endured, and the effects of their wounds, had been much weakened. Yet under all these trying circumstances, almost with-

---

Questions.—7. What took place the next day? 8. What is said of Maryland regiment in battle of White Plains? 9. Who was wounded?

out field officers, the Maryland line displayed its wonted valor at White Plains, and won new laurels for its State.

10. In the attack on Fort Washington, we again find the Marylanders distinguishing themselves. Posted among the trees, Rawling's riflemen, the hardy sons of the Maryland and Virginia mountains, poured upon the advancing column a murderous fire. The Hessians broke and retired. Again they were brought to the attack, and again repulsed with dreadful slaughter. The Maryland riflemen remembered the destruction of their brethren at the battle of Long Island by the Hessians, and did not forget to avenge it.

11. A single battalion of riflemen, whose weapons, from frequent discharges, had become foul and almost useless, could effect little, when opposed to five thousand men with the bayonet. They could not hope for victory, but they won great glory.

12. The fort was compelled to surrender.—Among the captives were Major Otho H. Williams, Lieutenants Luckett, Lingan, Davis and Evans. Some few Marylanders escaped across the river. The loss of the enemy was nearly twelve hundred, more than half of which was inflicted by Rawling's Maryland and Virginia riflemen.

Questions. — 9. What further is said of the Maryland line? 10. What is said of the attack on Fort Washington? 11. What of the riflemen? 12. What was the result? What was the loss of the enemy?

13. The victories of Trenton and of Princeton, during this celebrated retreat, were successful strategetic movements, rather than battles. They served to show the master-mind of Washington, but there was little of that hard fighting that shews the stuff the men were made of; hence in them, there are no particular instances of heroic deeds to record.

14. The campaign of 1776, was a dark and bloody one, but full of glory to the Maryland line; which, a powerful régiment in the month of August, was now reduced to a mere handful of men, under the command of a captain. In the battles from Brooklyn, Long Island, to Princeton, the *old* or first line was almost annihilated.

CHAPTER VI.

THE NEW CONSTITUTION AND STATE GOVERNMENT—*Convention—Division of Frederick County—Supplies for the Army—Constitution agreed to—Division of the Government—Qualifications for Voters—First State Legislature—Inducements to Enlist—The First Governor—Inauguration.*

1. An election having been held for delegates to a new convention to form a new constitution, this body assembled on the 14th of August, 1776, and

Questions.—13. What is said of the battles of Trenton and of Princeton? 14. What is said of the campaign of 1776? 1. For what was a new convention called?

organized, by unanimously electing Matthew Tilghman, President. The committee, appointed to prepare and report a declaration of rights, and form of government, was composed of Messrs. Tilghman, the President, Carroll, Paca, Carroll of Carrollton, Plater, Chase and Goldsborough.

2. On the 6th of September, the convention divided Frederick county, cutting off from it the counties now named Washington and Montgomery. The pressure of public business prevented the consideration of the bill of rights, and the constitution, which the committee had reported. This subject, therefore, was postponed, that they might give their attention to the condition of the troops, and the deficiency of all the material of war.

3. Ample supplies were determined upon, the committee of safety was ordered to import four thousand stand of arms, as many gun locks, fourteen cannons, twenty tons of powder, and forty tons of lead, to be purchased with wheat, tobacco, flour and other Maryland produce.

4. The quota of troops set down by Congress, to be furnished by Maryland, was eight battalions, numbering four thousand men, one-tenth of the whole army. This was larger in proportion than that levied on the northern States; still, Maryland,

---

Questions.—1. What committee was formed, and who composed it? 2. What counties were set off? What was said of the bills proposed by the committee? 3. What was the committee ordered to do? 4. What was Maryland's quota? What is said of this quota?

in her zeal for the general welfare, made no effort to get her quota reduced, but immediately took steps to furnish the troops.

5. On the 8th of November, after much deliberation, the new constitution of the State was finally agreed to, and elections were ordered to carry it into effect. The election took place in November 25th, 1776.

6. The government was composed of three distinct branches—the legislative, the executive, and the judiciary. The legislative authority was vested in a Senate and House of Representatives. The House of Delegates was composed of members from the counties, from Baltimore, and from Annapolis. The Senate consisted of fifteen members. The executive authority was in the hands of the governor. The judiciary was composed of the courts of the State.

7. Every voter was required to be the owner of fifty acres of land in the county in which he resided, or to possess property within the State to the value of thirty pounds current money. Delegates must own property to the value of five hundred pounds; Senators a thousand pounds; and the governor must possess a freehold of lands and tenements, of the value of a thousand pounds, and have resided three years within the State, prior to his election.

Questions.—5. When was the State constitution finally agreed to? 6. How was the government divided? 7. What were the qualifications of voters? Of senators? Of governor?

By the bill of rights, the conscience was left as free and untrammelled as in the days of Leonard Calvert.

8. The first State Legislature, met on the 5th of February, 1777. The first business that occupied their attention was the recruiting service. During the retreat from Long Island, the Maryland troops had been so reduced, that Smallwood's battallion, and the seven independent companies, which had entered the service fourteen hundred strong, had been worn down to a mere captain's command, and in the face of this great loss, it required corresponding exertions to fill up the quota of eight battalions.

9. To favor enlistments, every recruit was exempted from arrest for debts under twenty pounds, and his property was entirely freed from attachment and execution. To provide blankets for the soldiers, every family was obliged to give up one-half of their surplus articles of that kind for the use of the army.

10. On Friday, the 21st of March, 1777, Thomas Johnson was proclaimed first republican Governor of Maryland. The announcement was hailed by a salute from the military. Annapolis was the scene

---

Questions.—7. What about freedom of conscience? 8. When did the first State legislature meet? What was the condition of Maryland troops? 9. What was done to favor enlistments? How were blankets provided? 10. Who was first republican governor of Maryland?

of great festivities on the inauguration of the new government. The general and county committees of safety surrendered up their powers and ceased to exist. The State was under the law of the constitution.

CHAPTER VII.

CAMPAIGN OF 1777—*Increase and Division of the Maryland Line—Battle of the Brandywine—Deborre—Battle of Germantown—Success of the Marylanders—John Eager Howard—Marylanders not supported—Howe's Attack.*

1. The Maryland line, having been increased to seven battalions, was divided into two brigades. One, composed of four battalions, was placed under command of Smallwood, now promoted to the rank of Brigadier General. The commander of the other was General Deborre, a French officer, in the service of the confederacy.

2. On the 25th of August, the British army landed at the head of Elk river, and began their march upon Philadelphia. The Americans took post behind the Brandywine, and on the 10th of September, the British advanced to force their

---

Questions.—1. How was the Maryland line divided? Who were the officers? 2. When and where did the British land? Where did the Americans post themselves?

position. The Maryland line constituted a part of the division which was ordered to meet Cornwallis. But before the line could be formed, the Maryland division was attacked by the enemy. Deborre's brigade broke after a slight resistance, and subsequently the whole gave way. The Maryland line, while it behaved gallantly, scarcely sustained its ancient reputation—nor equalled its subsequent glory, when led by its own chiefs in the South.

3. Deborre was a foreigner, unpopular with his men, and entirely without their confidence. Gen. Smallwood and Col. Gist, leaders whom they would follow against any odds, were absent at the head of the militia. The troops had lain the night before on their arms, had slept but little, they had been in line all day without food, and were hurried into action only half-formed, after a rapid march, and sudden change of position.

4. The next fight in which we find the Maryland troops, was the battle of Germantown. This battle, though unsuccessful, was one that redounded very much to the credit of Washington and the American arms. Why it was not successful is not known. An unaccountable panic seized the Americans after orders to retreat had been given by the officers of the enemy.

Questions.—2. What is said of Deborre's brigade? 3. What is said of Deborre? What of the troops? 4. Where do we next find the Maryland line?

5. A regiment from the second Maryland brigade was detached to drive in the enemy's pickets. The pickets were reinforced by all the light infantry.—The attacking regiments, however, maintained their ground firmly, until the whole Maryland Division was brought to their assistance. They advanced in gallant style, and with such resolution, that the light infantry were driven from the field, after a sharp action, and their encampment fell into the hands of the victorious line.

6. In the pursuit, a company under Capt. Daniel Dorsey, was engaged with a body of the enemy. As the Maryland Division was pressing on, being already in advance of the rest of the army, Col. Hale attempted to disengage and bring up Dorsey's company, but was disabled by accident.

7. The command of his regiment devolved upon Major John Eager Howard, who immediately hurried the men forward through the camp of the light infantry, and captured two six-pounders. Being now fired upon by the enemy, who had taken shelter in a strong building, Col. Hazen, then in command at the left of the Maryland line, halted in the rear of that position.

8. The remaining regiments of the line under Sullivan, pursued the flying light artillery, and came upon the main body of the enemy drawn up

---

Questions.—5. What is said in this section? 6. What happened in the pursuit? 7. Upon whom did the command devolve? What did he do? 8. What did the remaining regiments do?

to receive them. A severe conflict followed. Sullivan at once ordered his Marylanders to advance upon them. They obeyed without hesitation. The enemy after a sharp resistance retired.

9. The firing at the dwelling house gave rise to the fear that the enemy was in force in that quarter, and the morning being dark and hazy, it was impossible to discover the exact position of either the British or American forces. The result was a considerable confusion, through which, the Maryland line—assisted by a regiment of North Carolinians and part of Conway's brigade—were now left open on their flank. Having pursued the enemy for a mile beyond the house, and having expended all their ammunition, they found themselves unsupported by any other troops, and, as the enemy were rallying on the left to attack them, were compelled to retire. They, however, brought off their cannon and their wounded.

10. Early in December, Howe marched his forces out of Philadelphia, as if to attack the American army. On the seventh, he approached near the main army. Washington, believing a general engagement at hand, threw Gist, with the Maryland militia, and Colonel Morgan's rifles forward, to attack their front and flank. The assault was made with great spirit, and after a severe

---

Questions.—9. What is said of the firing at the dwelling house? What further is said of the Maryland troops? 10. What is said of Howe? Repeat the section?

skirmish, the enemy's advanced parties were driven back. Being reinforced, they, in their turn compelled Gist and Morgan to retire.

11. Washington withheld his reinforcements, and prepared to defend his camp, and Howe, finding it impossible to take him at disadvantage, retired to the city. His loss in the action with the Maryland militia, was one hundred killed and wounded; that of the militia was seventeen wounded, and of the rifles, twenty-six killed and wounded.

12. While Washington was wintering at Valley Forge, the Maryland line, under Smallwood, was stationed at Wilmington. They succeeded in capturing a British brig, in the Delaware, laden with stores and provisions, which made their winter quarters comfortable, when compared to those of Valley Forge.

CHAPTER VIII.

1778 and 1779.—MORE TROOPS DEMANDED—*Disaffection—British Evacuate Philadelphia—Battle of Monmouth—General Lee—Washington's Reliance on Maryland Officers—Landing, and Retreat of British Troops.*

1. On the 17th of March, 1778, the legislature again assembled at Annapolis. Congress had

---

Questions.—11. What did Howe now do? What was his loss? What, of the militia? 12. Where did Smallwood winter?" 1. When did the legislature again meet?

called on the several States for an increase of their forces. The quota demanded from Maryland was two thousand nine hundred and two men.

2. While this quota was filling, Count Pulaski, a gallant Pole, was busily engaged forming his legion partly in this State and partly in Delaware.

3. He succeeded in raising a corps which did good service to the country. He perished in storming a battery at Savannah.

4. The drain upon Maryland was very great, in some parts of the State a great degree of disaffection still continued, and the population was scanty. Yet with all these drawbacks, before the other States had well moved in the matter, except New Jersey, the Maryland line was raised to its full number.

5. The severe winter spent by the army at Valley Forge, had almost exhausted the State. The northern and southern States had been very slow in sending their proportion of the provisions; the army, had, therefore, to depend largely upon Maryland, and it was feared that her resources were nearly consumed. But the energy of the governor in aiding the quartermaster's department, and the patriotism of the people were equal to the emergency.

Questions.—2. What is said of Count Pulaski? 3. What further is said of him? 4. What is said of the condition of Maryland? 5. What of the encampment at Valley Forge? What of the States north and south?

6. As the spring advanced, the British prepared to retreat from Philadelphia. Many were anxious to drive the enemy from the city, but the weakness of the American army rendered it too dangerous to make the attempt. None of the States, except Maryland and New Jersey, had filled up their quotas, although constantly urged by Washington to do so.

7. On the 18th of June, 1778, the British army evacuated Philadelphia, and crossed the Delaware. They had encamped at Monmouth Court House, in a strong position. Washington determined to attack them the moment they began to retire from the posts, and directed Lee to carry this design into execution.

8. General Lee having taken upon himself to judge of the propriety of engaging on the ground he occupied, ordered his troops to retire. At the first sound of the artillery, Washington moved on with the troops to support the advance. After a speedy march of five miles, he came upon Lee in full retreat, without having made an effort to maintain his position.

9. The crisis required promptness of action. Stopping only long enough to administer a stern

---

Questions.—6. What did the British prepare to do? What is said of the quotas of the State? 7. When did the British evacuate Philadelphia? Where did it encamp? What did Washington determine to do? 8. What is said of Gen. Lee? What did Washington do? 9. What further did he do and say?

and even fierce rebuke to Lee, Washington turned to Ramsay, who commanded a Maryland battalion, and Col. Stewart, commanding a regiment, and called to each of them that he "was one of the officers he should rely upon to check the enemy that day."

10. The enemy now opened their artillery upon Ramsay and Stewart, who were soon sharply engaged with the infantry. Though compelled to fall back before superior numbers, the obstinate defence made by the Marylanders, gave Washington time to draw up his lines of battle.

11. As soon as the scale of victory began to turn, Washington ordered up Patterson's division and Smallwood's brigade to secure the day. The British were driven back. But night coming on, the battle had to be suspended, and in the morning it was found that the British had retreated.

12. In November, the Maryland line was marched to Middlebrook, New Jersey, where Washington had established his head-quarters.

13. In February, 1779, the British landed a body of troops in New Jersey, with the design of taking Elizabethtown. Smallwood, with the Maryland line, and St. Clair, with the Pennsylvania division, were immediately ordered forward.

Questions.—10. Upon whom did the enemy open? What is said of the Marylanders? 11. What did Washington do? What further is said? 12. Where did the Maryland line now go? 13. What is said in this section?

The British, however, retreated without venturing a battle.

14. In July, the army was concentrated at West Point, New York. The Maryland line formed its right wing.

CHAPTER IX.

1779 AND 1781—*Maryland's Quota Large and always Full — Early Harvests — Arrival of French Fleet — Paper Money—Pensions to Troops—Depreciation of Currency —Confiscation—Tax—The Price of Liberty.*

1. Maryland had always kept its quota of troops full, and at one time its quota was one-third more than any other State, except Delaware, according to proportions fixed by congress.

2. But it was not only for men that the State was looked to; its wheat, ripening before that of the other wheat-growing States, was always required for the first supplies of the army. It was also bought up by the north for the use of the States, in that section.

3. This gave rise to a commerce that had to be protected from the British fleet. Maryland was, therefore, obliged to keep up a marine force of her

---

Questions.—1. What of the Maryland quota? 2. What besides men was required from Maryland? 3. What did this give rise to?

own. The fleet consisted of the ship Defence and several galleys, a sloop of war, and four barges.

4. The prize money, arising from captures made by these vessels, was distributed among the victorious crews, and was an incentive to exertion, which increased their usefulness.

5. The arrival of the French fleet, however, at a later period, rendered it unnecessary to maintain this force. The distressed condition of the finances made the reduction of the marine very desirable, as thereby the State was relieved of a great expense, and the men were employed as a portion of the State's quota for the campaign.

6. The expenses of the war increased so rapidly that it was found impossible to keep up with them by taxation. To furnish money, therefore, to pay the troops and to supply the necessities of trade, the States resorted to the means with which this generation is so familiar, namely, of issuing bills of credit, or paper money, which were made legal tender for the payment of debts.

7. The difference between the nominal value of this paper money and specie, was so great that forty dollars in paper were worth only one dollar in gold, or silver. An officer having been dis-

---

Questions.—3. What did the State fleet consist of? 4. What is said of the prize money? 5. What is said of the arrival of the French fleet? What was done with the marines? 6. To what did the State resort to raise money? 7. What is said of the value of this paper money?

patched to Baltimore to buy cloth for coats, after great difficulty, bought fifteen yards, for fifteen hundred pounds.

8. To ensure a just payment of the troops, the legislature of Maryland resolved that the officers of the Maryland line, who should serve to the close of the war, should be entitled to half-pay during life, to commence after the expiration of their pay from congress. This provision was also extended to their widows, during widowhood.

9. Thomas Johnson, having served three years as governor, was succeeded by Thomas Sim Lee. The depreciation of the currency, and the consequent high prices of provisions, compelled the legislature to enact very stringent laws against speculators, who bought up the necessities of life, in order to grow rich upon the distresses of the army.

10. It was also determined, as a matter of relief, to confiscate the estates of all those who had adhered to the royal cause. Their property was sold as that of British subjects, found within the State, as fair spoil of war. That injustice might not be done, an opportunity was allowed to the owners to come in and take the oath of allegiance to the State, prior to the first of March, 1782. This measure of confiscation, necessary as it was, was not passed without reluctance and serious opposi-

---

Questions.—8. What did the legislature do? 9. Who succeeded Gov. Johnson? What laws did the legislature pass? 10. What measure of relief was determined upon? What opportunity was given the disaffected?

tion, but the tax was one hundred pounds of paper money for every hundred pounds worth of property, nominally the whole worth of their property, but as paper money was worth only one-fortieth, the real tax was two and a half per cent. on all property, amounting often to more than half of the owner's income.

11. This tax was endured the more cheerfully because it was part of the price of liberty, and men knew that no price was too dear for that blessing. It was not a tax to support a party or a power, nor was it a tax to pay the cost of conquest; yet, even with all these advantages in its favor, the currency was in effect repudiated, and the governor's salary had to be paid in wheat, at the rate of forty-five hundred bushels per year.

CHAPTER X.

THE CONFEDERATION — *Delay of Confederation — Difficulty of adjusting Public Lands — Clause secured by Virginia—Maryland Objects—Compromise proposed by New York—Sovereign States—Maryland's efforts in the Common Cause.*

1. Early in the revolutionary struggle, a plan was introduced into congress for the confederation

---

Questions.—10. What rendered this act necessary? 11. What is said of the tax? How was the governor's salary paid? 1. What plan had been proposed in congress?

of the colonies. The matter had to be deferred from time to time, to give way to the pressing needs of the army.

2. One source of difficulty was the adjustment of the question of the public lands. Maryland was determined not to relinquish her claim to a portion of them, and was the last to hold out. Virginia claimed the unsettled territory of the west; Maryland maintained that if the dominion of those lands should be established by the blood and treasure of the United States, such lands ought to be considered as common property.

3. Virginia had succeeded in securing, in the articles of confederation, a clause, "that no State should be deprived of her territory, for the benefit of the United States." Maryland would not give in her adherence while that clause existed.

4. The compromise proposed by New York was, that each State should limit its western boundary, and cede to congress its claim to lands beyond it, in the purpose of erecting new States hereafter, and for no other purpose whatever. This effected a settlement and the articles of confederation were signed on the first day of March, 1781.

5. This was the germ of the Union. Each State preserved its separate and distinct sover-

---

Questions.—2. What was one source of difficulty? What position did Maryland take? 3. What clause had Virginia secured? 4. What compromise was offered, and by whom? 5. What is said in this section?

eignty. The United States, being the creation of the States, could not be greater than the power that created it. It could only exercise *acts* of authority delegated to it. It was the agent to exercise the power belonging to the States.

6. Questions were to be decided not by the people at large, but by the States themselves, a majority of them being required to carry a question.

7. The States agreed that congress, which represented them in their collective capacity, alone should exercise certain acts of sovereignty,—such as declaring war, laying imposts, and coining money,—which were essential for the common good.

8. Though Maryland had held aloof from the confederation, she had not relaxed her efforts in the common cause. At the very time when she was contending for her own rights with Virginia, her sons were fighting on the soil of this sister State for its defence, shedding their blood without stint upon every battle-field—the Maryland line and the Virginia regiments, side by side, bearing the brunt of the hard-fought southern campaigns. Her valor in the field, and her wisdom and firmness in the cabinet, have left their impress upon the country, however they may be ignored by partial writers of its history. Her valor in the

---

Questions.—6. How were questions to be decided? 7. What did the States agree to? 8. What is said of Maryland? What is said of her valor and firmness?

field either determined the victory, or saved the army in many a hard fought struggle, and her firmness in the cabinet gave rise to the formation of those States which this day constitutes the pride and power of the Republic—the great West.

CHAPTER XI.

THE MARYLAND LINE SOUTH—*Maryland Line sent to Reinforce the Southern Department—Passage through Maryland—Gates' Folly—Route marked by De Kalb—Changed by Gates—Battle at Camden—Dreadful Charge of the Marylanders — The whole British force brought against the Maryland Line—Virginia Militia.*

1. During the year 1779, the southern army had been unfortunate. Georgia and South Carolina were re-conquered by the enemy, and North Carolina was invaded.

2 In this critical state of affairs, it was resolved by congress that the Maryland and Delaware lines should be dispatched to reinforce that department.

3. In April, 1780, they were accordingly detached, under the command of Maj. Gen. De Kalb, and, after marching through New Jersey and Pennsylvania, embarked at the head of Elk river.

Questions.—1. What is said in this section? 2. What did congress resolve? 3. Under whose command were they placed?

4. The first and second brigades passed through the State early in May. They numbered about two thousand men, and most of that gallant and veteran army looked for the last time upon their beloved State. Yet proudly conscious of their noble bearing, and the honor they had won for it, they cheerfully marched on to new fields of glory.

5. The south was calling for their aid, and these men, who had shewn their prowess at the north—some, sharers with Gist of the bloody day upon Long Island, some, who fought at Harlem Heights, White Plains, Fort Washington, and through five severe campaigns—were hastening thither to cross their bayonets with British steel again.

6. The legislature directed the sum of three thousand dollars to be paid to each officer, and, to welcome their passage through the State, gratuities were distributed among the non-commissioned officers and privates.

7. On their march, they were overtaken and joined by Genl. Gates, who had been appointed to the command of the southern department.

8. The broken remains of the cavalry, which had served the preceding campaign, had been withdrawn to North Carolina to recruit. Its officers desired Gates to use his influence to fill his corps.

Questions.—4. What is said of their passage through the State? 5. What is said in this section? 6. How were they welcomed? 7. By whom were they joined? 8. What is said of the cavalry? What did the officers desire?

He refused to do so, thinking he had a sufficient force for his purpose. He learned to regret his folly.

9. De Kalb had already selected a route for the army, somewhat circuitous, but through a fertile country, where provisions and supplies could be obtained. Gates changed the course to a more direct one, but through a barren and exhausted district.

10. The result was disastrous; the men were compelled to live on green corn and unripe fruit, producing sickness and death. The horses, destitute of forage, were unable to support the forced marches, and the whole army, when it approached the enemy, was broken down, and scarcely fit for service.

11. The first battle in which they were called to engage was at Camden. Lord Cornwallis, the leader of the British, and Genl. Gates, had formed the design of surprising each other, and the advance parties of each met at half past two o'clock in the morning.

12. After some skirmishing, as if by mutual consent, both armies ceased their fire, and drawing back awaited the dawning of day. The artillery opened on both sides at day-break. To teach the

---

Questions.—9. What had DeKalb done? What did Gates do? 10. What was the result? 11. What was the first battle they were called upon to engage in? 12. When did the battle commence?

Virginia militia to stand the fire of the enemy, Col. Otho H. Williams, of Maryland, with a party of volunteers, moved in their front against the British artillery, to draw and sustain their fire. Cornwallis immediately threw forward his veteran corps. The Virginia militia, scarcely waiting to deliver one fire, threw down their arms and fled. One regiment of North Carolina militia followed their shameful example. Another North Carolina regiment, however, cheered by the firm bearing of the Marylanders, maintained its ground.

13. At the moment the left wing broke, Cornwallis elated with success, ordered a charge to be made on the right. But Gist's brigade was immovable. For a while the terrific struggle seemed of doubtful issue—"bold was the pressure of the foe," exclaims an eye witness, "firm as a rock the resistance of Gist—now the Marylanders were gaining ground."

14. The gallant Howard, at the head of Williams' regiment, impetuously broke upon the enemy, and drove the opposing corps before him. At this moment, Webster, second in command of the enemy, brought his veteran guards upon their flank. They were instantly met by the second Maryland brigade under Smallwood.

Questions.—12. What did Col. Williams do? What did Cornwallis? What, the Virginia militia? Who followed? 13. What is said in this section? 14. What is said of Howard? Of Webster? Who met him?

15. Finding his flank once more protected, and his Marylanders bearing up with unflinching valor, the brave De Kalb, although outnumbered two to one, resolved to make one great and final effort with the bayonet. Dreadful was the charge. The two lines seemed mingled with each other, the weaker going down before the stronger. The veteran troops of Cornwallis were beginning to give way; a single corps of cavalry would have completed the victory. The folly of Gates in refusing to recruit that arm of the service, when entreated to do so, rendered this impossible.

16. The advance movement left Smallwood's brigade exposed on the flank, which was immediately attacked by the enemy. But Gist and DeKalb continued to maintain their ground.—Cornwallis, alarmed at the unexpected resistance of the Maryland line, and having before experienced its desperate valor with the bayonet, now brought his whole force upon it. The whole British army was poured upon these two devoted brigades.

17 Eight hundred men stood their ground unsupported, and surrounded by more than two thousand British regulars, but fighting on with unflinching hearts. The cavalry was suddenly

---

Questions.—15. Describe the charge of the Marylanders? What rendered their charge useless? 16. How were the Marylanders left? What did Cornwallis have to do? 17. What is said in this section?

thrown upon their front and rear; the inequality was too great. These gallant men were compelled to fly.

18. The loss was severe. De Kalb was slain. The North Carolinians lost four hundred men taken prisoners, sixty killed and wounded. But the Maryland line and the Delaware regiment suffered most. The Virginia militia, to the regret of all, escaped with the loss of only three men.

19. The thanks of congress were voted to Gist and Smallwood for their exemplary skill and bravery on this disastrous day. Lieut. Col. Williams was everywhere in the heat of the battle, and Lieut. Col. Howard gave proofs of that cool and daring courage which distinguished him as one of the first and bravest of Maryland's sons.

Questions.—18. What is said of the loss? What, of the Virginia militia? 19. What did Congress do? What is said of Williams and Howard?

CHAPTER XII.

THE BATTLE OF COWPENS—*Recruiting—Consolidation of the Line—Col. Williams—General Morgan retreats before Tarleton—Makes a Stand—Marylanders Sustain the Battle—Victory—Col. Howard.*

GEN. OTHO WILLIAMS.

1. Smallwood and Gist remained at Charlotte with about one hundred and fifty officers and men to rally their scattered soldiers. By certain cool and skilful measures Smallwood succeeded, in about ten days, in collecting upwards of seven hundred non-commissioned officers and men, which number was increased by the recapture of a hundred and fifty continental prisoners taken at Camden. They were recaptured by Marion, on their way, under escort, to Charleston.

Questions.—1. What did Smallwood and Gist now do? How many did they collect?

2. The seven Maryland regiments of the old line, were reduced into one, to be called the first Maryland, and placed under Colonel Otho H. Williams. The officers who thus lost their commands were ordered back to Maryland to take charge of recruiting stations. General Smallwood was retained in the army. General Gates was superseded by General Greene.

3. Smallwood's detachment was drawn into the main army; and a chosen body of troops, four hundred of whom were of the old Maryland line, under Colonel Howard, was placed under the command of Morgan, to operate on the western quarter.

4. Cornwallis, learning the movements of the American forces, determined to strike a blow at Morgan, before he could be joined by the hardy mountaineers of the west.

5. He dispatched about one thousand men under Lieut. Col. Tarleton, to pursue him, while he, himself, put the main body in motion to cut off his retreat, if he should escape that active officer.

6. Morgan retreated with reluctance, although he was compelled to do so by the advance of Cornwallis, parallel to his route. Having at length gained sufficient time to risk an action with Tarleton, and having been joined by Gen'l Pickens with

---

Questions.—2. How were the regiments of the Maryland line reduced? Under whom was the regiment placed? 3. What was done with Smallwood's detachment? What, with Howard's? 4. What is said of Cornwallis? 5. Whom did he dispatch? 6. What did Morgan do? When did he determine to venture a battle?

a body of five hundred militia, he determined to await the coming of the enemy.

7. The ground was open and favorable to Tarleton, whose cavalry outnumbered that of Morgan three to one. As the enemy advanced, Morgan addressed his men; he directed the militia to deliver but two or three volleys, and then to retire and form behind the main line. He reminded the Marylanders of their past glory, and that victory was largely dependent upon them.

8. Tarleton advanced rapidly. The skirmishers delivered their fire, and fell back. The British pressed with loud shouts, upon the first line, which, undismayed, poured in a close and destructive fire. The enemy continued to advance with the bayonet, and the militia having only rifles retired in haste.

9. Believing the victory in their grasp, the enemy charged upon the continentals. They were met with unshaken firmness. The conflict was desperate, and for a time seemed doubtful, but the unconquerable spirit of the Marylanders at length prevailed, and the enemy began to falter. Being reinforced by the reserves, they again advanced.

10. Howard ordered his flank company to change front, but mistaking the order it fell back,

---

Questions.—7. What is said in this section? 8. What is said in this section? 9. How was the charge of the enemy met? 10. What is said in this section?

upon which the line commenced to retire. Morgan directed it to retreat towards the cavalry and assume a new position.

11. The British, thinking this movement was precursor of a flight, rushed forward with impetuosity and in disorder, to complete the triumph. Howard had not yet reached the position marked out by Morgan, but perceiving their condition, he suddenly faced about, and poured in upon the astonished enemy a close and murderous fire, and then cheering his men, broke in upon them with the bayonet.

12. The charge was terrible and decisive; and the day was won. The slaughter of Camden was repaid; the whole British infantry was killed or taken. The enemy's cavalry had pursued the retreating militia to their horses, and had begun to sabre them when Col. Washington charged upon them, and drove them before him.

13. Never was a complete or more glorious victory. The force of Morgan did not much exceed eight hundred men—only half of whom were regulars—and only eighty cavalry—while that of Tarleton reached a thousand, comprising three hundred and fifty cavalry. This force was entirely destroyed.

Questions.—11. What did the British think? What did Howard do? 12. What is said of the charge? What further is said? 13. What was the force of Morgan? What was Tarleton's?

14. "The weight of the battle fell upon Howard, who sustained himself admirably in those trying circumstances, and seized with decision the critical moment to complete with the bayonet the advantage gained by his fire." Yet he had won the battle without orders; and after he had swept the field by his glorious charge, Morgan rode up to him and said severely: "You have done well—for you are successful—had you failed, I would have shot you."

15. At one moment, Howard held in his hands the swords of seven British officers, who had surrendered to him. Congress awarded him a silver medal.

16. Morgan's aid on this memorable day was a young Maryland officer, Major Edward Giles, who distinguished himself, and was one of the five officers named in the resolution of thanks passed by Congress in 1781.

Questions.—14. Who deserves the credit of the victory? What did Morgan say? 15. How many British officers surrendered to Howard? 16. Who was Morgan's aid?

CHAPTER XIII.

BATTLE OF GUILFORD COURT HOUSE—*Greene's Retreat—Williams Covers the Retreat—Battle—Cornwallis' Desperate Resort—George Fox's Remark—Americans gain Possession of Strongholds—Unsuccessful Attack on Ninety-Six.*

GEN. JOHN EAGER HOWARD.

1. Greene, not finding himself strong enough to compete with Cornwallis, who had been reinforced, commenced his retreat from the Yadkin to the Dan. This retreat was remarkable for its masterly manœuvres, its rapid marches and severe duty. At times the two armies were within musket shot of each other.

2. Had Williams' corps, which was in the rear, become involved with the advance of the enemy,

Questions.—1. What was Greene compelled to do? What was this retreat remarkable for? 2. What would have been the result of conflict?

the strength of the army might have been destroyed, and Greene, no longer covered with light troops, would have fallen an easy victim to Cornwallis.

3. The burden of the retreat, therefore, fell upon Williams, and nobly did he bear it Scarcely a single man was killed or captured, in the face of an active, energetic and superior enemy, whose van for days was constantly in sight of the retiring rear.

4. Having crossed the Dan, Greene rested his army and recruited. Being reinforced, he thought he could venture an engagement with Cornwallis, which he did in the battle of Guilford Court House, on the 18th of February, 1781. In this fight the first Maryland regiment checked the left wing of the enemy, but the second, which had just been raised, fled.

5. The battalion of guards, which had turned the second Maryland, was now attacked by Col. Howard. Like a torrent the old Maryland regiment broke through their ranks, driving them headlong from the field with terrific slaughter.

6. To save his favorite corps from utter annihilation, and to arrest the progress of the pursuers, Cornwallis was compelled to open his artillery upon

---

Questions.—3. Upon whom did the burden of the retreat fall? 4. Where did Greene rest and recruit? What battle did he venture? 5. Describe the charge of Howard's battalion? 6. What was Cornwallis compelled to do?

them, although every discharge swept through his own men. The Maryland brigade lost in this fight one hundred and fifty-four officers and men. The British General lost nearly one-third of his men.

7. The enemy remained masters of the field, but the victory was almost as destructive to Cornwallis as a defeat. George Fox, in the British House of Commons, said of it, "another such victory will ruin the British army."

8. Six days afterward, February 25th, Greene was surprised at Hobkirk's hill. The first Maryland regiment, worn down by sufferings, emaciated from the scantiness of their food, and brought suddenly to a charge when only half-formed, was seized with panic and fled. They rallied, but too late to retrieve the day.

9. Notwithstanding the defeat at Guilford Court House, the Americans succeeded in gaining possession of all the strongholds in the south, with the exception of Charleston and Ninety-Six. This latter post Greene now hastened to invest.

10. Learning that Lord Rawdon was approaching at the head of two thousand men to relieve Ninety-Six, Greene determined to attempt it by assault. The resistance was desperate and successful, and Greene was forced to retire.

Questions.—7. What is said of victory? What did George Fox say in parliament? 8. What is said of Hobkirk's hill? 9. What did the Americans succeed in gaining? 10. What is said of Ninety-Six.

CHAPTER XIV.

BATTLE OF EUTAW SPRINGS—*Disposition of the Troops—Maryland Line charges the Buffs—Desperate Struggle—Marylanders Complimented on the Field—State Threatened with Invasion—La Fayette in Baltimore—Defence of the Bay—Washington's Design—Washington at Annapolis.*

1. On the 21st of August, Greene broke up his encampment, and hastened to the south to seek the enemy now under the command of Lieut. Col. Stewart. He overtook them at Eutaw Springs.

2. Greene advanced in two lines—the militia in front, the continentals in the rear. The Maryland brigade under Col. Williams, seconded by Lieut. Col. Howard, was on the left wing.

3. The militia advanced with spirit, and opened a heavy fire upon the enemy, which was soon briskly returned; but they maintained their ground until the British troops pressed close upon them.

4. The North Carolina troops were immediately ordered up to cover their retreat and check the advance of the enemy. This corps, consisting of newly raised regiments never before in action, pushed forward in good style and the conflict became warmer.

Questions.—1. When did Greene return south? Where did he overtake the enemy? 2. What was the position of the troops? 3. What is said of the militia? 4. What, of the North Carolina militia?

5. Greene now brought up the Maryland and Virginia lines, which advanced with a shout, and poured in a destructive fire upon the enemy. Stewart called up his reserve; the North Carolinians began to fall back, when Greene ordered the Marylanders and Virginians to charge with the bayonet.

6. At trailed arms, cheering vehemently, these two gallant brigades, led on by Williams, Howard and Campbell, rushed upon the enemy heedless of the close and deadly fire, which was repeatedly poured in upon them, as they advanced at a rapid pace. The shock was terrible.

7. Howard's regiment was received by the Buffs, an Irish corps, which had just joined the army; and here the fiercest struggle ensued. Neither would yield; but, crossing bayonets their ranks mingled together, opposing files sank down, each pierced with the bayonet of his antagonist.

8. Thus they were found, grappled in death and transfixed together upon the field of the slain, marking the spot where the Marylanders and Buffs had met in deadly conflict. The officers fought hand to hand. So bloody a strife could not continue long. The rest of the British line gave way, and the gallant Buffs, unable to maintain the conflict with the veteran Marylanders,

---

Questions.—5. Whom did Greene now bring forward? 6. Describe the charge? 7. By whom was Howard's regiment received? 8. What is said of this struggle? Who gave way?

broke and fled. Greene rode up and complimented the Marylanders and their commander in the midst of the action.

9. The victory was complete, and the British were compelled to retreat. Having obtained an unassailable position, the pursuers were recalled, bringing with them three hundred prisoners and two cannons, one of which was captured by Lieut. Duval, of the Maryland line.

10. Greene attributed his success to the free use of the bayonet by the Maryland and Virginia troops. The thanks of congress were voted to each of the corps engaged.

11. The spirit of the hostile army was broken, and the royal supremacy in the south may be said to have terminated, overturned in a great part by the bayonets of Maryland.

12. Whilst the Maryland line was thus gloriously occupied in the south, its native State seemed, for a time, threatened with invasion. Arnold, the Traitor, had been detached to Virginia, at the head of an active body of British troops. Cornwallis hastened into Virginia, and forming a junction with the forces there, took the command of the whole upon himself.

13. La Fayette was at once dispatched by General Washington to Virginia, with a small

---

Questions.—8. What did Greene do? 9. What is said of the victory? 10. To what did Greene attribute the victory? 11. What is said of the hostile army? 12. What invasion threatened Maryland? 13. Who was despatched to make head against Cornwallis?

force to make head against Cornwallis. He passed through Maryland on his way, and was hospitably received by the merchants of Baltimore.

14. Being invited to a ball, he was there observed to be grave and sad. On being questioned by the ladies, as to the cause of his gloom, he replied he could not enjoy the gayety of the scene, whilst his poor soldiers were without shirts, and destitute of the necessities of a campaign. "We will supply them," exclaimed these patriotic women.

15. The pleasures of the ball-room were exchanged for the labors of the needle, and on the next day they assembled in great numbers to make up clothing for the soldiers. The husbands and fathers furnished the materials. The distresses of his corps were relieved. The history of this city during the last few years has proved that the women of the present day, whose kind hearts and fair hands have contributed to alleviate the wants of the suffering, are worthy descendants of those noble women of the revolution.

16. Great efforts were made to organize a force to repel an invasion, which the open condition of the bay might invite. The glory of the southern battles had re-awakened the spirit of the people of Maryland, and the measures proposed were promptly carried out. Provision was made for

---

Questions.—14. What anecdote is related of La Fayette? 15. What was done the next day? 16. What is said of the defence of the bay?

the defence of the bay, and several severe actions took place with the straggling cruisers of the enemy. A regiment was ordered to join La Fayette in Virginia.

17. Washington, having formed the design of destroying Cornwallis, was now anxious to concentrate as strong a force as possible in that quarter, while the French fleet seized the mouth of the bay to cut off the retreat of the enemy.

18. On the 8th of September, Washington passed through Baltimore, where he was received with every mark of respect. An address was presented to him on behalf of the people, and the city was illuminated.

19. On the 19th of October, 1781, Cornwallis surrendered with his whole force of seven thousand men. In this hard contested siege, a portion of the Maryland troops was engaged, maintaining the honor of the State and the fame of the old Maryland line.

20. In a letter to Governor Lee, of Maryland, Washington says, "my present engagements will not allow me to add more than my congratulations on this happy event, and to express the high sense I have of the powerful aid which I have derived from the State of Maryland."

Questions.—17. What design had Washington formed? What was done in order to carry out this plan? 18. When did Washington pass through Baltimore? 19. When did Cornwallis surrender? 20. What does Washington, in his letter to Gov. Lee, say?

21. On Washington's passing through Annapolis, to join the army in the north, that venerable city was crowded to overflowing with happy spectators, and presented one constant scene of enthusiastic rejoicing.

22. Maryland had the honor of first "saluting him as the PATRIOT, the HERO, and the SAVIOUR OF HIS COUNTRY." She had been the first to propose him for that station which resulted in liberty to his country, and in the admiration of all posterity to himself. She was the first to announce to him the gratitude of the nation, and to confer upon him those titles which were to render his name universal and immortal.

Questions.—21. What is said of Washington's passage through Annapolis? 22. How did Maryland salute him?

CHAPTER XV.

The Close of the Revolution—*New Paper Issues—Tory Conspiracy—Plot Exposed—Execution of Leaders—Success or Failure—Commissioners from England—Spirited Resolution of Maryland Legislature—Close of the War.*

1. The Legislature had made every effort to prepare for the campaign of 1781. Knowing the impossibility of meeting the necessary expenses by means of the usual paper money, they determined to have recourse to the patriotism of the wealthier citizens.

2. There was a large amount of confiscated land unsold, that had belonged to British subjects. The Legislature determined to issue two hundred thousand pounds in notes, secured by these confiscated lands, which were pledged to the amount of four hundred thousand pounds.

3. The wealthy and patriotic planters and merchants agreed to take at their par, or nominal value, such amounts as they subscribed for. As the security was sufficient, nearly the whole amount was subscribed. For a time the scheme was successful, but such was the want of confidence in paper money of any kind, that in three months, even these

---

Questions.—1. What is said of the legislature? 2. How did the legislature proceed to raise money? 3. Did the plan succeed? Did the paper money retain its value?

bills had depreciated to less than half their nominal value.

4. An extensive alarm was created by the discovery of a conspiracy to excite an insurrection of the disaffected within the State.

5. At the opening of the campaign of 1781, a design was formed of invading the western frontier from Canada. A body of British troops was to strike at Fort Pitt; and Col. Conolly, already once baffled in his designs in Maryland, was to assemble a tory force to co-operate with him.

6. Large numbers had been enrolled in Frederick county, when the conspiracy was discovered at Frederick. It is said that a British officer in disguise was to meet a messenger of the conspirators at a designated place, and put into his hands papers containing every information concerning its progress.

7. The British officer was deterred from attending at the appointed place, and the papers fell into the hands of an American officer, who by a singular coincidence was at that moment standing where the tory expected to meet his correspondent.

8. The plot and the names of the leaders were at once exposed, and efficient measures were instantly taken. The leaders were arrested and convicted. Seven were brought to trial before a

---

Questions.—4. What alarm was excited? 5. What design was formed? 6. & 7. How was the conspiracy discovered? 8. What was done with the leaders of the plot?

commission presided over by Judge Hanson, found guilty and sentenced to death.

9. Three of their number were executed in the Court-house yard of Frederick. They persisted, to the last, that they were only guilty of doing their duty as lawful subjects of the King of England, and asserted that their judges were more truly deserving the name of rebels and traitors.

10. Had the result of the revolution been different, a different name would have been given to their fate—which they met with firmness; for whilst one side stigmatized them as traitors, the other mourned over them, and honored them as true and loyal martyrs. Success makes a revolution glorious, the want of it leaves the reproach of disgrace upon the unfortunate. Without success the patriots of the Maryland line would have been called traitors and rebels to this day, and the name of tory, now a reproach, would be proudly assumed as a token of loyalty.

11. As soon as the arrival of commissioners from Great Britain, with power to make either peace or war with the revolted colonies, was announced, the Maryland Legislature unanimously resolved, that "though peace with Great Britain and all the world, was an object truly desirable, war with all its calamities was preferable to national

---

Questions.—9. How many were executed? What did they insist upon to the last? 10. What is said in this section? 11. What did the Maryland legislature resolve?

dishonor. That this State could never consent to treat with Great Britain, except upon the footing of an equal, and would never enter into any treaty with that power, which would sully its own honor or violate its obligations to France, its great and good ally."

12. The bay-shores were still infested by armed galleys and barges, manned by tories and refugees, who plundered and sometimes murdered the inhabitants. The Legislature determined to re-establish the marine, and by its rigorous measures the commerce of the bay was relieved, and the inhabitants of its shores were protected.

13. The war was now at an end. Throughout the whole contest, Maryland had been distinguished for its zeal in support of the common cause. Besides those enlisted in the independent corps, the State companies, and the marine and naval forces, she had furnished during the war, to the Continental army, fifteen thousand two hundred and twenty-nine men, and five thousand four hundred and seven militia.

Questions.—12. What is said of the bay-shores? 13. What of the war? What of Maryland, during the war?

CHAPTER XVI.

THE MARYLAND LINE—*Their Sufferings—The First to use the Bayonet—Their Battles—Their Losses.*

1. No troops in the Continental army had rendered better service, endured more fatigue or won greater glory than the Maryland line. In proportion to their number, no body of men suffered more severely.

2. They were the first to use the bayonet against the experienced regulars of the enemy, and that in the earliest battle—and throughout the succeeding struggles of the war, they were most often called on to lead with that bloody weapon into the ranks of the foe. They seldom shrank from the encounter.

3. At Long Island, a fragment of a battalion shook, with repeated charges, a whole brigade of British regulars. At White Plains, they held the advance columns at bay. At Harlem Heights, they drove the enemy from the ground. At Germantown, they swept through the hostile camp, with their fixed bayonets, far in advance of the whole army. At Cowpens, and at Eutaw, their ranks with unloaded muskets bore down all opposition. At Guilford, and at Camden, though the victory was not theirs, they fought with a courage

---

Questions.—1. What is said of the Maryland line? 2. What were they the first to do? 3. Mention the several battles in which they distinguished themselves?

that won the admiration and surprise of the enemy, aud brought from Fox, in the House of Commons, the exclamation: "one more such victory and the British army is ruined." Everywhere they used the bayonet with terrible effect.

4. Entering into the war two strong battalions, they were soon reduced to a single company.—Again swelled up to seven regiments, they were again thinned by their losses to a single regiment, and before the campaign was well passed, they were once more recruited to four full battalions of more than two thousand men.

5. Two of their Colonels, Williams and Howard, were considered the best officers of their grade in the army. Grunby, Hall, Smith, Stone, Ramsey and Ford, were equal to any others in the whole continental service.

CHAPTER XVII.

SEAT OF GOVERNMENT—*Annapolis Offered—Action of Congress—Washington determines to Resign—Reception at Annapolis—Resignation.*

1. It was now an interesting question where the seat of national government should be placed.—The central position of Maryland drew attention

---

Questions.—4. What is said of their losses? 5. What of their officers? 1. What was now a question?

in this quarter, and the corporation of Annapolis addressed a memorial to the legislature in 1783, offering the city to the general government.

2. The legislature, therefore, offered to the government the use and possession of the State House for their sessions. Other inducements were offered to make Annapolis the permanent seat of government. Congress determined to fix the capital in Maryland, yet deemed it more prudent to select some other place than that already occupied by the State legislature.

3. They resolved to select a point upon the Potomac, near Georgetown, but for the present, accepted the accommodations tendered them by the State.—They, therefore, adjourned from Princeton to Annapolis. The legislature welcomed them with great cordiality, gave up one of their halls for their use. Governor Paca surrendered the government house to their president.

4. General Washington had already notified the several States of his intention to resign his commission, and retire to private life. He now hastened to Annapolis, where he arrived on the 17th of December, to consummate his purpose.

5. He was met a few miles from the city by Generals Gates and Smallwood, with the most distinguished citizens of Maryland. He was greeted

---

Questions.—1. What is said of the position of Maryland? 2. What did congress determine? 3. What did the legislature do? 4. What is said of Washington? 5. How was he received?

with enthusiasm by the people. Every one vied in doing him honor.

6. At twelve o'clock, on the 23d of December, the gallery, and a great part of the floor of the hall of congress, were filled with ladies, with public functionaries of the State, and with general officers. The members of congress were seated and covered, as representatives of the sovereignty of the union. The gentlemen present were standing uncovered.

7. After a decorous silence of a few minutes, Washington rose, and in a dignified and impressive manner, delivered a short address. When he had concluded, he placed into the hands of the President that great commission, under which he had achieved the liberty and independence of America, "commending the interests of our dearest country to the protection of Almighty God, and those who have the superintendence of them, to his holy keeping."

Questions.—6. Describe the scene in the State House? 7. What did Washington do? What did he say?

8. The editor of the Maryland Gazette, who was present, says: "Few tragedies ever drew so many tears from so many beautiful eyes, as the moving manner in which his Excellency took his final leave of congress."

9. Then calmly, as if he had not just resigned the highest place in his country's gift, and broken the sword of his own power for its lasting good, that great man retired from that hall which had thus been consecrated forever by this noble scene.

CHAPTER XVIII

1783-1789—DEBT—*Public Improvement—Susquehanna Canal—Potomac Company—Population of Baltimore—Colleges—Constitution of the United States Adopted.*

1. The great difficulty the country now had to contend with was the debt incurred both by the general government and the several states. The treasury was empty and credit was gone. So great was the scarcity of money that taxes had to be paid, to a great extent, in merchandise, or, as it is called, in kind.

Questions.—8. What is said by an eye-witness? 9. Repeat this section? 1. What great difficulty had the country to contend with? How had taxes to be raised?

2. Maryland was the most prompt of the States to take efficient measures to raise money, and restore her credit; and looking forward to her future growth, she laid the foundations of those public works which have contributed so materially to her subsequeut prosperity.

3. "The Proprietors of the Susquehanna Canal" were incorporated in 1784. The object of this company was to construct a canal from the Pennsylvania line, along the Susquehanna to tidewater.

4. In the same year, the Potomac Company was organized. The object of this organization was, "the opening and extending of the navigation of the Potomac." The idea originated with the greatest men of the day, and General Washington took great interest in it. It would open a highway for the already increasing travel from the Atlantic to the west.

5. The Potomac Company was subsequently merged in the Chesapeake and Ohio Canal Company, and the designs for rendering the river navigable were abandoned, and other plans adopted.

6. The removal of the dangers and impediments which had obstructed commerce during the war, gave the city of Baltimore a new impulse. In

---

Questions.—2. What is said of Maryland? 3. What company was incorporated? 4. What other company? 5. Into what was the Potomac company subsequently merged? 6. What gave Baltimore a new impetus?

1782 it only numbered eight thousand inhabitants, but from that time it has moved on with rapidity and power, and is now regarded as one of the most prosperous cities in the Union.

7. As early as 1782, Washington College, at Chestertown, on the Eastern Shore, was incorporated. In 1784, St. John's College at Annapolis was instituted. These two colleges, at which many of the principal men of the State have been educated, were in 1805 united under the name of the University of Maryland.

8. On the expiration of the term for which William Paca was eligible, in 1785, Maj. Gen'l Smallwood was elected governor. Though he was honored by the people of Maryland with the highest office in their gift, yet, his memory seems nearly forgotten. He is buried in a lonely grave, on his paternal estate, now in the hands of strangers. He who won so much glory for Maryland lies unhonored, without a stone to mark the spot, or an enclosure to protect his last resting place from desecration.

9. During the administration of Smallwood the Constitution of the United States was adopted. It was acceded to by Maryland on the 28th of April, 1788, by a vote of sixty-three to eleven.

Questions.—6. How many inhabitants had it in 1782? 7. What college was established in 1782? In 1784? 8. Who was elected governor in 1785? What is said of him? 9. What important step was taken during his administration?

CHAPTER XIX.

THE FEDERAL CONSTITUTION—*Needs of the Country—Convention Proposed — Disputes — The Constitution a Compromise—Capital—District of Columbia—Property Qualifications for Voting Removed—The Ballot substituted for vivâ voce.*

1. The old articles of confederation were found not adapted to the wants of the country in its new condition. There was need of a more centralized power, by which the States could be brought into closer union, and the general government could act more efficiently for the general good.

2. A convention of all the States, to devise some means to give stability to the confederation, having been proposed, the legislature of Maryland elected five delegates to represent the State.

3. The convention met at Philadelphia, and agreed upon the present Constitution and form of government of the United States, which was laid before Congress. That body immediately directed that copies should be transmitted to the several legislatures to be submitted to a convention of delegates, chosen in each State by the people.

4. The condition of the country was such, that every one acknowledged the necessity of immediate

---

Questions.—1. What is said of the confederation? What did the country need? 2. What was proposed? 3. Where did the convention meet? What did the convention present to congress? What was the action of congress? 4. What two parties were there in the country?

change. But there were two parties; one was desirous of strengthening State authority, fearing that too great centralization of power would ultimately destroy State independence and popular liberty itself, by leaving minorities entirely at the mercy of majorities; the other hoped to derive from an efficient general government, unity and stability, which would ensure prosperity at home, and respect abroad.

5. The Constitution was a happy compromise. The popular majorities were represented in the House of Representatives, and State sovereignty was represented in the Senate. This protected the weak from the strong. It is the remark of an ancient philosopher, and history confirms the truth of it, that "the weak always desire what is equal and just: but the powerful pay no regard to it."

6. The immense popular majorities of a large State, regarding only their own interests, could control legislation to the disadvantage of the smaller States; but in the Senate the smallest State is equal to the largest. Hence, under ordinary circumstances, the necessities of concurrent majorities would prevent unjust legislation, and the strong would be compelled to listen to the weak, and respect their rights.

Questions.—5. What is said of the constitution? How? 6. Explain further?

7. This most admirably contrived compromise and compact called the Constitution, was ratified by the Maryland convention. A certificate of their ratification was signed by the members, on the 28th of April, 1788.

8. On the 2d of July, 1788, the ratification of the constitution by nine States, was laid before the old Congress, then still in session, and preparations were immediately made to carry it into effect. The States were directed to appoint their electors to cast their votes for president and vice-president. The vote of Maryland was cast for Washington for president, and Robert Hanson Harrison for vice-president.

9. The general government had not yet adopted any permanent capital. After having hesitated between the Potomac and the Delaware, Congress concluded to accept the proposition of Maryland, and the Potomac was selected.

10. Commissioners were appointed in 1790; the district was laid out on both sides of the Potomac, embracing nearly equal portions of Virginia* and Maryland, including Georgetown and Alexandria, and called the "Territory of Columbia." The new

*The Virginia portion was afterwards ceded back to that State.

Questions.—7. When did Maryland ratify the constitution? 8. When was the ratification laid before congress? Who was the first president? 9. Had the capital been adopted yet? 10. When were commissioners appointed?

city, whose site was selected for the Federal Metropolis, was named Washington.

11. On the 18th of September, 1793, the corner stone of the north wing of the capitol was laid by Washington in person.

12. Prior to 1801, no person was allowed to vote unless he possessed a certain amount of property. It was thought necessary that there should be a property qualification in voters, in order to give them a personal interest in the management of public affairs.

13. The first States to break through this custom were Vermont and Maryland. In Maryland there was great opposition at first to the extension of the right of suffrage, on the part of the senate. But it was contended that property was not the only interest at stake in the community, or to be effected by its government and legislation. The rights of life, liberty and character, are to be regarded as paramount to those of mere property.

14. It is not always the property holders who have interest enough in the general welfare, in the hour of danger to the commonwealth, to stake their lives or liberty in its defence. But being powerful in the State, by reason of their wealth, the danger is that they will use that power for their own ag-

---

Questions.—10. What site was selected? 11. When and by whom was the corner stone of the capitol laid? 12. What was necessary prior to 1801? 13. What States were the first to break through this custom? What was contended in favor of enlarged suffrage? 14. What is said of property holders?

grandizement, indifferent to the rights, or even the sufferings of the masses, who alone can protect them in their wealth.

15. Hence the people of Maryland insisted that the power of wealth, in producing class legislation, should be checked by the power of numbers, every one of whom had life, liberty and character at stake, and they succeeded in passing a law giving the right of suffrage to every free white male citizen, twenty-one years of age, who had resided twelve months in the State, and six in the county prior to the election.

16. The ballot and the ballot-box were also substituted for *vivâ voce* vote. In 1809, all clauses of the State constitution requiring property qualifications for office holders, were repealed.

CHAPTER XX.

1812—WAR WITH ENGLAND—*Declaration of War—Two Parties—The Position of New England—Of Maryland—Riot in Baltimore—Hartford Convention—Admiral Cockburn—His Deeds—Defence of Havre de Grace.*

1. Difficulties, which arose from the jealousy of England and her haughty spirit, and which led to an interference with the commerce of America, and

Questions.—15. What did the people of Maryland insist upon? 16. What method of voting was introduced? 1. What led to difficulties with England?

an infringement on her rights as a nation, at last resulted in a declaration of war. This was made by the United States, on the 11th of June, 1812.

2. There were two political parties in the country, known as the Federal and Democratic. The former, as its name implies, favored a strong central government, the latter adopted the theory of State-rights. The Federal party opposed the war.

3. The New England States, at first, were quite eager for it, because the measures adopted to prevent so great a calamity, interfered with their commerce. They looked upon war as a remedy for the evil, but finding the remedy worse to them than the evil, they were thenceforth bitterly opposed to war, as both wicked and expensive.

4. Maryland, and the agricultural States generally, thinking the honor of the republic, as well as its commerce, were at stake, favored active hostilities. The legislature of Maryland voted an address to the President of the United States, declaring they were ready to submit to all the hardships and dangers of war, rather than permit outrages upon the honor of the country to pass unpunished.

5. The "Federal Republican," a newspaper published in Baltimore, made such a violent attack upon the administration and the war measures, that

---

Questions.—1. When was war declared? 2. What two political parties? 3. What is said of the New England States? 4. What of Maryland? 5. In what lawless manner did the people of Maryland show their zeal?

a riot was the result; the office of the paper was torn down, and one person was killed.

6. In New England, on the other hand, where the Federalists were in the majority, opposition to the war was popular. The Massachusetts legislature proposed to call a convention of delegates from the several States of New England, to meet and enquire what ought to be done. This was called the Hartford Convention.

7. It is claimed by the New England historians that the objects of this convention were patriotic, and that "as the mists of passion fade away this becomes more apparent." Whether so, or not, it is certain the convention was considering the propriety of withdrawing New England from the Union, for, in its journal it says, "whenever it shall appear that these causes of our calamities are radical and permanent, a separation by equitable arrangement will be preferable to an alliance by constraint, among nominal friends, but real enemies." The somewhat unexpected close of the war prevented further action.

8. Divided by these elements of internal discord the United States went into the war. Whether owing to this want of unanimity on the part of the people, or to want of skill on the part of the officers, the first year of the war was one of misfortune.

Questions.—6. How did New England shew its hostility? 7. What is claimed by the New England historians? What is certain? 8. What effect had these dissensions on the war?

9. Maryland bore part in the deeds of the war only through her privateers. Her soldiers and sailors were distributed throughout the Federal army, and were not, as formerly, distinguished in a separate corps.

10. In 1813, Admiral Cockburn made his appearance in the Chesapeake with four ships of the line and six frigates. He directed his operations against detached farm houses and seats of private gentlemen, unprepared for defence; these were robbed, and the owners treated in the rudest manner. The cattle, which could not be carried away, were destroyed; the slaves were armed against their owners, and persuaded to attack defenceless families.

11. Although it was impossible to station a force at each farm house to repel these incursions, yet the spirited citizens of Maryland formed bodies of cavalry, which were stationed at intervals along the shore. In several instances Cockburn and his ruffians were bravely repelled by a collection of neighbors, under no authority and without a leader.

12. Cockburn took possession of several islands in the Bay, particularly Sharp's, Tilghman's and Poplar Islands, whence he could make a descent upon the neighboring shores.

Questions.—9. How did Maryland bear her part? 10. When did Admiral Cockburn arrive? What was his conduct? 11. How did the Marylanders protect their shore? 12. What places did Cockburn seize?

13. Among the places that suffered by this famous or infamous Admiral, were Frenchtown, Havre-de-Grace, Fredericktown, (on the Eastern Shore), and Georgetown, which were taken, plundered and burned.

14. Frenchtown was a small village, consisting of six dwelling houses, two store houses and several stables. It was of some importance, however, as a place of deposit on the line of packets and stages between Baltimore and Philadelphia.—Against this village he sent a force of five hundred marines. A small party of militia from Elkton collected to oppose him, but moved off as the Admiral approached.

15. Havre-de-Grace was, at that time, a neat village, containing about twenty or thirty houses. The attack on this place was made on the third of May, before day-light. The approach of the enemy was announced by cannon shot and the firing of rockets. The inhabitants, roused from their sleep, leaped up in the greatest consternation. The more courageous repaired to the beach, where a few small pieces of artillery had been planted on a kind of battery.

16. On the approach of the barges, nineteen in number, they all, with the exception of an old citizen of the place, an Irishman named O'Neill, fled.

Questions.—13. What towns were plundered and burnt? 14. What is said of Frenchtown? 15. What is said of Havre-de-Grace? What of its attack? 16. What is said of O'Neill?

O'Neill manned a gun himself and kept up a fire on the approaching enemy until he was disabled by a wound in the thigh, received from the recoil of the cannon which he was firing. He then continued the fight with two muskets, until he was captured by the enemy.

17. Cockburn's men no sooner landed than they set about plundering and destroying. The houses were burned, the women had their clothes torn from their backs, the horses were maimed and the stage coaches were broken to pieces. The church edifice was defaced but not burned. The house of Commodore Rodgers was also saved. Most of the women and children of the place had collected here, and at their earnest solicitation the torch was not applied.

18. The enemy now divided his force into three parts. One remained at Havre-de-Grace; one party followed the road to Baltimore for several miles, plundering the farm houses, and robbing the travellers on the road of their clothes and money; the other proceeded up the river, committing similar outrages.

19. On the sixth, they returned to their fleet, taking O'Neill with them They threatened to hang him as a British subject found in arms; but the determination of the Americans to execute two

---

Questions.—17. What was the conduct of Cockburn's men? 18. What did the enemy now do? 19. What did they do with O'Neill.

British sailors in reprisal, induced them to spare his life.

20. Fredericktown and Georgetown were two beautiful villages on the Sassafras river, situated opposite each other, one in Kent, the other in Cecil county. On the sixth, placing himself at the head of six hundred men, in eighteen barges, he ascended the river towards Fredericktown. Col. Veazy had collected here about fifty militia.

21. On the approach of the barges, which immediately commenced a heavy fire, the greater part of the militia fled. Veazy, with a few dauntless spirits, kept his ground, and maintained a steady fire until the enemy was so near that he was compelled to retreat. The houses were plundered and burnt. Georgetown was then treated in a similar manner.

22. Men of the stamp of Cockburn, who do not regard the tender years of childhood, nor the weakness of women, who illuminate the skies with incendiary fires of peaceful hamlets, who, instead of alleviating the horrors of war, make it the means of gratifying their passions and their avarice, are not considered as true specimens of the soldier. It is not to be wondered at, therefore, that we do not find him exposing himself to any risks. He threatened Annapolis, but finding it prepared for defence, retired. He approached

---

Questions.—20. What is said of Fredericktown and Georgetown? 21. Describe the attack? 22. What is said of men like Cockburn?

Baltimore, but five thousand citizens were in arms, and he shrunk from the encounter. He preferred the safe and profitable, though at that time thought inglorious, warfare of destroying or carrying off private property. If he won no laurels, he at least could console himself with the tobacco and furniture which he stole.

CHAPTER XXI.

BATTLE OF BLADENSBURG.

1. The termination of the European war, which was waged at this time against Napoleon, enabled England to supply a powerful land force to invade the interior.

2. Anticipating that Baltimore or Washington would be made the points of attack, a new military district, composed of Maryland, the District of Columbia, and part of Virginia, was formed, and on the fifth of July, 1814, the command was given to Gen'l Winder.

3. The forces assigned to him were some fragments of regulars—less than five hundred, mostly raw recruits, and some two thousand militia from the District of Columbia. He had, also, authority

---

Questions.—1. What enabled England to send more forces to this country? 2. What new military district was formed, and why? 3. What forces were assigned to Gen. Winder?

to call upon the State of Maryland, in case of invasion, for six thousand militia, upon Virginia for two thousand, and upon Pennsylvania for five hundred.

4. Gen. Winder proposed to call out this militia, and to form a camp of three thousand men between the Eastern Branch and the Patuxent, and to mass the remainder in Washington. Had his plan been carried into execution the cities of Baltimore and Washington would safely have bid defiance to the enemy. But his plan was opposed by the Secretary of War.

5. This army of over ten thousand men, existed only on paper. When the requisitions were made upon the States for their quota, the men were not forthcoming. At the beginning of August he had only about a thousand regulars upon whom he could depend, and about four thousand militia, the greater part of whom were quietly at their homes.

6. Such was the condition of affairs when, in the beginning of August, news reached Washington that a new and large British fleet, under Admiral Cochrane, had arrived. This fleet brought General Ross and four thousand of Wellington's troops. To this fleet Cockburn's squadron was added.

Questions.—4. What did Gen. Winder propose? 5. What is said of this army? How many were there at the beginning of August? 6. Who arrived at this time?

7. The American squadron in the Chesapeake had been placed under the command of Joshua Barney. He was blocked up in the Patuxent, where he succeeded, however, by the help of the militia, in repelling one or two attacks.

8. The enemy divided his force into three parts, sending one up the Potomac, under Captain Gordon, to open the way to the city of Washington; the other, under Sir Peter Parker, as if to threaten Baltimore; while the main body, under Commodore Cochrane, consisting of twenty-seven vessels, ascended the Patuxent as if to attack Commodore Barney's flotilla, but with the real intention of attacking Washington.

9. The enemy reached Benedict on the 19th of August, and on the next day landed six thousand regulars and seamen. On the 21st, they moved toward Nottingham, and on the following day reached Marlborough. The British flotilla, consisting of barges and launches, ascended the river, under Cockburn, keeping on the right flank of the army. On the 23d, the flotilla of Commodore Barney was set fire to by sailors left for the purpose, the Commodore, with his men, having already joined General Winder.

Questions.—7. What is said of the American squadron? 8. What were the movements of the enemy? 9. What place did the enemy reach? How many did they land? What is said of the British flotilla?

10. The enemy reached Bladensburg, a village about six miles from Washington, without opposition or resistance, on the 24th of August. The American forces here were re-inforced by a body of twenty-one hundred men, under Gen. Stansbury, including the fifth regiment, the favorite regiment of Baltimore, under Colonel Sterrett, together with several rifle companies, commanded by Maj. Pinckney, and two companies of artillery, under Myers and Magruder, as well as by the sailors and marines, already mentioned, under Com. Barney. It was determined to make a stand here, and risk a battle for the defence of the capital. The action commenced at one o'clock.

11. General Stansbury was stationed on the left of the road leading to Washington, with his artillery in a breast work near the bridge over the Eastern Branch, with the Baltimore volunteers in advance. Col. Beall, with eight hundred militia, was placed on the right of the road, and General Winder in person commanded the main body, a short distance in the rear. The heavy artillery, under Commodore Barney, was placed so as to command the road.

12. As soon as the enemy appeared in sight, they formed, and moved towards the bridge, but

---

Questions.—10. When did the enemy reach Bladensburg? By whom were the Americans re-inforced? What was determined upon? 11. What was the disposition of the troops? 12. What is said in this section?

were received with a destructive fire from the batteries and the Baltimore rifles, and driven back in disorder.

13. They immediately formed again and advanced a second time. The head of their column was again thrown into confusion, but they at length forced their way across the bridge and drove back General Stansbury's force, capturing one piece of artillery.

14. Col. Beall's militia retreated with great precipitation, and a detachment of Annapolis militia was thrown back in disorder on the main body.—The enemy now advanced briskly along the road, certain of an easy victory, when Barney's battery opened upon them in front, and Colonel Millar with the marines poured in a heavy fire upon their flank.

15. The first discharge of Barney's pieces swept across their columns with terrible effect. Moving obliquely to the left, to escape the range of the cannon, the British grenadiers fell upon Millar's marines. From these they received so warm a reception that the advance was driven back upon the main body in disorder.

16. The moment was critical, but from the want of a sustaining force, the Americans were unable

---

Questions.—13. Describe what further is said? 14. Who checked the advance of the British? 15. What was the effect of the discharges of artillery? How did they try to avoid it? 16. What prevented the Americans obtaining the victory?

to follow up the advantage, and Ross having rallied his men, extended his front so as to attack the marines in front and on both flanks. Being thus assailed, the marines could not hold their ground; Col. Millar having been wounded, Capt. Sevier ordered them to retire. Barney, no longer sustained by the infantry, was unable to maintain his position, though his gallant sailors worked the guns until they were surrounded and some of their number bayonetted at their posts. Then, only, they retired, leaving their gallant commander covered with wounds in the hands of the enemy, who, admiring his gallant resistance, treated him with great consideration.

17. The main body of militia and a body of regular cavalry and infantry, eager to join in the fight, in the moment of victory, by the folly of their officers, were ordered to retire. When once undisciplined troops look back, a panic seizes them; it was so at Bladensburg; an unwilling retreat became a rout.

18. Washington thus fell into the hands of the enemy, who burned the capitol, the president's house and all the public offices. They then returned to their shipping at Benedict, having lost in the expedition four hundred men, killed and wounded, and five hundred prisoners. The loss

---

Questions.—17. What is said in this section? 18. What did the British do at Washington? How many did the British lose? How many the Americans?

of the Americans was about thirty killed, fifty wounded, and one hundred and twenty taken prisoners.

19. The squadron under Capt. Gordon ascended the Potomac as far as Alexandria, which was plundered of all the merchandise of every description, whether in town, or removed within the past ten days.

20. Sir Peter Parker, who ascended the Chesapeake, was not so fortunate as the other officers. He landed at night, in the neighborhood of Moor's fields, near Belair, Kent county, with the view of surprising a party of militia under Col. Reed. In this he was disappointed, for the militia, having heard the approach of the barges, were prepared to receive them. Sir Peter Parker landed with two hundred and thirty men. The militia under Colonel Reed consisted of one hundred and seventy men. Sir Peter was repulsed, and soon after died of his wounds.

Questions.—19. What is said of the squadron under Capt. Gordon? 20. What was Parker's success?

BATTLE OF NORTH POINT.

CHAPTER XXII.

BATTLE OF NORTH POINT.

1. General Ross now turned his eyes upon Baltimore. Anticipating his design, the governor had ordered the militia of the State to hold themselves in readiness, and large bodies were marched to the city for its defence. About seven hundred regulars, several volunteer and militia companies from Pennsylvania and Virginia, increased their strength to about fifteen thousand men.

Questions.—1. Where did Ross now turn? What had the governor ordered? Who had assembled?

2. They were commanded by General Samuel Smith, who had distinguished himself in the revolution by his gallant defence at Fort Mifflin. One division of the army was confided to General Winder, the other to General Stricker.

3. As soon as it was announced that the British were approaching the city, the militia flocked in from all quarters in such numbers, that neither arms, ammunition nor provisions could be supplied them, and the services of many were necessarily declined.

4. The fleet threatening Baltimore consisted of about forty vessels—the largest of which anchored across the channel—and landed troops at North Point, about fourteen miles from the city.

5. On the 12th, eight thousand troops were ready for marching, and sixteen bomb vessels proceeded up the Patapsco, and anchored within two and a half miles from Fort McHenry.

6. The defences of the city consisted of this fort, commanded by Lieut. Col. Armistead; two batteries were erected on the south side, one at the Lazaretto, under Lieut. Rutter, the other a six gun battery under Lieutenant Steuber. Lines of entrenchment were hastily thrown up; along these

---

Questions.—2. By whom commanded? How were the divisions commanded? 3. What was the effect of the announcement of the approach of the British? 4. What did the fleet consist of? How many troops were landed? 5. What is said in this section? 6. Of what did the defences of the city consist?

breastworks were stationed about four thousand men.

7. As the British advanced towards the city, General Stricker was ordered forward with three thousand two hundred men, to oppose their progress. He took a position about eight miles from the city, his right resting on Bear Creek, and his left covered by a marsh.

8. In a skirmish with the rifles, who were thrown in the advance, the British commander, Gen. Ross, was killed. Among these rifles were two apprentice boys, named Wells and McComas. There is a tradition that these boys, concealed behind some bushes, fired upon the General as he was advancing, and that then rising to see the effect of their shot, themselves received the fire of a whole platoon. Their remains are buried in the City of Baltimore.

9. General Brook, the second in command, continued to advance, and, at half-past three, action commenced with the main body by a heavy cannonade.

10. The fifty-first regiment having fallen into confusion, while executing an order, failed to keep its ground, and by its retreat the American force was reduced to about one-third of the enemy.—Notwithstanding this disparity the line maintained

---

Questions.—7. Who was ordered forward? 8. Who was killed? What is said of Wells and McComas? 9. Who succeeded him? 10. What is said of the fifty-first?

its ground with the greatest firmness, pouring in a destructive fire upon the advancing columns of the enemy. The artillery opened with terrible effect upon the left, which was opposed to the gallant fifth, which sustained the laurels won at Bladensburg. The front ranks of the enemy were frequently observed throwing themselves upon the ground to avoid the unerring fire that was poured upon them.

11. Finding his force unable to make head against the superior strength of the enemy, and having given them a severe check, Gen. Stricker ordered his line to retire to the position occupied by the reserve. This position being too exposed, he fell back nearer to the city.

12. The enemy did not attempt pursuit, and the brigade assumed a position near the entrenchments, ready for another struggle with the invader. Although the American loss was heavy, it bore no comparison to that of the British. The loss of the former was twenty-four killed, one hundred and thirty-nine wounded, and fifty prisoners; that of the latter was nearly twice as great. The British lost their leader, General Ross, who had boasted that he would take up his winter quarters in Baltimore.

13. On the morning of the 13th, the British made their appearance within two miles of the

---

Questions.—10. What further is said? 11. What did Stricker now do? 12. Did the enemy pursue? What was the loss on each side? 13. Where did the British next appear?

entrenchments, on the Philadelphia road, as if endeavoring to gain the flank of the American position; but being baffled by Gen. Smith, they retired to their former position.

BATTLE MONUMENT.

CHAPTER XXIII.

BOMBARDMENT OF FORT McHENRY.

1. Having failed to take the city by land, the enemy hoped that an attack by water would be more successful, and on the evening of the 13th, the fleet began to bombard the fort.

Question.—1. What took place on the 13th?

2. The garrison was composed of three companies of United States artillery, and three volunteer city companies, under Capt. Berry, Lieut. Pennington and Capt. Nicholson, besides six hundred infantry; in all about one thousand men, under Col. Armistead.

3. The fleet being anchored two miles from the fort, and out of reach of its guns, the latter was compelled to receive the fire in silence. But a supposed advantage having been obtained, several vessels were brought within range. The batteries immediately opened upon them with such effect, that they were driven back to their former position.

BOMBARDMENT OF FORT MCHENRY.

Questions.—2. What composed the garrison? 3. What is said in this section?

4. During the night several rocket vessels and barges, with fourteen hundred men, supplied with scaling ladders, passed silently by the fort, and entered the Patapsco. Suddenly as they drew opposite the six gun battery, Lieut. Webster, its commander, opened upon them with terrible effect. The fort and ten gun battery, also poured in their fire. The havoc was dreadful. One of the barges was sunk, and the cries of the wounded and drowning, could be plainly heard upon the shore. The rest, having suffered a heavy loss, retreated to the fleet.

5. Just previous to the bombardment, Francis S. Key, Esq., had, under a flag of truce, gone on board of the enemy's fleet, to obtain the release of a friend who had been taken captive. He was himself detained until after the bombardment.—During the night he composed the national song, "THE STAR SPANGLED BANNER," descriptive of the scene which was passing, and of his own excited feelings.

6. Baffled by land and by water, the enemy determined to abandon the expedition. The troops were embarked on the 15th, and, on the 16th, the hostile fleet dropped down the Chesapeake, leaving the city filled with joy at her triumphant preservation, mingled with sorrow for the brave men who had died to defend her.

Questions.—4. What was done during the night? How were they received? 5. What national song was composed this night? 6. What is said in this section?

7. Early in the ensuing year, the war was closed. The treaty of peace was signed at Ghent on the 24th of December, 1814, and ratified by the United States, on 17th of February, 1815.

CHAPTER XXIV.

1815-1848 — REFORM — *Internal Improvements — Chesapeake and Ohio Canal — Rail Roads — Baltimore and Ohio Rail Road — Other Rail Roads — Colonization Society — Pecuniary Crisis — Mexican War.*

1. The people of Maryland began now to turn their attention to the affairs of their own State. Baltimore had grown very rapidly and under the existing constitution, her representation in the legislature was not proportioned to her population.

2. By the system of that day, a minority of the people could determine the choice of the senate, the governor and council, and the legislature.

3. The senate was not chosen directly by the people, but by electors, two from each county, and the governor was appointed by the legislature; thus the influence of ten small counties, if brought to bear, could overpower that of the larger.

Questions.—1. What is said of Baltimore? 2. What of the senate and governor? 3. How were they chosen?

4. After many years of fruitless efforts, a reform was effected. The election of the governor was given to the people, and his term of office fixed for three years. The council was abolished, and a secretary of State provided. The senate was reorganized and was to be elected by the people.

5. The constitution of the house of delegates was materially altered, and the number of delegates was distributed more in accordance with the population of the several counties and towns.

6. In 1823, the subject of internal improvements became an absorbing theme in Maryland. The immense mineral resources of the western part of the State, the iron and the coal made it important that the designs of the Potomac Company should be completed. But after repeated efforts, it was found that the mode of navigation proposed by the Potomac Company was insufficient.

7. It was, therefore, proposed to incorporate a new company, to which the old one should surrender its privileges, for the purpose of making a canal along the river to its head, and thence to the Ohio. In pursuance of this plan, the Chesapeake and Ohio Canal Company was incorporated in 1824.

8. This canal had its terminus at Georgetown. The city of Baltimore naturally feared that the

---

Questions.—4. What change was made? 5. What change in the house of delegates? 6. What is said of internal improvements? 7. What new company was formed? 8. What is said of Baltimore?

trade with the west would be drawn from her. As she had no means of competing by canal or water routes with the interior, her attention was drawn to railways.

9. At this time, rail roads were an untried novelty. In England, the engineers and capitalists were agitating the subject of this means of transportation between Liverpool and Manchester,—the first passenger rail road ever constructed,—and simultaneous with this movement the leading citizens of Baltimore were contemplating the organization of a company to build the Baltimore and Ohio Rail Road—the first in this country.

10. The first persons to propose this measure were George Brown, Esq., and his associate, Philip E. Thomas, Esq. The far-reaching sagacity of these men, and the wonderful results that have developed themselves in connection with this road, render their names as worthy of honorable mention as those of any that grace the history of Maryland.

11. In February, 1827, these men called a meeting of the citizens of Baltimore, and a memorial was, at once, presented to the legislature: in ten days after a charter was granted.

12. A rail road was also projected from Baltimore to York, Pennsylvania, and an act of

---

Questions.—9. What of rail roads? 10. Who were the first to propose the Baltimore and Ohio Rail Road? 11. When was the first meeting called? 12. What other road was projected?

incorporation was obtained, under the title of the "Baltimore and Susquehanna Rail Road." The title was subsequently changed to "Northern Central Rail Road." The "Western Maryland Rail Road" was also projected, but for many years it was suspended. The Washington Branch of the Baltimore and Ohio Rail Road was also built.—This branch has proved very profitable to the State.

13. During this period, the American Colonization Society was formed, for the purpose of establishing colonies on the western coast of Africa, and of settling there those emancipated blacks, who should be willing to return to the land of their forefathers. A branch of this Association was immediately formed in Maryland. Finding that, by its connexion with the National Society, it was liable to the vexatious interference of Northern abolitionists, it determined to form an independent organization, and plant a separate colony under the name of "Maryland," in Liberia. This society received aid from the State, by an annual appropriation of one thousand dollars.

14. In 1837, a great financial crisis occurred. There was great distress in all parts of the country. Suspensions and failures in business became of every day occurrence. In addition to private distress, the national treasury itself was plunged into a state of bankruptcy.

Questions.—13. What is said of the Colonization society? 14. What occurred in 1837?

15. Of course, Maryland did not escape. Her liabilities were very great, as the State had subscribed very liberally to the public improvements. It was found that, on the first of December, 1840, there would be a deficit in the treasury of six hundred thousand dollars—an amount almost twice as great as the whole revenue of the State.

16. Instead of following the example of some of the other States, by repudiating her debts, it was resolved that a direct tax should be levied on the property of the people; as a means of revenue, it also adopted the stamp system on all pecuniary obligations. By the energetic measures recommended by Governor Pratt, she redeemed her credit, and her financial condition has ever since been highly prosperous.

17. In the Mexican war, which broke out in 1845, Maryland was represented by many brave and distinguished heroes, among whom was Maj. Samuel Ringgold, who, at the head of his battery of light artillery, had distinguished himself throughout that conflict. He was killed at Point Isabel, in Texas, May 11th, 1846. He is buried in Greenmount cemetery, near Baltimore.

18. Colonel Wm. H. Watson distinguished himself at the battle of Monterey. He fell a victim to his ardor. Struck by a cannon ball, he sunk in

---

Questions.—15. What is said of Maryland? 16. How did she relieve herself of her difficulties? 17. What is said of the Mexican war? Of Major Ringgold? 18. What is said of Col. Watson?

the arms of Capt. Oden Bowie one of his comrades, since made Governor of this State, and expired.

19. Lieut. Randolph Ridgeley, who distinguished himself at the battle of Resaca de la Palma, and who had passed unscathed through so many scenes of blood, was instantly killed by being thrown from his horse.

20. In the battles of the valley of Mexico, the Maryland company of Voltigeurs was distinguished in the storming of the Castle of Chapultepec, where they were thrown in the advance. Captain John Eager Howard, grandson of the hero of Cowpens, was the first officer to cross the parapet, and to leap down amidst the bayonets of the foe, slaying several of the enemy with his own hand. Capt. Archer and Lieut. Swan were also distinguished for their courage.

21. Thus stood Maryland in 1848. Its credit established; its property redoubled; its internal improvements hastening to completion; its metropolis growing with a rapidity almost beyond precedent; its commerce, agriculture and manufactures flourishing and improving, and its people proud of its past history, were welcoming home those gallant sons who had so sustained her reputation with the brave *old Maryland Bayonet.*

Questions.—19. What is said of Lieut. Ridgeley? 20. What is said of the Maryland company in the battles of the valley of Mexico? Of Howard? 21. What is said of Maryland in 1848?

The Thomas viaduct on the Patapsco.

CHAPTER XXV.

RE-SURVEY OF MASON AND DIXON'S LINE—*New Constitution—Completion of Baltimore and Ohio Rail Road —Its Communication with Europe—Southern Boundary Line of the State—Commission appointed to Retrace the Line.*

1. Very little of interest occurred after the Mexican war, until the civil war of 1861. In 1849, a revision was made of the boundary line between Maryland and Pennsylvania. The re-survey was made by commissioners appointed by the States of Maryland, Delaware and Pennsylvania. So accu-

Question.—1. What is said of the re-survey of Mason and Dixon's line?

rate was the work of Mason and Dixon, that the change involved by the corrections amounted to less than two acres, which were added to the area of Maryland.

2. In 1851, a State Convention was appointed to form a new constitution. By this constitution lotteries were made illegal; imprisonment for debt was abolished; the judiciary was made elective; and, the fees of the officers were not allowed to exceed three thousand dollars; all in excess of this amount was to be paid into the State treasury. Other changes were made, but they were not of a permanent character.

3. On the first day of January, 1853, the Baltimore and Ohio Rail Road was finished to the Ohio river. It had been promised two years before, that it should be completed on that day, and true to the time appointed, the first passenger train from Baltimore arrived at the bank of Wheeling Creek.

4. Thomas Swann, Esq., subsequently governor of the State, was president of the road at that time. It was to his boldness, eloquence and confidence, sustained by the skill, experience, energy and caution of the chief engineer, Benjamin H. Latrobe, Esq., that this work was carried through its difficulties to a successful completion—a work

---

Questions.—2. State some of the changes made by the Constitution of 1851? 3. When was the Baltimore and Ohio Rail Road completed? What had been promised two years before? 4. Who was president of the road at that time? To what was the completion of the road due?

whose importance to Maryland, and particularly to Baltimore, can never be over-estimated.

5. Upon its completion, Mr. Swann resigned. The presidency of this corporation, which exercises so controlling an influence over the whole business of Maryland, and even of neighboring States, has fallen into able and trustworthy hands. Such judicious connections have been made with western roads, that the distance between the seaboard and the great west, finds its shortest line along the Baltimore and Ohio Rail Road, which is, therefore, destined to form a part of the great highway between the two Oceans.

6. Availing themselves of this fact, the company have made direct communication with Europe, by means of two lines of steamers, one to Liverpool and the other to Bremen. By the exercise of energy and tact, Baltimore was, in 1868, in this way, the only American owner of Trans-Atlantic steamers, and that, too, without the aid of government subsidy.

7. The southern boundary line of this State was described in the charter as "a right line drawn from the promontory, or head-land, called *Watkins' Point*, unto the main Ocean on the East." In 1661, a dispute arose as to the precise location of Watkins' Point.

Questions.—5. When did Mr. Swann resign? Who is the present president? What connections have been made? 6. What is said of communication with Europe? 7. How was the southern boundary of the State described in the charter? When did a dispute arise?

8. This dispute was settled by articles of agreement between Philip Calvert, commissioner for Maryland, and Edmund Scarbrugh, commissioner for Virginia, in the year 1668. (See page 74.) By this agreement, Watkins' Point was defined to be the *whole body of land* between the north side of the Pocomoke bay and the south side of Annamessex bay, now Big Annamessex river.

9. The commissioners ran what was intended to be an east line, from "the extremest part of the westernmost angle of the said Watkins' Point."

10. All of the existing maps of Maryland and Virginia being incorrect, the points named did not conform with the provisions of the charter; and, the time and manner of the early settlement of the boundary line being almost forgotten, the old question of the locality of Watkins' Point was revived. In 1858, Thomas J. Lee, Esq., was appointed commissioner for Maryland, in conjunction with a commissioner from Virginia, "to retrace and mark the boundary between Smith's Point, at the mouth of the Potomac, and the Atlantic."

11. The commissioners, in retracing the line from Watkins' Point, discovered that it did not run east. By the agreement in 1668, it was intended to be an east line, or a parallel of latitude; and

---

Questions.—8. How was the dispute settled? 9. What was the line intended to be? 10. What is said of the maps of Maryland? Of the settlement of the dispute? When was a commission appointed to retrace the line? Who was appointed for Maryland? 11. What did the commissioner discover?

such a line would add about twenty-three square miles to Maryland. But as the error in the line was probably due to not taking into the account the variation of the compass, and as its direction was fixed by marks, the commissioners simply renewed such landmarks as were either lost or destroyed, and did not look to any change in the present limits of the State.

NEAR VIEW OF THOMAS' VIADUCT.

Questions.—11. What is the probable cause of this error Did they propose any change?

CHAPTER XXVI.

CHARACTER OF THE PERIOD — *Election of Lincoln — Southern Views of the Government — Northern Views — The Feelings of Maryland — Its Geographical Position — Not prepared to Secede — Slave Property — Excitement — Riot in Baltimore.*

1. The period upon which we are about to enter is one of great gloom. It was characterized by that civil war, from the effects of which the whole country is still suffering.

2. The election in 1860, of Abraham Lincoln as president of the United States, by the anti-slavery party, alarmed the people of the South for the safety of their institutions. They declared that the compact of the constitution had been violated by previous acts of the Northern States, and that their rights, both political and personal, were now in danger. They, therefore, asserted and exercised the right of separation from the Union.

3. There had always existed two parties in the country, differing in their ideas of the fundamental principles of the government; one had favored a strong central, or a federal government, the other, as was mentioned in the chapter on the Federal Constitution, fearing that too great centralization

---

Questions.—1. What is said of this period? 2. What was the effect of the election of Lincoln? 3. What two parties had always existed?

would ultimately destroy State independence, and popular liberty, asserted the States Rights doctrine.

4. Although Massachusetts, as early as 1811, was perhaps the first to avow and maintain that withdrawal from the Union was the "privilege of all and might be the duty of some," the States-rights party had its strength mostly in the Southern States.

5. The State in which he was born; the laws under whose protection he lived; the institutions by which he was surrounded; the common interests and sympathies of his section; the scenes of his childhood; his home; the history of his State as a State, in which he had so much pride, and of which he himself, or his ancestors were a part; these made for the Southerner his country, these claimed and received his allegiance.

6. The interests, the sympathies, and the habits of thought of the Northerners were different, and, in many respects, opposed to those of the Southerners. The population of that section was greatly modified by immigration, and its bulk increased far beyond the natural increase by births.

7. This vast army of foreigners, with their descendants, had no social or historic associations

---

Questions.—4. What State first asserted the right of secession? Where was the States-rights party the strongest? 5. What is said of the people of the South? 6. What, of the North? 7. How did the foreigners regard the country?

connected with the State which chance, interest, or necessity had determined as their future home, and it is natural that they should look upon the country as a unit; not as a union of several States, but as a consolidated nation. And thus when the Federal Government determined to resist, with all its power, the act of secession on the part of the Southern States, the old party divisions in the North were, to a great extent, obliterated, and nearly all united on the idea of a national unity.

8. The people of Maryland were devoted to the union, and loyal to the Constitution; but the sympathies of the majority of the State were upon the side whose interests and institutions were identical with their own. These people looked upon the preparations of the Federal Government as a violation of the Constitution, and as an unlawful aggression upon the rights of the Southern people.

9. The geographical situation of Maryland rendered it desirable to the Southern States that she should join them. The Federal Capital was within her border, and should Maryland secede, Washington would become the capital of the Southern Confederacy. But this geographical position, on the other hand, operated to deter her from that step. On the north and east she was bounded by Pennsylvania and Delaware whence, as there was

---

Questions.—7. At the breaking out of the war which side did they espouse? 8. What is said of the people of Maryland? 9. What, of its geographical situation?

no barrier to prevent an invasion, she could be overrun by the Northern forces. The South, to meet these forces, would be compelled to send adequate numbers to the borders of Maryland, and thus this State would be the battle-ground of the two sections.

10. Notwithstanding their sympathy with the Southern brethren, and their belief that the Southern States were exercising a natural and constitutional right, the people of this State were not yet prepared to think they had sufficient cause to leave the Union, but thought they should contend for their rights in the Union, and, therefore, were not willing to make their territory desolate in order to enforce an act of which they doubted the wisdom.

11. Again, many thought her large slave property would, in the event of Maryland's seceding, immediately leave for the neighboring free State of Pennsylvania, and thus, beside depriving her citizens of property valued at fifty millions of dollars, the State would be left comparatively bare of labor for the cultivation of the soil. She would cease to be a slave State, and hence have less interest in a a union with slave States, and at the same time would be in a hostile position towards the free States. There were also not an inconsiderable

---

Questions.—9. What other effect had this geographical situation? 10. Did the people of Maryland think the act of secession a wise one? 11. What other cause deterred Maryland from uniting with the South?

minority, with the Governor at their head, who looked upon secession as treason, and upon all acts or words looking that way as treasonable.

12. A feeling of intense excitement, therefore, pervaded all classes, especially in the city of Baltimore. Many prominent men had expressed their views on both sides, and meetings had been held in favor of uniting with the South, and also against any such step. On neither side, however, was there any organization. Great efforts were made to induce Governor Hicks to call an extra session of the Legislature. The Governor opposed this, thinking it involved a seizure of Washington, and the prevention of the inauguration of President Lincoln. The Governor was supported in his course by a large number of citizens on the Eastern Shore and in the Western counties. The Southern counties, however, and the city of Baltimore were emphatic in their denunciation of the executive.

13 When in obedience to the President's call for seventy-five thousand volunteers, the sixth Massachusetts regiment reached Baltimore, on April 19th, 1861, a disposition was manifested to interfere with their passage through the city. After some of the troops had been transported by car

---

Questions.—12. What was the state of feeling? What was the governor desired to do? Why did the governor oppose this? Who supported, and who denounced him? 13. What happened on the 19th of April?

to the Washington Depot, obstructions were placed upon the track in the city, which stopped the progress of the remainder. These alighted and proceeded to march to the Washington Depot.

14. As the police authorities had no knowledge that troops were expected that day, until within an hour of their arrival, but a short time was allowed to make proper arrangements to preserve order. The marshal of the police, Geo. P. Kane, Esq., immediately called out a large portion of his force, which came, in squads, to the Washington depot.

15. Whatever disturbance there may have been in that neighborhood having been quelled by the police, an alarm was given that there were more troops at the Philadelphia depot, and that the mob was tearing up the track. Having sent a hasty summons to a body of police to follow him to the scene of the riot, the Mayor, Geo. Wm. Brown, Esq., proceeded alone to the Philadelphia depot. When he reached the obstructions on the track, he ordered the few policemen that were on the ground to remove the obstructions, and his authority was not resisted. When he approached the troops, he found an attack upon them by a mob had already commenced. He immediately placed himself by the side of the officer in command, and marched with him, doing what he could by his presence and personal efforts to allay the tumult.

Questions.—14. What is said in this section? 15. What did the mayor do? Where did he place himself?

16. Missiles were, notwithstanding, thrown at the troops, and some of them were injured. The soldiers fired upon the crowd, with fatal effect upon distant and innocent spectators. An intense and irrepressible feeling was at once aroused; one of the mob seized a musket from a soldier and fired. Fire-arms were then freely used on both sides.—Three of the Massachusetts regiment were killed.

17. At this moment, Marshal Kane, with about fifty policemen, from the direction of the Washington depot, rushed to the rear of the troops, and formed a line across the street, with their drawn revolvers, checking and keeping off the mob. Under the escort of this body of policemen, the troops finally reached the Washington depot.

18. The police authorities insisted that they had both the disposition and the power to prevent the riot had timely notice been given of the arrival of the troops, and that, had it not been for the efficiency of the marshal and his men, the bloodshed would have been great.

19. In the meanwhile, another body of troops arrived at the Philadelphia depot. These troops were protected by the police until they were sent back to Havre-de-Grace, whence they were taken in transports to Annapolis. From Annapolis they marched to the Washington rail road and were thence transported in cars to the Federal capital.

Questions.—16. State what happened? 17. Who appeared at this time? 18. What did the police authorities declare? 19. What is said of another body of troops?

20. The Governor of Massachusetts telegraphed to the Mayor of Baltimore to have the killed sent forward to him. The Mayor, in promising to do so, reminded the Governor that the Massachusetts soldiers were considered as invaders of the soil of Maryland. He also told the Governor that the wounded were tenderly cared for, and said: "Baltimore will claim it as her right to pay all the expenses incurred."

21. By night, the excitement in the city was so great that it was regarded by the police authorities as impossible that soldiers from other States could pass through the city without a fierce and bloody conflict at every step, and that great loss of life, and possibly the destruction of the city itself might ensue.

22. As the readiest method of averting such a calamity was by stopping the immediate arrival of more troops from the North, it was suggested that, to this end, the bridges on the roads leading to the city should be disabled. Governor Hicks having agreed to these views, and given his consent thereto, instructions were issued for carrying them into effect.

23. On the 21st, Gen'l B. F. Butler arrived with troops off Annapolis. He requested permission

---

Questions.—20. What did the governor of Massachusetts do? What was the reply? 21. What was the condition of the city? 22. What was thought the best method of averting the calamity? 23. Who arrived on the 21st?

from Governor Hicks to land his forces. The Governor, in his message to the General Assembly, says he refused his consent. The troops, however, were landed. The Governor protested against this act, as well as against the forcible seizure of the Annapolis and Elk Ridge rail road.

24. Great excitement prevailed on the same day in Baltimore. A body of troops, on their way to the South, had been stopped at Ashland Station, on the Northern Central rail road, by the destruction of the bridge. Many of the citizens, both of the city and county, armed themselves to resist their passage. The troops returned to their State, and were sent forward by another route, the President having agreed with the Governor of the State and the Mayor of Baltimore, that no more troops should be sent through that city.

25. Among the troops that were compelled to return, was the Seventh regiment of New York, the favorite corps of that city. Their trip to Washington was regarded by these gay young men as a party of pleasure, and they were surprised to find that they were to be resisted in Baltimore by those with whom, in former days, they had exchanged hospitalities.

26. It was the remark of the officers of this regiment that, if the fortunes of war should bring

---

Questions.—23. State what further is said? 24. What was the condition of Baltimore? What did the troops do? 25. What regiment was among those compelled to return? What is said of them? 26. What remark was made by their officer?

them in conflict with their old friends of Baltimore, at the first fire, they would present arms; at the second, they would defend themselves. As this regiment was never under fire, it cannot be known whether the gallantry of their deeds would equal the courtesy of their language.

27. The exasperation felt towards Baltimore in Northern States was intense and universal. Attacks were threatened, not only by troops in the service of the General Government, but also by independent organizations, sworn to the perpetration of all kinds of excesses.

28. The people of the North regarded secession as treason, and the acts of the 19th and 21st of April, by the people of Baltimore as aiding and abetting treason. The South regarded the right of separation from the Union as a sovereign right, and while denying the charge of treason, retorted that the acts of the Federal Government were aggressive, tyrannical, and a usurpation of power subversive alike to political and personal liberty. Each side may have acted conscientiously, but neither side had charity sufficient to make allowance for the different views of the nature and relations of the General Government to the States that had prevailed ever since the adoption of the Constitution.

Questions.—26. Was this regiment ever under fire? 27. What is said of the feeling towards Baltimore in the north? 28. What is said in this section?

29. The people of Maryland, while opposed to the *policy* of secession, generally conceded the *right* of a State to secede. Believing that the Federal Government had no right to wage war against a State for the purposes of subjugation or conquest, they refused to regard those as guilty of treason who struck a blow at the invaders of their soil, on their way to slay their kindred.

CHAPTER XXVII.

MEETING OF LEGISLATURE — *Governor's Message—Address to the People—Military Departments—Scott's Campaign against Baltimore—Butler's Occupation of Baltimore—Non-Resistance of Baltimore—Habeas Corpus—Case of John Merryman.*

1. Washington being now safe from the supposed seizure by the Southern sympathisers in Maryland, there was no reason why Governor Hicks should decline to call an extra session of the Legislature. But as Annapolis was now in possession of the Federal troops, by a proclamation, dated April 24, he appointed Frederick as the place of meeting.

2. Accordingly, that body met at Frederick on the 26th. The Governor, in his message, briefly

---

Questions.—29. What view did Marylanders take? 1. What is said of calling an extra session of the legislature? 2. When did it meet and where?

detailed the startling events that had induced him to summon them together, and stated his views of the proper course to be pursued by Maryland in the present crisis.

3. His convictions were, "that the only safety of Maryland lay in preserving a neutral position between the North and the South; that he could not counsel Maryland to take sides against the General Government until it shall commit outrages upon us that would justify us in resisting its authority; that the geographical position of the State forces it to declare for Union and Peace, if it would not have every material interest of its people destroyed."

4. On the 27th, the day after their assembling, the Senate and House of Delegates issued an address to the people, stating that the fear that their deliberations might result in committing the State to secession, was groundless, and that they had no constitutional authority to take such a step.

5. In the meanwhile, the General Government had created the military department of Annapolis. This department embraced the country twenty miles on each side of the Washington rail road, as far as Bladensburg. Gen'l Benj. F. Butler was placed in command of it, with ample discretionary power to make him a sort of military dictator.

Questions.—3. What were his convictions? 4. What did the legislature do on the 27th? 5. What is said of the military department? Who was in command?

6. General Scott, at that time Lieut. Gen'l of the United States army, devised a grand campaign against Baltimore. His plan was to send a column of three thousand men from Washington; another, of the same number from York, Pennsylvania, and a third column of three thousand men from Perryville, or Elkton, by land, or by water, or both, and a fourth, of equal strength, from Annapolis.

7. Either the military education of Gen'l Scott was in his way, or he was totally ignorant of the condition of affairs in Baltimore. However willing the people may have been to resist the Government in sending troops to coerce States, they were utterly without arms or organization to carry any such wish into execution.

8. General Butler, however, knew very well how utterly unprepared the city was to make opposition even to a single regiment, if brought unexpectedly to the citizens, and prepared for any emergency. He, therefore, asked permission to take a regiment or two from Annapolis and march to the Relay House on the Baltimore and Ohio rail road. The request was granted.

9. On the 4th of May he issued orders for two regiments and a battery of artillery to be ready to march at two A. M. The troops were in Washington city. In two hours after starting, they were at the Relay House.

Questions.—6. What was Gen. Scott's plan against Baltimore? 7. What is said of this plan? 8. What is said of General Butler? 9. What order did he issue on 4th of May?

10. Not only the utter inability to resist the passage of troops, but even the want of disposition to do so on the part of the citizens, was shewn by the fact that on the 8th of May, Col. Patterson landed at Locust Point with twelve hundred men. There was no other demonstration than the usual assembling of a crowd to witness the soldiers. Marshal Kane was present with a body of police, and tendered the services of the officers of the civil law. His offer was accepted, and there was no disturbance.

RELAY HOUSE, *Washington Junction, B. & O. R. R.*

11. Butler remained at the Relay House for a week. On the 13th, in the night, when those who

---

Questions.—10. Was there any ability to resist troops? Who landed at Locust Point? 11. How long did Butler remain at the Relay House, and then what did he do?

were not in bed, were kept in doors by a violent rain storm that was raging, he marched with a thousand men to Federal Hill. Lieut. Gen. Scott called this "a hazardous occupation of Baltimore," and regarded it as a "God-send that it was without conflict."

12. Scott, whether he really thought that Butler had acted with temerity, or whether he was annoyed to find himself so deceived about the condition of affairs in the city, insisted upon the recall of General Butler.

13. Butler was succeeded by General Cadwallader, and the troops were temporarily withdrawn. Afterwards, Duryée's Zouaves occupied Federal Hill and built a strong earthwork, whose cannon commanded both the town and Fort McHenry.

14. The first act of resistance to the civil law on the part of the military, was on May 14th. On that day, Judge Giles, of the United States District Court, issued a writ of *habeas corpus* for the release of a man confined in Fort McHenry.—Major Morris refused to obey.

15. The most noted case, however, of a refusal to obey the writ of *habeas corpus*, was that of John Merryman, of Baltimore county, who was cast into Fort McHenry, on May 25th.

Questions.—12. What did Scott insist upon, and why? 13. By whom was Butler succeeded? 14. What was the first act of resistance to the civil law by the military? 15. Which was the most noted case?

16. Mr. Merryman was charged with holding a commission as Lieutenant in a company avowing its hostility to the General Government; with being in communication with the army at the South, and with varions acts of treason. His counsel had an interview with the commander of the Fort, and requested that he might be permitted to see the papers under and by which Mr. Merryman was detained in custody. The request was refused.

17. Mr. Merryman at once forwarded a petition to Roger B. Taney, Chief Justice of the Supreme Court of the United States, praying for a writ of *habeas corpus* to be issued, commanding General Cadwallader to produce the petitioner in Court and shew cause for his detention. The writ was issued for May 27th. General Cadwallader's response to the writ was a letter to the Chief Justice stating the charges against the accused; that *he* was satisfied of the guilt of the prisoner, and that he was duly authorized by the President of the United States to suspend the writ of *habeas corpus*. He concluded his letter to the Chief Justice by giving *his* views of that venerable officer's duty in the case.

Questions.—16. What was Mr. Merryman charged with? 17. What did Mr. Merryman do? What was Gen. Cadwallader's response?

CHIEF JUSTICE TANEY.

18. The Chief Justice immediately ordered that an attachment forthwith issue against Gen'l Cadwallader, for contempt in refusing to produce the body of John Merryman, according to the command of the writ of *habeas corpus*. On the day appointed for the return, the Marshal replied that he had proceeded to the fort to serve the writ, that he was not permitted to enter the gate, and that he was informed, "there was no answer to his card."

19. The Chief Justice remarked in court that the detention of the prisoner was unlawful upon two grounds:

1. That the President, under the Constitution, cannot suspend the privilege of the writ of *habeas corpus*, nor authorize any military officer to do it.

2. That "a military officer has no right to arrest and detain a person, not subject to the rules and articles of war, for an offence against the laws of the

---

Questions.—18. What did Chief Justice Taney do? What was the effect? 19. What did the Chief Justice decide?

United States, excepting as subject to the control of the judicial authority; and that it is the duty of the military to immediately deliver over persons so arrested, to the civil authority, to be dealt with according to law. It is, therefore, very clear that John Merryman is entitled to be set at liberty and discharged immediately from imprisonment."

20. The Chief Justice subsequently reduced his opinion to writing, and filed it with the archives of the Court. In this opinion he recited the history of the arrest, as given in the petition, and said that Gen'l Cadwallader in his return did not deny any of the facts alleged in the petition, but had stated that the prisoner was arrested by order of General Keim, of Pennsylvania; that it was not alleged in the return that any specific act, constituting an offence against the laws of the United States, had been charged against the prisoner, upon oath, but that he appeared to have been arrested upon charges of treason and rebellion without proof, and without the names of witnesses being given, or the acts specified, which, in the judgment of the military officer, constituted these crimes.

21. After discussing the constitutional right of the President to suspend the writ of *habeas corpus*, the Chief Justice uses the following language: "Such is the case now before me; and I can only say that if the authority which the Constitution has

---

Questions.—20. State what is said in this section? 21. What language did the Chief Justice use?

confided to the judiciary department, and judicial officers may thus, upon any pretext, or under any circumstances, be usurped by the military power at its discretion, the people of the United States are no longer living under a Government of laws, but every citizen holds life, liberty and property at the will and pleasure of the army officer in whose military district he may happen to be found."

22. After stating that his constitutional power had been resisted by a force too strong for him to overcome, and suggesting the possibility that the military officer may have misunderstood his instruction, and exceeded the authority intended to be given him, and stating his intention to have a copy of the proceedings transmitted to the President of the United States, he thus concludes: "It will then remain for that high officer, in fulfilment of his constitutional obligation 'to take care that the laws be executed,' to determine what measures he will take to cause the civil process of the United States to be respected and enforced." The Chief Justice declared that the prisoner was improperly held, and was entitled to his liberty.

23. The Legislature of Maryland passed a resolution declaring "that we deem the writ of *habeas corpus* the great safe-guard of personal liberty, and we view with the utmost alarm and indignation the exercise of despotic power, that has dared

---

Questions.—22. What further did he say? 23. What resolution did the legislature pass?

to suspend it in the case of John Merryman, now confined in Fort McHenry."

24. Within six months no less than one hundred prisoners of State, to whom the privilege of *habeas corpus* had been denied, were confined in Fort La Fayette, N. Y., alone; and in December, the commanding officer read a document to the prisoners, to the effect that the United States would not recognize any one as attorney for political offenders, and that all applications through this usual method would be regarded as sufficient reason for detaining them in custody. They must make their application to the State Department, or in other words, to their accusers.

25. The Attorney General of the United States, and a prominent lawyer of Philadelphia, published answers to the Chief Justice's decision. The number of replies to those answers that appeared throughout the North, shewed the deep interest taken in the subject of personal freedom, and that the minds of many, even in the strife of the hour were startled from the fancied security to their liberties.

26. Mr. Merryman was subsequently released on bail, but was never tried, although on two occasions he demanded this right. On the first occasion, May, 1863, the case was dismissed by the

---

Questions.—24. Were others deprived of their civil rights? 25. Who published replies to Chief Justice Taney's decision? 26. What further is said of Mr. Merryman?

orders of the Attorney General of the United States. In June, however, he was re-indicted, and held so until 1867, when by the direction of the United States District Attorney, the case was finally dismissed.

CHAPTER XXVIII.

LEGISLATIVE PROCEEDINGS — *Arrest of Winans — The Report on Federal Relations — Resolutions Passed — Governor's Denial of the Right of Senate to make Enquiries.*

1. Shortly after the assembling of the Legislature in their extra session, Ross Winans, a member of the House of Delegates, was arrested in the presence of the Governor of State by an armed force under orders of the Federal Government.

2. The General Assembly passed resolutions condemning in the strongest terms this act, and declaring "the same to be subversive of the most sacred guarantees of the Constitution, and in flagrant violation of the fundamental principles of free government."

3. Other important resolutions were passed by the Legislature. The Committee on Federal Rela-

---

Questions.—1. Who was shortly afterwards arrested? 2. What resolutions did the legislature pass?

tions, composed of S. T. Wallis, J. H. Gordon, G. W. Goldsborough, Jas. T. Briscoe and Barnes Compton, presented a report and resolutions which were adopted.

4. The report contended "that the President in calling upon the militia of other States to enforce the laws of the United States in those States where the execution thereof was obstructed, was unconstitutional, and a summons to the people of the two sections to shed each other's blood. It further declared that the war was chiefly obnoxious to the people of Maryland because it was one of sectional aggression and domination; that the dominant section had seized upon the name, and flag, and resources of the General Government to establish its dominion over the other section; that the name and sacred memories of the Union were prostrated; that it was a war waged against a people of our own name and blood, who sought peace and kindly relations with us, and who only asked to be let alone, and to govern themselves; that subjugated provinces could not be sister States; that a government maintaining its authorities by armies, could not be other than the most uncontrollable of despotisms; that the South had entrenched itself upon the principle of self-government, and that unless the American Revolution was a crime, the Declaration of Independence a falsehood, and every

---

Questions.—3. & 4. What is said of the report on Federal relations?

patriot and hero of 1776 a traitor, the South was right and the North was wrong upon that issue."

5. The report further discussed the constitutional right of the President, and insisted "that the lawless outbreak in Baltimore on the 19th of April, was primarily the fault of those who marched the Massachusetts soldiery through that city upon an illegal and unconstitutional errand." The report then discussed the Governor's proposition of neutrality, and pronounced it futile, saying "that the only possible position of the State was an attitude of submission." It discouraged the calling of a convention, "since the military occupation of the soil by Northern troops, against the wishes of its people, and the solemn protest of the Governor, would render futile any attempt at the performance of an act of sovereignty."

6. The resolutions proposed by the committee, and adopted by the legislature, were in accordance with the views in the report, viz: "that the State of Maryland registers her solemn protest against the war which the Federal Government has declared upon the Confederate States; that it anxiously desires the restoration of peace between the belligerent sections, and implores the President of the United States to accept the olive branch held out to him, and in the name of God and humanity to cease the unprofitable strife; that it desires, and

---

Questions.—5. What further did the report discuss? 6. What resolutions were passed?

gives her assent to, a recognition of the Confederate States; that the military occupation of the State was in violation of the Constitution; and, finally, that it was inexpedient to call a Sovereign Convention of the State, or to take any measure for the organizing of the militia." A committee was appointed to lay these resolutions before the President of the Southern Confederacy, and if possible to obtain a general cessation of hostilities until the meeting of Congress in July. The committee consisted, from the Senate, of Messrs. Brooke, of Prince George's County; Yellott, of Baltimore City; Lynch, of Baltimore County, and McKaig, of Alleghany County. From the House of Delegates, Messrs. Harding, of Montgomery; Goldsborough, of Caroline County; Compton, of Charles, and Morgan, of St. Mary's County.

7. Governor Hicks having changed his attitude of neutrality, and taken that of open hostility to the South, and fearing that the arms belonging to the militia might be used against the Federal authorities, had them seized and sent to Fort McHenry.

8. Early in June, the Senate ordered that the Governor be requested to furnish that body with a statement of the facts which induced him to reclaim these arms, and why they were sent to

---

Questions.—6. What committee was appointed? 7. What is said of Gov. Hicks? 8. What order did the senate pass?

Fort McHenry; and also what security he had for the restoration of said arms, when demanded by the proper authorities of Maryland.

9. The Governor, in his message, denied the right of the Senate to make the enquiries, but said that "he was satisfied that many of them had been carried beyond the limits of Maryland for disloyal purposes; that he had good reason to believe more would be carried off for a like purpose; that he had placed them in Fort McHenry as a place of security; that his guarantee for their return was in the honor of the United States Government and its loyal officers."

10. This message of the Governor was submitted to the committee on judicial proceedings, who reported that "the action of the Governor was a palpable usurpation of authority, which ought not to be tolerated; and that if the Governor was right in assuming the position he did, there is no power in the State to question his authority or stay his hand."

11. The Legislature passed a resolution that the Governor be requested to return to the armories of the State the arms, that had been removed, and that he return to the militia the arms reclaimed from them." It does not appear to have been done.

Questions.—9. What reply did the Governor make? 10. To whom was the message submitted, and what was the report? 11. What resolution was passed by the legislature?

CHAPTER XXIX.

PROVOST MARSHALS—*Arrest of Kane—Arrest of Police Commissioners—Habeas Corpus—Military Occupation of Baltimore—Action of Legislature.*

1. The administration of General Cadwallader, as commander of the department, having been thought too mild by the Federal authorities, he was superseded, on June 8th, by General N. P. Banks.

2. On the 27th of the month, General Banks ordered a large body of soldiers, armed and supplied with ball cartridges, to march from Fort McHenry into the city and arrest Marshal Kane, and incarcerate him in Fort McHenry.

3. Gen'l Banks issued a proclamation announcing that it was not his design to interfere with the legitimate government of the people of Baltimore, or Maryland, but that the government regarded the Chief of the Police as at the head of a force hostile to its authority and acting in concert with its enemies. For this reason he arrested him and detained him in custody.

4. The suspension of the writ of *habeas corpus* rendered it impossible for any competent tribunal to decide whether the government was correct in

---

Questions.—1. What is said of Gen. Cadwallader? 2. What did Gen. Banks do? 3. What proclamation did he issue? 4. What was the effect of the suspension of the *habeas corpus*?

in its opinion, either in this instance, or in many others that occurred. The people of Maryland were powerless to prevent interference with the exercise of the functions of the civil courts by the military, and the people of the other parts of the Union, though many of them saw a threatening danger, were willing, for a time, to sacrifice their liberties for the accomplishment of an object dearer to them than liberty, trusting to be able to reclaim all they had yielded, after they had gained the object for which they were struggling.

5. Mr. Kane, after a tedious confinement at Fort Warren, Massachusetts, was released on bail. His bail bond having expired, and not being called on to appear on the appointed day, he left the State.

6. Col. J. R. Kenly was appointed Provost Marshal by the military commander, "to superintend and cause to be executed the police laws provided by the laws of Maryland." Colonel Kenly took possession of the headquarters of the Police Commissioners.

7. The Commissioners of Police, however, having maturely considered their duties and obligations under the law, protested against the proceedings of Gen'l Banks as an arbitrary exercise of military power, not warranted by any provision of the Constitution, and declared that they did not recognize

Questions.—5. What further is said of Kane? 6. Who was appointed Provost Marshal, and what did he do? 7. What did the commissioners of police do?

the right of any of the officers and men of the police force to receive orders from any other authority than from the Board of Police Commissioners.

8. On the 1st of July, at 3 o'clock in the morning, all the members of this board, excepting the Mayor, were arrested and taken to Fort McHenry. They were transferred to Fort Lafayette, in New York harbor, and on the 6th of August, Judge Garrison, of Brooklyn, issued a writ directing Col. Burke to produce the persons in court. Colonel Burke declined on the authority of an order from Lieut. Gen'l Scott. As in the instance of Gen'l Cadwallader, Burke was cited to answer for contempt of court. He did not appear, and on the 22d of August, Judge Garrison, "submitting to inevitable necessity," dismissed the proceedings. The prisoners were subsequently removed to Fort Warren.

9. When the morning of July 2d, dawned, the principal places of the city of Baltimore were found occupied by masses of artillery and infantry. The Court House, the Exchange, and many public places belonging to the city, were appropriated to the use of the troops, who thronged the streets and squares by night and by day.

Questions.—8. What was done with these commissioners? What further is said of them? 9. What is said of the city of Baltimore?

10. Meanwhile, Mr. Brown, the Mayor of the city, expressed his readiness to Gen'l Banks to undertake the management of the police. Gen'l Banks declined, but appointed Mr. G. R. Dodge Provost Marshal, in place of Col. Kenly, who was relieved at his own request.

11. On the appointment of Dodge, the military were removed from the heart of the city. On the 21st of July, Congress, in spite of the protests and solemn remonstrances of the Senators and Representatives from Maryland, passed a bill appropriating one hundred thousand dollars for the payment of the police organization of Baltimore employed by the United States."

12. The reports and memorials of the Police Commissioners to the Legislature, were referred to a joint committee of the Senate and House of Delegates. This committee submitted a report denouncing the act of the United States authorities as a revolution and usurpation "in the garb of government, and depending for its legitimacy upon bayonets;" asserting that the State under such dominion was no longer in the Union, in effect, whatever she might be in name. "She has no constitution, no government, no laws that she can call her own. She is ruled by external and arbitrary power. Her people are no longer free."

Questions.—10. What did the mayor propose? 11. What is said in this section? 12. What was the report of the committee?

13. The Legislature passed a series of resolutions pronouncing these acts a gross and unconstitutional abuse of power, and a revolutionary subversion of the Federal compact. They appealed, in the most earnest manner, to the whole country to come to the rescue of the free institutions of the republic, and ordered copies of their resolutions to be forwarded to the Senators and Representatives in Congress, and also to the Governors of the several States, and to the Legislatures. These resolutions were passed August 6th. On the next day, the Legislature adjourned to meet on the 17th day of September.

CHAPTER XXX.

ARREST OF THE LEGISLATURE—*Elections—General Dix—Candidates—Success of the Union Candidate—Oppression—Case of Judge Carmichael—Invasion of Southern Army — Conduct of Troops — Orders of Lee — South Mountain and Antietam — General Wool.*

1. This Legislature never met again. On the 11th of September, the Secretary of War issued orders to General Banks to arrest all, or a part of the members. On the morning of the 13th, the Provost Marshal, George R. Dodge, arrested the

---

Question.—13. What resolutions were passed? 1. What happened on September 11th?

Mayor of Baltimore, and the members of the Legislature from Baltimore city, and also those from Baltimore county. As fast as the members arrived in Baltimore, on their way to Frederick, they were arrested. Other members, and the officers of the Legislature were seized in Frederick.

2. No charge was ever made against these men; they were confined for fourteen months, and when discharged were as ignorant as on the day of their arrest, on what account they had been deprived of their liberty. The orders of the Secretary of War to Gen'l Banks were, that "the passage of any act of secession must be prevented. If necessary all or any part of the members must be arrested." There is no evidence that any such act was contemplated. Among the baggage of one of the members, it is said were found papers that *looked like* amendments to a secession ordinance, which, however, had never been proposed.

3. On November 6th, the regular election for Governor and Legislature took place. On the 28th of October, the Secretary of War had issued an order to Gen'l McClellan, that, in order to have a full vote in Maryland, he should grant a furlough to the soldiers of the first, second and third regiments of the Maryland volunteers. These soldiers were sent home at the expense of the government.

Questions.—2. What were the orders of the Secretary of War? What further is said in this section? 3. What election took place? What order had the Secretary of War issued?

4. General Dix, who had succeeded General Banks in command of the department, issued an order to the Provost Marshal of Baltimore, "to have the polls unobstructed," saying, "we have shewn that we can control Maryland by force; we now wish to shew we can control it by the power of opinion."

5. A States-Rights and a Union candidate for Governor were proposed. The latter, A. W. Bradford, Esq., was chosen by a majority of over thirty-one thousand votes. The whole number of votes cast was nearly eighty-four thousand. The number cast at the presidential election, a year before, was about ninety-eight thousand. A presidential election always brings out a larger vote than any other, and during the year many of the voters had left. Some were fearful that Baltimore was not a safe place of residence, and had gone North; others had gone to join the Southern army.

6. It would seem, therefore, that the majority of the voters in the State were not only adverse to any movement to join her fortunes to the Southern Confederacy, but were even willing to commit themselves to the policy of the administration in coercing the seceded States. But on the other hand, it was claimed that the returned soldiers boasted that they had voted as often as they

---

Questions.—4. What was Gen'l Dix's order? 5. What candidates? Who was elected? What further is said in this section? 6. What is said in this section?

pleased, and, that any one wearing the uniform of a Federal soldier, voted without question, whether he were a citizen or not.

7. Among the first acts of the new Legislature, after making provision for the relief of the families of the Massachusetts soldiers, who were killed and wounded by the rioters on the 19th of April, was the passage of resolutions, which were presented to the United States Senate on the 2d of January, 1862, declaring the unalterable attachment of the people of Maryland to the Union, but that their loyalty was untouched by any shade of servility, and that they regarded with jealousy all attempts to make the war for the restoration of the Union the means of interfering with the domestic institutions of the States; that, notwithstanding the necessity might exist for the resort to extraordinary measures, yet, the dangers of a departure from the ordinary forms of law, which are the protection of individual rights, ought never to be forgotten. The resolutions also expressed their approval of the President's course thus far in the conduct of the war, and their confidence in his honesty and firmness.

8. Notwithstanding the decided stand in behalf of the Union—which, by preserving the capital of the Republic to the Federal Government in the

---

Questions.—7. What were the first acts of this legislature? 8. What had Maryland done for the Federal Government?

beginning of the war, had saved that government from total overthrow, and, notwithstanding this decided majority for the Union candidates, the United States, while calling Maryland a loyal State, yet acted upon the theory that she would, if supported by the Southern army, unite with the South, and pressed her hard with its military hand.

9. General Dix was very strenuous in his efforts to break up all communication with the South.—To prove his efficiency, he instituted a system of midnight arrests and domiciliary visits. Parties, whether old men or delicate women, were seized, and in a few hours hurried away, and carried beyond the Federal lines in Virginia, to find friends, food and shelter as best they might. The celerity with which the military orders were executed, afforded no time to examine into the truth of any of the charges, and in cases where lenity was shewn, it was not on the score of innocence, or doubt of guilt, but was due to the personal influence of such as might have the ear of the military commander. Among the arrests that caused great sensation, was that of the Hon. Richard B. Carmichael, Judge of the Talbot county court, on a charge of treason. The arrest was made when the Judge was presiding on the bench. The Judge refused to acknowledge the authority by which he

---

Questions.—8. How was she treated by that government? 9. What is said of Gen'l Dix? What is said of these arrests? Who was among those arrested?

was arrested, and resisted the officer detailed to seize his person. The officer then struck him several times upon the head with his pistol, cutting and wounding him. The arrest having been made, he was placed on a steamer and carried to Fort McHenry and placed as a prisoner in charge of Col. Morris, commanding the post.

10. In September, 1862, the Southern army, under Gen. Lee, entered Maryland. It crossed the Potomac near Point of Rocks, and quietly entered Frederick. "These soldiers were in a destitute condition in respect to clothes and shoes, yet the most scrupulous regard was had to private property. They had no tents, and no baggage wagons. If enduring great hardships without a murmur, and most bravely and heroically fighting, are evidences of good soldiers, seldom has the world witnessed better than those who composed the army of Gen. Lee."*

11. Gen. Bradley Johnson, a former citizen of Frederick, was appointed Provost Marshal, and an address was issued to the people of Maryland, stating that the army came as friends, and not as enemies; that they did not purpose to interfere with non-combatants, or to disturb private property, or to inquire into the opinions of citizens;

* Appleton's Annual Gazetteer.

Questions.—10. What happened in September, 1862? 11. What is said of Gen'l Bradley Johnson?

and that whatever stores they required would be paid for. At night, the soldiers were all ordered to their camps outside the city.

12. On the 8th, Gen. Lee issued an address recounting the grievances under which Marylanders were suffering, inviting them to throw off their yoke, to accept the assistance of his army, and once more enjoy freedom of thought and speech. The response was not equal to the expectations of Gen. Lee. There was as yet no certainty that Lee would maintain his position, and owing to the divided state of opinion,—a man's enemies were often of his own household,—any demonstration in favor of the Southern troops would be sure to be visited by military punishment, after the departure of Lee.

13. The battle, therefore, that was preparing, was that which was to determine the destiny of Maryland, if not of the United States. Had it been successful, the United States troops would have been withdrawn to the main army, and Maryland, free to make her choice, with whatever side she united, would become the fighting ground of the contending hosts, and probably have been ground to atoms between them. It was too late for Maryland to unite with the South, even if it had been her wish to do so.

Questions.—12. What orders did General Lee issue? 13. What is said of the approaching battle?

14. Lee was met by McClellan. The first battle was fought at South mountain, on the 14th. Three days after, on the 17th, the celebrated battle of Antietam was fought. Night brought an end to the battle with the advantage on the side of the Federal troops. Gen. McClellan devoted the next day to recruiting his troops before renewing the attack, but on the night of the 18th, Gen. Lee withdrew his forces across the Potomac, and returned to Virginia.

15. Gen. Dix was succeeded by Gen. Wool, an old army officer, who had rendered distinguished services to the country in the Mexican war. Although his rule was less galling than that of his predecessor, the arrest of citizens without legal process was carried on to a greater extent in Maryland, than in any other State. Among those arrested were Thos. H. Gardner, Clerk of the Criminal Court; Col. Thos. R. Rich, Aid to the Governor; Alfred Evans and Thomas Sewall.

16. These parties were a committee appointed at a large Union Mass Meeting, in Baltimore, to investigate charges of disloyalty and official corruption. While making their report to the vice-presidents of the meeting they were arrested by a company of soldiers under an officer of Gen. Wool's

---

Questions — 14. What is said of the battle of Antietam? 15. By whom was General Dix succeeded? What is said of his rule? Who were arrested? 16. Who were these parties, and what was the effect of their arrest?

staff, and sent to Fort Delaware. Immediately a great outcry was raised by those who had been most zealous in procuring military arrests. Gen. Wool's course was denounced as tyrannical, arbitrary and unlawful. He was denounced as a favorer of the secessionists, and petitions were circulated among the active friends of the government for his removal. The President released these men.

CHAPTER XXXI.

MILITARY DEPARTMENTS—*General Schenck—His Vigorous Rule—Col. Fish—Arbitrary Arrests —Imprisonment of Col. Fish—Invasion of Lee—Alarm in Baltimore—Martial Law—Battle of Gettysburg—Seventh Regiment— Gen'l Schenck's Fourth of July Order—Enrolment of Negroes.*

1. In a division of the country into departments, a part of Maryland now lay in the middle military department, which embraced several of the contiguous States, with head-quarters at Baltimore. Gen. Wool was severely censured for leniency towards Baltimoreans, by the people and press of the North.

Questions.—1. What is said in this section?

2. His successor, Gen. Robert C. Schenck, was obnoxious to no such complaint. The strictness of the military vigilance in Baltimore, will long be remembered by those who knew for the first time what it was to live under a government, in the making of which they had no part, and to criticise which was a crime visited by arrest and imprisonment.

3. Spies were every where, and every man was at the mercy of his enemy. No oath or process of law was necessary to deprive a man of his liberty. Any one, whether instigated by patriotism, avarice or revenge, had only to charge another with disloyalty, or seditious language, or uttering treasonable sentiments, and the Provost Marshal, Col. Fish, would have him, or her, arrested.

4. As Gen. Schenck's time was occupied, according to one of the papers of the day, in the interest of the commanding General, "he could not be expected to give such matters a thorough investigation," and therefore, the parties "must cultivate a spirit of contentment." In the month of July, 1863, no less than three hundred and sixty-one arrests were made. The nature and foundation of the charges in many instances were known only to Col. Fish. By his command, a lady, Mrs. Sterrett, was arrested in this way by Lieut. Marcus

---

Questions.—2. Who was Gen'l Wool's successor, and what is said of his rule? 3. What is said in this section? 4. What is said of Gen'l Schenck? How many were arrested in July?

Sterling. She was seized in her house, hurried in a carriage, placed on a steamer and sent South, without any examination at the simple dictation of the subordinate to a man "who could not be expected to give such matters thorough" or even any "investigation."

5. One man was arrested because he had gunpowder in his pocket; two, for using abusive language to some negroes; another, because he rendered assistance to some wounded prisoners. Two women were arrested upon the same charge; another for throwing some pieces of bread in the cars to Southern prisoners. Several were imprisoned for charging too much hack hire to Federal officers.

6. A young man, a native of Baltimore, having joined the Southern army, was mortally wounded, and after his death had been buried by the Federal soldiers. At the instance of his mother, his remains were brought to Baltimore, and his friends desired to give him a Christian burial in the lot of the family. Gen. Schenck promised they should not be molested if the proceedings were conducted without display. As soon as the services were over, several military officers appeared and arrested the male attendants of the funeral.

7. Mr. B. H. Richardson, a gentleman over sixty years of age, his son, and several others were

---

Questions.— 5. Describe the arrests in this section? 6. What happened at a funeral? 7. What is said of Mr. Richardson?

arrested, for publishing in their paper a poem called the Southern Cross. They were not allowed to communicate with any one. The wording of the order precluded them from receiving a change of clothing, or having an interview with the members of their families, or of receiving assistance of any kind. They were sent South. Through the intervention of some friends, the commanding General found time to attend to the matter, and allowed him to take some money with him in his exile.

8. Hundreds were arrested upon the vague charge of disloyalty and uttering treasonable sentiments; some were sent to Fort McHenry, some to Washington, some North, and some South. The outrages of the Provost Marshal, his dishonesty and corruption, became so rank that he was convicted of felony, and sent to the Albany Penitentiary. In a few months, however, he was quietly pardoned and discharged.

9. In June of this year, Gen. Lee again entered Maryland. A false alarm having been raised that a body of Southern cavalry were within seven miles of the City of Baltimore, a great excitement prevailed.

10. In expectation of an attack, the city authorities had taken steps to fortify the city by means

---

Questions.—8. Upon what charge were many arrested? What became of Col. Fish? 9. When did Lee again enter Maryland? What is said of the alarm in Baltimore? 10. What was done in Baltimore?

of barricades, composed of large casks filled with stones, and surmounted with a sort of board fence. On the occasion of this alarm, men went about shouting, "to arms, to arms;" the military were under arms all night, and several thousand citizens collected at the barricades.

11. The next day, Gen'l Schenck declared martial law. No person was allowed to leave the city without a pass. Gunboats were also brought to bear upon the city.

12. The Confederate forces, however, were not moving towards the city. Gen'l Lee issued very stringent orders that his men should respect private property, and not make the helpless and innocent suffer. The Baltimore and Ohio Railroad, however, being regarded as government property, was injured through a range of eighty miles, between Harper's Ferry and Cumberland. Bridges and water stations were burned, and machinery and telegraphs were destroyed.

13. The Confederate army passed through Maryland to Pennsylvania. Having met the Federal army at Gettysburg, it was defeated, and returned to Virginia. The battle raged during the 1st, 2d and 3d days of July.

Questions.—11. What did General Schenck do? 12. What were General Lee's orders? What did the Confederates destroy? 13. Where did the Confederate army meet the Federal army, and what was the result?

14. During the absence of the fighting soldiers, who were needed in the field, the seventh regiment of New York returned to Baltimore, to act as a sort of provost guard, or military police. Their neat uniforms and cleanly appearance, as well as their social position with those of their own party, formed a striking contrast to the men who had gone to the front of the battle. They were of great service in executing military arrests and enforcing the military enactments, such as the closing of club-houses, instituted whether for social intercourse, mental improvement, or the cultivation of art.

15. On the 2d of July, Gen'l Schenck issued an order prohibiting the citizens from keeping arms in their possession. Houses were searched, and every kind of gun, whether warlike or sporting, was seized and carried away. On the 3d, another proclamation from Schenck required every house in the city of Baltimore to display a national flag on the following 4th, under threat of being regarded as disloyal if the order was not obeyed.

16. As this display was upon compulsion, it was no evidence of the real sentiments of the people, but only tended to deepen a lately awakened antipathy to a goverment that, little more than a year before, had the support of the majority of the

---

Questions.—14. What is said of the seventh regiment? 15. What was Gen'l Schenck's order of 2d July? What, of 3d? 16. What is said in this section?

people of the State. They were beginning to feel the tyranny of a consolidated government.

17. Whether by accident or otherwise, the barn of an enrolling officer was burned down. Gen. Schenck immediately issued an order for an assessment of three thousand dollars upon "persons known to be disaffected to the loyal government, who reside within six miles from where the barn was burnt." In like manner, innocent parties were made to bear the loss of fourteen hundred dollars, in Anne Arundel County.

18. Great difficulty existed in making up the quota of troops required from the State. There was a great disinclination on the part of the citizens to enlist in a war so unpopular with them. The State, moreover, was greatly exhausted of her young men, from their determination that if they had to fight at all, they would fight on the side their principles and sympathies inclined them, and their joining the Southern army. To meet this difficulty, the Government determined to enlist the negroes. At first, only the free blacks were received, but subsequently, slaves also. In many cases the officer entered upon farms and took away whole families, women and children included. An asylum for the latter was opened at Washington.

Questions.—17. What order of Gen'l Schenck is mentioned in this section? 18. Why was it difficult to make up the quota of troops required from the State? What was done about the negroes?

CHAPTER XXXII.

DIVISION IN THE UNION PARTY—*Election—Extraordinary orders issued at Chestertown—Gov. Bradford's Proclamation—Military suppression of the Proclamation, and control of the Polls—Gov. Bradford's comment.*

1. About this time, a division took place in the Union party of the State. One section demanded the immediate emancipation of the slaves. The other, a conservative party, thought that the aggressive policy of the administration party would retard, rather than facilitate, a restoration of the Union; and that this course was developing the fact that the paramount and leading issue of the war was not for the Union, but for emancipation.

2. The contest for State officers in the coming election was between these two divisions of the Union party. The conservative Union men in one of their county conventions, expressed their views in a series of resolutions. Among them was one containing the following words: "That we are opposed to the exercise by the General Government of all unauthorized powers, deeming it of little consequence if the Constitution is to be sacrificed, whether it is to be effected by usurpation or rebellion."

Questions.—1. What is said of the division of the Union party? 2. What views had the conservative Union party expressed?

3. The day of the election was Tuesday, November 4th. Late in October, General Schenck issued an order to the effect "that there were evil disposed persons, who have either been engaged in rebellion against the government, or have given aid and encouragement to others so engaged, who may embarrass the approaching election, or through it, force enemies of the United States into power." The order required the Provost Marshal, and other military power, to "arrest such persons found at, or hanging about, or approaching any place of election, and that those officers shall support the judges of election in requiring an oath of allegiance to the United States, as the test of citizenship."

4. A Lieutenant Colonel of Dragoons, who was sent by Gen. Schenck to enforce this order at Chestertown, issued an order of his own, excluding from the election all who were not prepared to give "a full and ardent support of the whole Government ticket, upon the platform of the Union League Convention."

5. Two days before the election, Gov. Bradford issued a proclamation protesting against any such invasion of the privileges of the ballot box, and so offensive a discrimination against the rights of a loyal State.

6. He stated this extraordinary order of Gen. Schenck had been issued without any notice to, or consultation with the constituted authority of the State, and at a time when the result of the election could in no way endanger the Government, or the peace of the community.

Questions.—3. What did Gen'l Schenck issue? 4. What order was issued at Chestertown? 5. What proclamation did Governor Bradford issue? 6. What did he say?

7. The Governor considered the order particularly oppressive, as *all* the Congressional candidates, with, perhaps, one exception, were loyal to the Federal Government, and because persons were not only to be arrested *at* the polls, but *approaching* them; and, he enquires, "who is to judge whether voters thus on their way to the place of voting, have given aid or encouragement to persons engaged in rebellion?" "The Provost Marshal, and other military officials were made the sole and exclusive judges;" "an extent of arbitrary discretion the most odious, and more especially offensive, from the fact that two of the five Provost Marshals were candidates for important offices, and sundry of their deputies for others."

8. The proclamation further stated "that the order was without justification; it was obnoxious by the means appointed for its execution; it was offensive to the sensibilities of the people and the authorities of the State, who had given such repeated proofs of their devotion to the Government."

9. The Governor then reminded the judges of election that they were clothed with the necessary authority and power to preserve the peace; that it was their special duty to give information to the officers of the civil law of all infractions of the State laws on the subject of elections, and that by these laws it was forbidden for any military officer to bring any troops within the view of any place of election, during the time of the election; that they are required by oath to permit all persons to vote who "shall, according to the directions contained in the Constitution and Laws, be entitled to

---

Questions.—7. Why did he think the order particularly oppressive? 8. What did the proclamation further state? 9. Of what did the Governor remind the judges?

do so; that it is the judgment of the judges of election alone that must determine the right of any person to vote when offering himself for that purpose; that they must discharge their duty undeterred by an order to Provost Marshals to report them at head-quarters."

10. The President revoked the first part of Gen. Schenck's order, and substituted another, which, however, had the obnoxious feature of requiring the presence of the military at the places of election. As there was no change in the general principles of the order, the Governor made no change in his proclamation.

11. A correspondence took place between the Governor and the President, in which the latter justified the action of Gen. Schenck. The reply of the Governor was a complete and spirited answer, and refutation to every position taken by the President.

12. The military authorities immediately sent orders to the Eastern Shore, directing the circulation of the proclamation to be suppressed. The public papers were forbidden to publish it; and lest the steamers from Baltimore might carry it, they were prevented from leaving the port. In his message to the Legislature, the Governor states that the officer who had himself landed in Kent County, commenced his operations of arresting and sending across the bay some ten or more of the most estimable and distinguished of its citizens, including some of the most uncompromising loyalists of the Shore. The jail of the county was entered,

---

Questions.—10. What did the President do? What further is said? 11. What is said of the correspondence between Gov. Bradford and President Lincoln? 12. What steps did the military take? What did the Governor state in his message? What was done on the Eastern Shore?

the jailer seized, imprisoned, and afterwards sent to Baltimore, and prisoners confined therein were set at liberty. The "Government ticket" was designated by its color, and armed with that a voter could run the gauntlet of sabres and carbines that guarded the polls, whether a lawful voter or not. In fact, voters were invited to avail themselves of the opportunity to establish their loyalty "by giving a full and ardent support to the whole Government ticket," and it asserted that many known sympathizers with the rebellion, whether to avert suspicion from themselves or for other reasons, voted; while others, loyal to the union, but adverse to the administration ticket, were not allowed even to approach the polls. The color of the ticket in their hands was the test of their right to vote.

13. In one district, the military officer took his stand at the polls and declared that none but the "yellow ticket" should be voted, and excluded all others. In another district, a similar officer examined every ticket, and unless it was the favored one, the voter was compelled to take an oath unknown to the laws of the State, and administered by an alien to its soil. In another, after one vote was taken, the polls were closed, and the judges were arrested, and sent out of the county, and military occupation taken of the town. The ticket favored by the military was elected. The administration and opposition parties in Congress were nearly equal, hence the strenuous exertions to secure from Maryland and West Virginia, where the military had control, the return of men pledged to the support of the administration. By forcing these States to the administration side, that party

---

Questions.—12. What is said of the "Government ticket?" What was the test of the right to vote? 13. What is said in this section?

secured ninety-eight out of one hundred and eighty-five members of Congress, or a majority of eleven.

14. The Governor, in calling the attention of the Legislature to the abuses, says: "a statement of them presents a humiliating record, and that unless it indeed be a fallacy to suppose that any rights whatever remain to the State, or that any line whatever marks the limit of Federal power, a bolder stride across that line, that power never made even in a rebel State, than it did here on the 3d of November. A part of the army which the people had supplied for a very different purpose, was engaged on that day in stifling the freedom of elections in a faithful State, intimidating its lawful officers, violating the constitutional rights of its citizens, and obstructing the usual channels of communication between them and their Executive."

CHAPTER XXXIII.

CONSTITUTIONAL CONVENTION—*General Lew. Wallace — Questions to Candidates and Voters — Paramount Allegiance — Abolition of Slavery— The Constitution made Operative before its Adoption — Difference of Opinion between the Executive and Judicial Branches —Soldiers' Vote—Inquisition of Voters—Investigation of the Vote.*

1. The success of the government party in the election for legislature for 1864, ensured the calling of a convention to remodel the Constitution of the State, with the view of extinguishing slavery in her borders.

Questions.—14. What did the Governor say in his message? What did he say a part of the army was engaged in? 1. For what purpose was a convention called?

2. A bill was passed calling upon the people to decide whether there should be a convention or not, and, at the same time, to elect the members of that convention should the affirmative receive the largest vote. There was a provision in this bill, that "if any military or armed force of the United States shall appear at the polls, or in any way interfere with the elections, the election shall be set aside and a new one held, from time to time, as long as the grievance shall continue."

3. Gen'l Lew. Wallace, who was now in command of the middle department, and whose administration was a continuance of the acts that had characterized Gen'l Schenck's, issued certain questions to be asked of the candidates for the Convention, and where the answers were not agreeable to him, the candidate was withdrawn.

4. A set of questions was also prepared and asked in some counties, which precluded a vast number from voting. The result of an election held under such circumstances was a majority of more than twelve thousand in favor of the Convention. Of ninety-eight members elected, sixty-eight were emancipationists. The Convention met on April 27th, Henry H. Goldsborough having been chosen President.

5. The Bill of Rights proposed by this Convention, contained two articles that met with very strenuous opposition. The first of the two declared that every citizen of the State owed paramount allegiance to the Constitution and the *government* of the United States. It was contended that this

---

Questions.—2. What bill was passed by the Legislature? What provision was in this bill? 3. What did Gen. Wallace do? 4. What other questions were prepared? 5. What article in the Bill of Rights was much opposed? Mention the arguments against it?

was a new doctrine, and could not be found embodied in any constitution of any of the States; that the States were always recognized as sovereign; that it is impossible, in the nature of things, for a sovereign to alienate its sovereignty, or to make the thing created greater than the creator; that the government created by these States was of a limited character; that to it has been delegated the performance of *acts* of sovereignty, but that the power remains with the people of States as States; that the Constitution of the United States itself recognized no such doctrine; that it subverted the intention of the founders of the Constitution and government by removing the checks to arbitrary power; that paramount allegiance to the government might prevent allegiance to the Constitution and involve a citizen or State in a loss of constitutional rights. It was further contended that the government consisted of three departments, the executive, the legislative and the judiciary, and should any two of these, for instance the executive and judicial, differ, as in the case of Merryman, who should decide to which obedience is due? and disobedience to which of them would constitute treason? Obedience will be enforced by the department having superior physical force, and disobedience to this physical force would be treason, and thus, individuals and States would eventually become the subject of an irresponsible military dictation.

6. On the other hand, it was contended that at the adoption of the Federal Constitution, the States had surrendered the sovereignty to the

Questions.—6. What arguments in favor of it?

people of the United States; that even if it were not so, and the fact were otherwise, the doctrine of States-rights was wrong in principle, as it made the Federal Union weak, and that it ought to be abolished in order that the power of the government might become consolidated, independent and efficient; that whatever danger there may be in centralization, of crippling individual action of the different parts, yet centralization is essential to the healthy activity, no less than the perfection of the body.

7. The other article that met with prolonged opposition was that of abolishing slavery. It, however, finally passed. This constitution also provided who should, and who should not vote on its adoption by the people, by prescribing an oath to be taken by every one offering to cast his ballot. It was objected that this was making the constitution operative before it was adopted by the people; that this new constitution had no vitality until it should be accepted by the people, and proclaimed by the Governor as the fundamental law of the State; that until this was done, the citizens were living under the constitution then existing; that the convention had been appointed to make a draft of a constitution, and when that was done, their functions were at an end; that they exceeded their powers when they limited the rights of the people and took away privileges they enjoyed under the then existing constitution; that what were claimed as precedents of other States to the contrary, were where the privileges were enlarged and not curtailed; that a people, through a sovereign con-

---

Questions.—7. What other article met with opposition? What else did this constitution provide? What objection was made to this?

vention, might demand rights not before enjoyed, but that it was contrary to the nature of a sovereign to deprive itself of its own immunities, and that, therefore, such precedents were without force.

8. Another article provided that the vote of the soldiers absent on duty, could be taken at their several camps. It was objected that here also the convention transcended their powers; that the existing constitution, which was the law, provided how elections should be held, and that votes must be cast at the polls in the county and district in which the voter resides; that the nature of military discipline was such that it could not be certain that the soldiers voted otherwise than as suited their commanders,—who were to be judges of the election,—and under their dictation.

9. The Governor was called upon to interpose his authority to prevent these infringements of the existing constitution, but he replied that he considered the question a judicial, and not a political one, and that he did not consider it his province to prevent the operation of what at least had the color of law. The remedy was in the courts. It was replied that the courts could not meet the difficulty until after the wrong had been inflicted, and that then there was no remedy; that the courts to whom the appeal would be taken, would themselves be the creation of the new constitution, if adopted.

10. After the election, but before the constitution went into operation, an application was made to the Superior Court for a *mandamus* requiring

---

Questions.—8. What other article met with opposition? 9. What was the Governor called upon to do? How did he regard the question? What was the reply to the Governor? 10. What measures were taken before the proclamation of the constitution?

the Governor to exclude all votes given outside the State of Maryland from the count on the adoption of the constitution. The court dismissed the application, and an appeal was taken to the Court of Appeals. This court decided that it was a political and not a judicial question, and that it was, therefore, a matter of executive and not judicial action. Each branch threw the responsibility of settling the question upon the other. It was, however, regarded as a foregone conclusion, that the constitution prepared was to be adopted.

11. A set of questions, which were to be answered under oath, was prepared for the judges to ask each voter. The questions concerned not only the acts and words of the voter, but entered even into his very inmost and secret thoughts.

12. Notwithstanding this inquisition, and the repugnance of men to subject themselves to a questioning so new and so abhorrent to the feelings of freemen, the vote against the new constitution was so large that it was supposed to have been rejected. When, however, the soldiers' vote was brought in from Virginia, it was found that the constitution had been adopted by 375 majority.

13. Before the proclamation of the new constitution, the Governor was requested to allow counsel to investigate the soldiers' vote. Several days were passed in the examination, but nearly all the objections were overruled by the Governor.

Questions.—11. What questions were prepared for the voters? 12. Did many vote against the new constitution? Whose vote caused the adoption of this constitution? 13. What was done before the new constitution was proclaimed? How were the objections treated?

CHAPTER XXXIV.

THE CONFEDERATES AGAIN IN MARYLAND—*Defeat of Wallace—Approach of Raiders to Washington—Excitement and Alarm at Washington—Timely Arrival of Troops—Gen'l Ord—Freedman's Rest.*

1. Early in July, of this year, a Confederate force appeared again in Western Maryland. Hagerstown having been occupied by them, a requisition was made on the inhabitants for $20,000 This money was paid, and the raiding party left.

2. In the orders of the commanding officer, it was required of the officers and men, when encamped, to remain in camp, and upon march, to observe silence, "the silly practice of whooping and hallowing is forbidden; destruction of fences and crops of farmers is positively prohibited, and such outrages will be paid for from the pay of the officers of the command nearest where such depredations may be committed."

3. A few days afterward, another body of Confederate cavalry entered Hagerstown and burned some buildings. In the evening of the same day, Gen. Wallace withdrew from Frederick to Monocacy Junction, and on the next day, the Southerners, under Gen'l Early, entered and levied a contribution on the inhabitants.

4. Having swept Gen. Wallace from their path, the Confederate force pushed towards Ellicott's Mills. Dividing their force, a portion of them went towards Baltimore, and burned the Governor's residence, sit-

Questions.—1. Where did the Confederates now come? 2. What were the orders of their commanding general? 3. What is said in this section? 4. What did the Confederates now do? What did another portion do?

uated within five miles of the city. Twenty-five miles of the Northern Central rail road were destroyed, and a train on the Philadelphia road was captured and burnt. The bridge over the Gunpowder was also partially burned. Another portion, under Bradley Johnson, crossed the country to Beltsville, on the Washington road. The troops posted there, four hundred in number, precipitately retreated without waiting to fire a shot. The Southern troops, after resting for three hours, followed, towards Washington, coming within eight miles of the city.

5. The defeat of Gen. Wallace, who was missing for several days, and the bold movement of these raiders, caused the greatest excitement in Washington, and throughout the North. The Federal city, at that time, was almost destitute of troops. Reinforcements were hurried forward from Petersburg, and the 19th army corps, sent from New Orleans to reinforce Gen. Grant before Richmond, appeared at this juncture in the Chesapeake Bay, and was at once sent to Washington.

6. This timely arrival saved Washington. Forty thousand troops were concentrated there. at about the same time the Confederate party arrived. Gen. Bradley Johnson, therefore, crossed the country during the night, and joined Gen. Early, who had halted before Fort Stevens, on Seventeenth street, on the outskirts of the city.

7. After some skirmishing here, Gen. Early withdrew and succeeded in recrossing the Potomac. A large proportion of the men of this command were Marylanders, and however cold their reception was in the Western part of the State, it

---

Questions.—5. What was the effect of the defeat of Wallace? What was the condition of Washington? How was it saved? 6. What is said in this section? 7. What is said of Gen'l Early? What, of his men, and of their reception?

cannot be denied that they were cordially received by the farmers of Prince George's county.

8. Gen'l Wallace was superseded in his command at Baltimore by Gen'l Ord, who had been an officer of the regular army. His administration was a short one. Finding, it is said, that the duties of the command were utterly repugnant to his feelings as a man and a soldier, at his own request, he was relieved. Gen'l Wallace was reinstated, and under him the old system of arbitrary arrests was continued.

9. In November, shortly after the new constitution became operative, Gen'l Wallace, assuming that the State would not carry out the provision of its own laws, issued an order placing the emancipated slaves under special military protection, creating a "Freedman's Rest," and notifying the people that if the voluntary contributions for the support of the negroes were not sufficient, he would levy upon those who sympathized with their Southern brethren, for the necessary funds to sustain the "Freedman's Rest."

10. If, in the language of Governor Bradford, "the statement of these acts presents a humiliating record," it must be borne in mind that this record is not the history of the State. The record of the acts of a government constitutes a history of the State when the government represents the State. But when the name of the State is seized upon for purposes aside from the good of the State, the record is only that of the individuals, or government that control by military power, but do not represent, the people.

Questions.—8. By whom was Wallace superseded, and what is said of him? 9. What new order did Wallace issue? 10. What is said of this record of events?

CHAPTER XXXV.

CONCLUSION OF THE WAR—*Gov. Swann's Instructions to the Registers—Difficulties with the Police Commissioners—The New Legislature—Election of Senator—He declines—His Substitute refused his Seat—New Constitution—Election of Gov. Bowie.*

1. The war having been concluded by the surrender of the Southern armies, the Provost Marshals were recalled, and the citizens were once more under the government of the civil law.

2. An effort was immediately made to have the Registry law declared unconstitutional. The courts, however, decided otherwise, and Gov. Swann, who was elected to succeed Gov. Bradford, in his message to the Legislature, discouraged any repeal or modification of the law.

3. But prior to the election of State officers in November, 1866, the Governor instructed the registers that the registry law was to be so interpreted that it should secure the citizen in his rights, and not deprive him of them, and that every one who presented himself, and would take the prescribed oath, should be registered without any further inquisition by way of questioning, excepting what is usual where fraud is suspected. The judges of the election were also to regard the registration of the voter as an evidence of his legal right to vote.

4. A difficulty, however, arose in Baltimore by the refusal of the judges of the election, in the charter election of October, to recognize the new registration. These judges were appointed by the Police Commissioners. The Governor, therefore, immediately removed the Commissioners and appointed others in their stead.

5. The difficulty at one time assumed a threatening aspect, and a riot appeared imminent. Threats were made, out of the State, of marching troops within the

---

Questions.—1. What is said in this section? 2. What effort was made? 3. What instructions did the Governor give to the registers? 4. What difficulty arose in Baltimore? 5. What threats were made?

borders to sustain the Police Commissioners in their refusal to vacate their office to the new Commissioners, and even to destroy the city.

6. The Governor issued a proclamation, threatening, in case of any such movement, to use the whole power of the State for its suppression, and the punishment of its authors. The Commissioners were cited to appear before the Governor to answer the charge of being guilty of illegal acts. The charges were sustained, and the Commissioners submitted to their removal.

7. New judges of the election having then been appointed, the November elections were held on the basis of the new registration, and a complete change was made in the Legislature.

8. This Legislature met January 2d, 1867. One of its first duties was to choose a United States Senator. By an existing law, it was required that one of the Senators in Congress should be from the Eastern Shore. In order to elect Gov. Swann who, under this law, was not eligible, the law was repealed, but immediately re-enacted, to resume its operation on the 1st of April. Mr. Swann was then elected. However, at the request of numerous prominent citizens that he should not leave the Executive chair, he declined the senatorship.

9. Subsequently, Philip F. Thomas, Esq., a former Governor of the State, was chosen to fill the vacancy. He was not allowed to take his seat in Congress, on the charge of having "given aid and comfort to those in arms against the United States." He had supplied his son, when about to go South and join the Confederate army, with some money. G. R. Vickers, Esq., was appointed in his stead.

10. The Legislature passed resolutions addressed to the Congress of the United States, to the effect that the Union being restored, each State is entitled to all the rights and immunities of all the others, and all have an equal right to participate in the administration of the government; that any attempt on the part of Congress

---

Questions.—6. What was the proclamation of the Governor? 7. What was, of appointing new judges of elections? 8. Who was elected to Senate of U. S. Did he accept? 9. Who was chosen in his place? 10. What resolutions did the Legislature pass?

to interfere with the elective franchise in any State would be a flagrant violation of the spirit of the Constitution, and an encroachment on the rights of the States.

11. The provision in the Constitution restricting the suffrage, authorized its own repeal by a two-thirds vote of the General Assembly. It was enacted by this Legislature, that all the rights of citizenship should be restored to the citizens.

12. A strong desire existed to abolish the constitution of 1864. But the existing constitution provided that a reference to the people of the matter of calling a convention for forming a new constitution could be made only when two-thirds of the General Assembly might think it necessary; and that in case of such necessity appearing, and the people deciding in favor of a convention, that the next Legislature should provide for calling the same.

13. The Legislature decided, however, that the power to refer to the people questions concerning the organic law, cannot be limited, and that any such limitations were in conflict with the Bill of Rights, which declares that the people have, *at all times*, the unalienable right to alter, reform or abolish their form of government.

14. A reference to the people was made in April, and resulted in favor of holding the convention. The convention met on the 8th of May, and selected Hon. Richard B. Carmichael, as their President.

15. In the Bill of Rights appended to the Constitution prepared by this convention, the article on "paramount allegiance to the Constitution and government of the United States" was modified so as to read, "The Constitution of the United States, and the laws made in pursuance thereof, are and shall be the supreme law of the State, and all the people of this State shall be bound thereby, anything in the Constitution and Laws of this State to the contrary notwithstanding." "The powers not delegated to the United States by the Constitution thereof, are reserved to the States respectively, or to the

---

Questions.—11. What is said in this section? 12. What desire existed? What proviso of the existing Constitution was there? 13. What did they desire? 14. When a reference to the people made? 15. What changes were made?

people thereof." "That the people of this State have the sole and exclusive right of regulating the internal government and police thereof, as a free, sovereign and independent State."

16. Another article declared that any departure from the constitution, either of the United States or of this State, whether in time of peace or war, under the plea of necessity, or any other plea, is subversive of good government, and tends to anarchy and despotism.

17. The constitution was adopted by a majority of 24,116. The first election under it took place in November, 1867. The rival candidates for the office of Governor were Oden Bowie, Esq., whose name has already been mentioned in connection with the Mexican war, and the Hon. H. L. Bond. Gov. Bowie was elected by a majority of 41,712 votes.

18. In 1870, in pursuance of the requirements of the Fifteenth Amendment of the Constitution of the United States, the negroes exercised the right of voting.

THE END

Questions.—16. What did another article declare? 17. By what majority was the new constitution adopted? When was the first election under the new constitution? 18. When did the negroes first exercise the right of voting?

GOVERNORS OF MARYLAND.

1777—Thomas Johnson.
1779—Thomas Sim Lee.
1782—William Paca.
1785—William Smallwood.
1788—John Eager Howard.
1791—George Plater.
1794—John H. Stone.
1797—John Henry.
1798—Benjamin Ogle.
1801—John Francis Mercer.
1803—Robert Bowie.
1806—Robert Wright.
1809—Edward Lloyd.
1811—Robert Bowie.
1812—Levin Winder.
1815—Charles Ridgeley, of Hampton.
1818—Charles Goldsborough.
1819—Samuel Sprigg.
1822—Samuel Stevens, Jr.
1825—Joseph Kent.
1828—Daniel Martin.
1829—Thomas King Carroll.
1830—Daniel Martin.
1831—George Howard.
1832—James Thomas.
1835—Thomas W. Veazey.
1838—William Grason.
1841—Francis Thomas.
1844—Thomas G. Pratt.
1847—Philip Francis Thomas.
1850—E. Louis Lowe.
1854—T. Watkins Ligon.
1857—T. Holliday Hicks.
1861—Augustus W. Bradford.
1865—Thomas Swann.
1867—Oden Bowie.
1871—William Pinkney Whyte.

APPENDIX.

The Constitution of Maryland,

ADOPTED BY THE CONVENTION WHICH ASSEMBLED AT THE CITY OF ANNAPOLIS, ON THE EIGHTH DAY OF MAY, EIGHTEEN HUNDRED AND SIXTY-SEVEN, AND ADJOURNED ON THE SEVENTEENTH DAY OF AUGUST, EIGHTEEN HUNDRED AND SIXTY-SEVEN.

DECLARATION OF RIGHTS.

We, the People of the State of Maryland, grateful to Almighty God for our civil and religious liberty, and taking into our serious consideration the best means of establishing a good Constitution in this State for the sure foundation and more permanent security thereof, declare:

ARTICLE 1. That all Government of right originates from the People, is founded in compact only, and instituted solely for the good of the whole; and they have, at all times, the inalienable right to alter, reform or abolish their Form of Government, in such manner as they may deem expedient.

ART. 2. The Constitution of the United States, and the Laws made, or which shall be made in pursuance thereof, and all Treaties made, or which shall be made, under the authority of the United States, are, and shall be the Supreme Law of the State; and the Judges of this State, and all the People of this State, are, and shall be bound thereby; anything in the Constitution or Law of this State to the contrary notwithstanding.

ART. 3. The powers not delegated to the United States by the Constitution thereof, nor prohibited by it to the States, are reserved to the States respectively, or to the people thereof.

ART. 4. That the People of this State have the sole and exclusive right of regulating the internal government and police thereof, as a free, sovereign and independent State.

ART. 5. That the Inhabitants of Maryland are entitled to the Common Law of England, and the trial by Jury, according to the course of that Law, and to the benefit of such of the English Statutes as existed on the Fourth day of July, seventeen hundred and seventy-six; and which, by experience, have been found applicable to their local and other circumstances, and have been introduced, used and practised by the Courts of Law or Equity; and also of all Acts of Assembly in force on the first day of June, Eighteen hundred and Sixty-seven; except such as may have since expired, or may be inconsistent with the provisions of this Constitution; subject, nevertheless, to the revision of, and amendment or repeal by, the Legislature of this State. And the Inhabitants of Maryland are also entitled to all property derived to them from, or under the Charter granted by His Majesty Charles the First to Cæcilius Calvert, Baron of Baltimore.

ART. 6. That all persons invested with the Legislative or Executive powers of Government are the Trustees of the Public, and, as such, accountable for their conduct: Wherefore, whenever the ends of Government are perverted, and public liberty manifestly endangered, and all other means of redress are ineffectual, the People may, and of right ought, to reform the old, or establish a new Government: the doctrine of non-resistance against arbitrary power and oppression is absurd, slavish and destructive of the good and happiness of mankind.

ART. 7. That the right of the People to participate in the Legislature is the best security of liberty and the foundation of all free Government; for this purpose, elections ought to be free and frequent; and every white male citizen, having the qualifications prescribed by the Constitution, ought to have the right of suffrage.

ART. 8. That the Legislative, Executive and Judicial powers of Government ought to be forever separate and distinct from each other; and no person exercising the functions of one of said Departments shall assume or discharge the duties of any other.

ART. 9. That no power of suspending Laws or the execution of Laws, unless by, or derived from the Legislature, ought to be exercised or allowed.

ART. 10. That freedom of speech and debate, or proceedings in the Legislature, ought not to be impeached in any Court of Judicature.

ART. 11. That Annapolis be the place of meeting of the Legislature; and the Legislature ought not to be convened, or held at any other place but from evident necessity.

ART. 12. That for redress of grievances, and for amending, strengthening and preserving the Laws, the Legislature ought to be frequently convened.

ART. 13. That every man hath a right to petition the Legislature for the redress of grievances in a peaceable and orderly manner.

ART. 14. That no aid, charge, tax, burthen or fees ought to be rated or levied, under any pretence, without the consent of the Legislature.

ART. 15. That the levying of taxes by the poll is grievous and oppressive, and ought to be prohibited; that paupers ought not to be assessed for the support of the Government; but every person in the State, or person holding property therein, ought to contribute his proportion of public taxes for the support of the Government, according to his actual worth in real or personal property; yet, fines, duties or taxes may properly and justly be imposed, or laid, with a political view for the good government and benefit of the community.

ART. 16. That sanguinary Laws ought to be avoided as far as it is consistent with the safety of the State; and no Law to inflict cruel and unusual pains and penalties ought to be made in any case, or at any time, hereafter.

ART. 17. That retrospective Laws, punishing acts committed before the existence of such Laws, and by them only declared criminal, are oppressive, unjust and incompatible with liberty; wherefore, no *ex post facto* Law ought to be made; nor any retrospective oath or restriction be imposed, or required.

ART. 18. That no Law to attaint particular persons of treason or felony, ought to be made in any case, or at any time, hereafter.

ART. 19. That every man, for any injury done to him in his person or property, ought to have remedy by the course of the Law of the Land, and ought to have justice and right, freely without sale, fully without any denial, and speedily without delay, according to the Law of the Land.

ART. 20. That the trial of facts, where they arise, is one of the greatest securities of the lives, liberties and estate of the People.

ART. 21. That in all criminal prosecutions, every man hath a right to be informed of the accusation against him; to have a copy of the Indictment, or charge, in due time (if required) to prepare for his defense; to be allowed counsel; to be confronted with the witnesses against him; to have process for his witnesses; to examine the witnesses for and against him on oath; and to a speedy trial by an impartial jury, without whose unanimous consent he ought not to be found guilty.

ART. 22. That no man ought to be compelled to give evidence against himself in a criminal case.

ART. 23. That no man ought to be taken or imprisoned or disseized of his freehold, liberties or privileges, or outlawed, or exiled, or, in any manner, destroyed, or deprived of his life, liberty or property, but by the judgment of his peers, or by the Law of the Land.

ART. 24. That Slavery shall not be re-established in this State; but having been abolished, under the policy and authority of the United States, compensation, in consideration thereof, is due from the United States.

ART. 25. That excessive bail ought not to be required nor excessive fines imposed, nor cruel or unusual punishment inflicted, by the Courts of Law.

ART. 26. That all warrants, without oath or affirmation, to search suspected places, or to seize any person or property, are grievous and oppressive; and all general warrants to search suspected places, or to apprehend suspected persons, without naming or describing the place, or the person in special, are illegal, and ought not to be granted.

ART. 27. That no conviction shall work corruption of blood or forfeiture of estate.

ART. 28. That a well regulated Militia is the proper and natural defence of a free Government.

ART. 29. That standing Armies are dangerous to liberty, and ought not to be raised, or kept up, without the consent of the Legislature.

ART. 30. That in all cases, and at all times, the military ought to be under strict subordination to, and control of, the civil power.

ART. 31. That no soldier shall, in time of peace, be quartered in any house, without the consent of the owner, nor in time of war, except in the manner prescribed by Law.

ART. 32. That no person except regular soldiers, marines, and mariners in the service of this State, or militia, when in actual service, ought, in any case, to be subject to or punishable by Martial Law.

ART. 33. That the independency and uprightness of Judges are essential to the impartial administration of Justice, and a great security to the rights and liberties of the People; Wherefore, the Judges shall not be removed, except in the manner, and for the causes, provided in this Constitution. No Judge shall hold any other office, civil or military, or political trust, or employment of any kind, whatsoever, under the Constitution or Laws of this State, or of the United States, or any of them; or receive fees, or perquisites of any kind, for the discharge of his official duties.

ART. 34. That a long continuance in the Executive Departments of power or trust is dangerous to liberty; a rotation, therefore, in those Departments is one of the best securities of permanent freedom.

ART. 35. That no person shall hold, at the same time, more than one office of profit, created by the Constitution or Laws of this State; nor shall any person in public trust receive any present from any foreign Prince or State, or from the United States, or any of them, without the approbation of this State.

ART. 36. That as it is the duty of every man to worship God in such manner as he thinks most acceptable to Him, all persons are equally entitled to protection in their religious liberty; wherefore, no person ought, by any Law to be molested in his person or estate, on account of his religious persuasion, or profession, or for his religious practice, unless, under the color of religion, he shall disturb the good order, peace or safety of the State, or shall infringe the laws of morality, or injure others in their natural, civil or religious rights; nor ought any person to be compelled to frequent, or maintain, or contribute, unless on contract, to maintain, any place of worship, or any ministry; nor shall any person, otherwise competent, be deemed incompetent as a witness, or juror, on account of his religious belief; provided, he believes in the existence of God, and that under His dispensation such person will be held morally accountable for his acts, and be rewarded or punished therefor either in this world or the world to come.

ART. 37. That no religious test ought ever to be required as a qualification for any office of profit or trust in this State, other than a declaration of belief in the existence of God; nor shall the Legislature prescribe any other oath of office than the oath prescribed by this Constitution.

ART. 38. That every gift, sale or devise of land, to any Minister, Public Teacher or Preacher of the gospel, as such, or to any Religious Sect, Order or Denomination, or to, or for the support, use or benefit of, or in trust for, any Minister, Public Teacher or Preacher of the gospel, as such, or any Religious Sect, Order or Denomination; and every gift or sale of goods, or chattels, to go in succession, or to take place after the death of the Seller or Donor, to or for such support, use or benefit; and also every devise of goods or chattels to or for the support, use, or benefit of any Minister, Public Teacher or Preacher of the gospel, as such, or any Religious Sect, Order or Denomination, without the prior, or subsequent, sanction of the Legislature, shall be void; except always, any sale, gift, lease or devise of any quantity of land, not exceeding five acres, for a church, meeting-house, or other house of worship, or parsonage, or for a burying-ground, which shall be improved, enjoyed, or used only for such purpose; or such sale, gift, lease, or devise shall be void.

ART. 39. That the manner of administering an oath or affirmation to any person, ought to be such as those of the religious persuasion, profession, or denomination, of which he is a member, generally esteem the most effectual confirmation by the attestation of the Divine Being.

ART. 40. That the liberty of the press ought to be inviolably preserved; that every citizen of the State ought to be allowed to speak, write and publish his sentiments on all subjects, being responsible for the abuse of that privilege.

ART. 41. That monopolies are odious, contrary to the spirit of a free government and the principles of commerce, and ought not to be suffered.

ART. 42. That no title of nobility or hereditary honors ought to be granted in this State.

ART. 43. That the Legislature ought to encourage the diffusion of knowledge and virtue, the extension of a judicious system of general education, the promotion of literature, the arts, sciences, agriculture, commerce and manufactures, and the general melioration of the condition of the People.

ART. 44. That the provisions of the Constitution of the United States, and of this State, apply, as well in time of war, as in time of peace; and any departure therefrom, or violation thereof, under the plea of necessity, or any other plea, is subversive of good Government, and tends to anarchy and despotism.

ART. 45. This enumeration of Rights shall not be construed to impair or deny others retained by the People.

CONSTITUTION.

ARTICLE I.

ELECTIVE FRANCHISE.

SECTION 1. All elections shall be by ballot; and every white male citizen of the United States, of the age of twenty-one years, or upwards, who has been a resident of the State for one year, and of the Legislative District of Baltimore City, or of the county, in which he may offer to vote, for six months next preceding the election, shall be entitled to vote, in the ward or election district, in which he resides, at all elections hereafter to be held in this State; and in case any county, or city, shall be so divided as to form portions of different electoral districts, for the election of Representatives in Congress, Senators, Delegates, or other Officers, then, to entitle a person to vote for such officer, he must have been a resident of that part of the county, or city, which shall form a part of the electoral district, in which he offers to vote, for six months next preceding the election; but a person, who shall have acquired a residence in such county, or city, entitling him to vote at any such election, shall be entitled to vote in the election district from which he removed, until he shall have acquired a residence in the part of the county, or city, to which he has removed.

SEC. 2. No person above the age of twenty-one years, convicted of larceny, or other infamous crime, unless pardoned by the Governor, shall ever thereafter be entitled to vote at any election in this State; and no person under guardianship, as a lunatic, or, as a person *non compos mentis*, shall be entitled to vote.

SEC. 3. If any person shall give, or offer to give, directly or indirectly, any bribe, present, or reward, or any promise, or any security for the payment, or the delivery of money, or any other thing, to induce any voter to refrain from casting his vote, or to prevent him, in any way, from voting, or to procure a vote for any candidate, or person proposed, or voted for, as Elector of President and Vice-President of the United States, or Representative in Congress, or for any office of profit or trust, created by the Constitution or Laws of this State, or by the Ordinances, or Authority of the Mayor and City Council of Baltimore, the person giving, or offering to give, and the person receiving the same, and any person who gives, or causes to be given, an illegal vote, knowing it to be such, at any election to be hereafter held in this State, shall, on conviction in a Court of Law, in addition to the penalties now, or hereafter to be, imposed by Law, be forever disqualified to hold any office of profit or trust, or to vote at any election thereafter.

SEC. 4. It shall be the duty of the General Assembly to pass Laws to punish, with fine and imprisonment, any person, who shall remove into any election district, or precinct of any ward of the City of Baltimore, not for the purpose of acquiring a *bona fide* residence therein, but for the purpose of voting at an approaching election, or, who shall vote in any election district, or ward, in which he does not reside, (except in the case provided for in this article,) or shall, at the same election, vote in more than one election district, or precinct, or shall vote, or offer to vote, in any name not his own, or in place of any other person of the same name, or shall vote in any county, in which he does not reside.

SEC. 5. The General Assembly shall provide by Law for a uniform Registration of the names of all the voters in this State, who possess the qualifications prescribed in this Article, which Registration shall be conclusive evidence to the Judges of election of the right of every person, thus registered, to vote at any election thereafter held in this State; but no person shall vote at any election, Federal or State, hereafter to be held in this State, or at any municipal election in the City of Baltimore, unless his name appears in the list of registered voters; and until the General Assembly shall hereafter pass an Act for the Registration of the names of voters, the Law in force on the first day of June, in the year eighteen hundred and sixty-seven, in reference thereto, shall be continued in force, except so far as it may be inconsistent with the provisions of this Constitution; and the registry of voters, made in pursuance thereof, may be corrected, as provided in said Law; but the names of all persons shall be added to the list of qualified voters by the officers of Registration, who have the qualifications prescribed in the first section of this Article, and who are not disqualified under the provisions of the second and third sections thereof.

SEC. 6. Every person elected, or appointed, to any office

of profit or trust, under this Constitution, or under the Laws, made pursuant thereto, shall, before he enters upon the duties of such office, take and subscribe the following oath, or affirmation: I, ———, do swear, (or affirm, as the case may be,) that I will support the Constitution of the United States; and that I will be faithful and bear true allegiance to the State of Maryland, and support the Constitution and Laws thereof; and that I will, to the best of my skill and judgment, diligently and faithfully, without partiality or prejudice, execute the office of ———, according to the Constitution and Laws of this State, (and, if a Governor, Senator, Member of the House of Delegates, or Judge,) that I will not directly or indirectly, receive the profits or any part of the profits, of [of] any other office during the term of my acting as ———.

SEC. 7. Every person, hereafter elected, or appointed, to office, in this State, who shall refuse, or neglect, to take the oath, or affirmation of office, provided for in the sixth section of this Article, shall be considered as having refused to accept the said office; and a new election, or appointment, shall be made, as in case of refusal to accept, or resignation of an office; and any person violating said oath, shall, on conviction thereof, in a Court of Law, in addition to the penalties now, or hereafter, to be imposed by Law, be thereafter incapable of holding any office of profit or trust in this State.

ARTICLE II.

EXECUTIVE DEPARTMENT.

SECTION 1. The Executive Power of the State shall be vested in a Governor, whose term of office shall commence on the second Wednesday of January next ensuing his election, and continue for four years, and until his successor shall have qualified; but the Governor chosen [d] at the first election under this Constitution, shall not enter upon the discharge of the duties of the office until the expiration of the term for which the present incumbent was elected; unless the said office shall become vacant by death, resignation, removal from the State, or other disqualification of the said incumbent.

SEC. 2. An election for Governor, under this Constitution, shall be held on the Tuesday next after the first Monday of November, in the year eighteen hundred and sixty-seven, and on the same day and month in every fourth year thereafter, at the places of Voting for Delegates to the General Assembly; and every person qualified to vote for Delegates, shall be qualified and entitled to vote for Governor; the election to be held in the same manner as the election of Delegates, and the returns thereof, under seal, to be addressed to the Speaker of the House of Delegates, and enclosed and transmitted to the Secretary of State, and delivered to said Speaker at the commencement of the session of the General Assembly, next ensuing said election.

SEC. 3. The Speaker of the House of Delegates shall then open the said Returns, in the presence of both Houses; and the person having the highest number of votes, and being constitutionally eligible, shall be the Governor, and shall qualify, in the manner herein prescribed, on the second Wednesday of January next ensuing his election, or as soon thereafter as may be practicable.

SEC. 4. If two or more persons shall have the highest and an equal number of votes for Governor, one of them shall be chosen Governor by the Senate and House of Delegates; and all questions in relation to the eligibility of Governor, and to the returns of said election, and to the number and legality of votes therein given, shall be determined by the House of Delegates; and if the person, or persons, having the highest number of votes, be ineligible, the Governor shall be chosen by the Senate and House of Delegates. Every election of Governor by the General Assembly shall be determined by a joint majority of the Senate and House of Delegates; and the vote shall be taken *viva voce.* But if two or more persons shall have the highest and an equal number of votes, then a second vote shall be taken, which shall be confined to the persons having an equal number; and if the vote should again be equal, then the election of Governor shall be determined by lot between those, who shall have the highest and an equal number on the first vote.

SEC. 5. A person to be eligible to the office of Governor, must have attained the age of thirty years, and must have been for ten years a citizen of the State of Maryland, and for five years next preceding his election, a resident of the State, and, at the time of his election, a qualified voter therein.

SEC. 6. In case of the death or resignation of the Governor, or of his removal from the State, or other disqualification, the General Assembly, if in session, or if not, at their next session, shall elect some other qualified person to be Governor for the residue of the term for which the said Governor had been elected.

SEC. 7. In case of any vacancy in the office of Governor, during the recess of the Legislature, the President of the Senate shall discharge the duties of said office, until a Governor is elected, as herein provided for; and in case of the death or resignation of the said President, or of his removal from the State, or of his refusal to serve, then the duties of said office shall, in like manner, and for the same interval, devolve upon the Speaker of the House of Delegates. And the Legislature may provide by Law, for the impeachment of the Governor; and in case of his conviction, or his inability, may declare what person shall perform the Executive duties; and for any vacancy in said office not herein provided for, provision may be made by Law; and if such vacancy should occur without such provision being made, the Legislature shall be convened by the Secretary of State for the purpose of filling said vacancy.

SEC. 8. The Governor shall be the Commander-in-Chief of the land and naval forces of the State; and may call out the Militia to repel invasions, suppress insurrections, and enforce the execution of the Laws; but shall not take the command in person, without the consent of the Legislature.

SEC. 9. He shall take care that the Laws are faithfully executed.

SEC. 10. He shall nominate, and, by and with the advice and consent of the Senate, appoint all civil and military officers of the State, whose appointment, or election, is not otherwise herein provided for; unless a different mode of appointment be prescribed by the Law creating the office.

SEC. 11. In case of any vacancy, during the recess of the Senate, in any office which the Governor has power to fill, he shall appoint some suitable person to said office, whose commission shall continue in force until the end of the next session of the Legislature, or until some other person is appointed to the same office, whichever shall first occur; and the nomination of the person thus appointed, during the recess, or, of some other person in his place, shall be made to the Senate within thirty days after the next meeting of the Legislature.

SEC. 12. No person, after being rejected by the Senate, shall be again nominated for the same office at the same session, unless at the request of the Senate; or, be appointed to the same office during the recess of the Legislature.

SEC. 13. All civil officers appointed by the Governor and Senate, shall be nominated to the Senate within fifty days from the commencement of each regular session of the Legislature; and their term of office, except in cases otherwise provided for in this Constitution, shall commence on the first Monday of May next ensuing their appointment, and continue for two years (unless removed from office) and until their successors, respectively, qualify according to Law; but the term of office of the Inspectors of Tobacco shall commence on the first Monday of March next ensuing their appointment.

SEC. 14. If a vacancy shall occur, during the session of the Senate, in any office which the Governor and Senate have the power to fill, the Governor shall nominate to the Senate before its final adjournment, a proper person to fill said vacancy, unless such vacancy occurs within ten days before said final adjournment.

SEC. 15. The Governor may suspend, or arrest any military officer of the State for disobedience of orders, or other military offence; and may remove him in pursuance of the sentence of a Court Martial; and may remove for incompetency, or misconduct, all civil officers who received appointment from the Executive for a term of years.

SEC. 16. The Governor shall convene the Legislature, or the Senate alone, on extraordinary occasions; and whenever from the presence of an enemy, or from any other cause, the Seat of Government shall become an unsafe place for the meeting of the Legislature, he may direct their sessions to be held at some other convenient place.

SEC. 17. To guard against hasty or partial legislation, and encroachments of the Legislative Department upon the co-ordinate Executive and Judicial Departments, every Bill which shall have passed the House of Delegates and the Senate, shall, before it becomes a Law, be presented to the Governor of the State; if he approve, he shall sign it; but if not, he shall return it, with his objections, to the House in which it originated, which House shall enter the objections at large on its Journal, and proceed to reconsider the Bill; if, after such reconsideration, three-fifths of the members elected to that House shall pass the Bill, it shall be sent, with the objections, to the other House, by which it shall likewise be reconsidered, and if passed by three-fifths of the members elected to that House, it shall become a Law. But, in all such cases, the votes of both Houses shall be determined by yeas and nays; and the names of the persons voting for and against the Bill, shall be entered on the Journal of each House, respectively. If any Bill shall not be returned by the Governor within six days, (Sundays excepted) after it shall have been presented to him, the same shall be a Law in like manner as if he signed it; unless the General Assembly shall, by adjournment, prevent its return, in which case it shall not be a Law.

SEC. 18. It shall be the duty of the Governor, semi-annually (and oftener, if he deem it expedient) to examine under oath the Treasurer and Comptroller of the State on all matters pertaining to their respective offices; and inspect their Bank and other Account Books.

SEC. 19. He shall, from time to time, inform the Legislature of the condition of the State and recommend to their consideration such measures as he may judge necessary and expedient.

SEC. 20. He shall have power to grant reprieves and pardons, except in cases of impeachment, and in cases, in which he is prohibited by other Articles of this Constitution; and to remit fines and forfeitures for offences against the State; but shall not remit the principal, or interest of any debt due the State, except, in cases of fines and forfeitures; and before granting a *nolle prosequi*, or pardon, he shall give notice, in one or more newspapers, of the application made for it, and of the day on, or after which, his decision will be given; and in every case, in which he exercises this power, he shall report to either Branch of the Legislature, whenever required, the petitions, recommendations, and reasons, which influenced his decision.

SEC. 21. The Governor shall reside at the Seat of Government, and receive for his services an annual salary of Four Thousand Five Hundred dollars.

SEC. 22. A Secretary of State shall be appointed by the Governor, by and with the advice and consent of the Senate, who shall continue in office, unless sooner removed by the Governor, till the end of the official term of the Governor from whom he received his appointment, and receive an annual salary of Two Thousand dollars, and shall reside at the Seat of Government; and the office of Private Secretary shall thenceforth cease.

SEC. 23. The Secretary of State shall carefully keep and preserve a Record of all official acts and proceedings, which may at all times be inspected by a committee of either Branch of the Legislature; and he shall perform such other duties as may be prescribed by Law, or as may properly belong to his office, together with all clerical duty belonging to the Executive Department.

ARTICLE III.

LEGISLATIVE DEPARTMENT.

SECTION 1. The Legislature shall consist of two distinct Branches; a Senate, and a House of Delegates, and shall be styled the General Assembly of Maryland.

SEC. 2. Each County in the State, and each of the three Legislative Districts of Baltimore City, as they are now, or may hereafter be defined, shall be entitled to one Senator, who shall be elected by the qualified voters of the Counties, and of the Legislative Districts of Baltimore City, respectively, and shall serve for four years from the date of his election, subject to the classification of Senators, hereafter provided for.

SEC. 3. Until the taking and publishing of the next

National Census, or until the enumeration of the population of this State, under the Authority thereof, the several Counties, and the City of Baltimore, shall have representation in the House of Delegates, as follows: Alleghany County, five Delegates; Anne Arundel County, three Delegates; Baltimore County, six Delegates; each of the three Legislative Districts of the City of Baltimore, six Delegates; Calvert County, two Delegates; Caroline County, two Delegates; Carroll County, four Delegates; Cecil County, four Delegates; Charles County, two Delegates; Dorchester County, three Delegates; Frederick County, six Delegates; Harford County, four Delegates; Howard County, two Delegates; Kent County, two Delegates; Montgomery County, three Delegates; Prince George's County, three Delegates; Queen Anne's County, two Delegates; Saint Mary's County, two Delegates; Somerset County, three Delegates; Talbot County, two Delegates; Washington County, five Delegates; and Worcester County, three Delegates.

SEC. 4. As soon as may be after the taking and publishing of the next National Census, or after the enumeration of the population of this State, under the Authority thereof, there shall be an apportionment of representation in the House of Delegates, to be made on the following basis, to wit: Each of the several Counties of the State, having a population of eighteen thousand souls, or less, shall be entitled to two Delegates; and every County, having a population of over eighteen thousand, and less than twenty-eight thousand souls, shall be entitled to three Delegates; and every County, having a population of twenty-eight thousand, and less than forty thousand souls, shall be entitled to four Delegates; and every County, having a population of forty thousand, and less than fifty-five thousand souls, shall be entitled to five Delegates; and every County, having a population of fifty-five thousand souls, and upwards, shall be entitled to six Delegates, and no more; and each of the three Legislative Districts of the City of Baltimore shall be entitled to the number of Delegates to which the largest County shall, or may be entitled, under the aforegoing apportionment. And the General Assembly shall have power to provide by Law, from time to time, for altering and changing the boundaries of the three existing Legislative Districts of the City of Baltimore, so as to make them, as near as may be, of equal population; but said Districts shall always consist of contiguous territory.

SEC. 5. Immediately after the taking and publishing of the next National Census, or after any State enumeration of population, as aforesaid, it shall be the duty of the Governor, then being, to arrange the Representation in said House of Delegates, in accordance with the apportionment herein provided for; and to declare, by Proclamation, the number of Delegates, to which each County, and the City of Baltimore may be entitled, under such apportionment; and after every National Census taken thereafter, or after any State enumeration of population, thereafter made, it shall be the duty of the Governor, for the time being, to make similar adjustment of Representation, and to declare the same by Proclamation, as aforesaid.

SEC. 6. The members of the House of Delegates shall be elected by the qualified voters of the Counties, and the Legislative Districts of Baltimore City, respectively, to serve for two years, from the day of their election.

SEC. 7. The first election for Senators and Delegates shall take place on the Tuesday next, after the first Monday in the month of November, eighteen hundred and sixty-seven; and the election for Delegates, and as nearly as practicable, for one-half of the Senators, shall be held on the same day, in every second year thereafter.

SEC. 8. Immediately after the Senate shall have convened, after the first election, under this Constitution, the

Senators shall be divided by lot, into two classes, as nearly equal in number as may be — Senators of the first class shall go out of office at the expiration of two years, and Senators shall be elected on the Tuesday next after the first Monday in the month of November, eighteen hundred and sixty-nine, for the term of four years, to supply their places; so that, after the first election, one-half of the Senators may be chosen every second year. In case the number of Senators be hereafter increased, such classification of the additional Senators shall be made as to preserve, as nearly as may be, an equal number in each class.

SEC. 9. No person shall [*be*] eligible as a Senator or Delegate, who at the time of his election, is not a citizen of the State of Maryland, and who has not resided therein, for at least three years, next preceding the day of his election, and the last year thereof, in the County, or in the Legislative District of Baltimore City, which he may be chosen to represent, if such County, or Legislative District of said City, shall have been so long established; and if not, then in the County, or City, from which, in whole, or in part, the same may have been formed; nor shall any person be eligible as a Senator, unless he shall have attained the age of twenty-five years, nor as a Delegate, unless he shall have attained the age of twenty-one years, at the time of his election.

SEC. 10. No member of Congress, or person holding any civil or military office under the United States, shall be eligible as a Senator or Delegate; and if any person shall after his election as Senator or Delegate, be elected to Congress, or be appointed to any office, civil or military, under the Government of the United States, his acceptance thereof, shall vacate his seat.

SEC. 11. No Minister or Preacher of the Gospel, or of any religious creed, or denomination, and no person holding any civil office of profit, or trust, under this State, except Justices of the Peace shall be eligible as Senator, or Delegate.

SEC. 12. No Collector, Receiver, or Holder of public money shall be eligible as Senator or Delegate, or to any office of profit, or trust, under this State, until he shall have accounted for, and paid into the Treasury all sums on the Books thereof charged to, and due by him.

SEC. 13. In case of death, disqualification, resignation, refusal to act, expulsion, or removal from the county, or city, for which he shall have been elected, of any person, who shall have been chosen as a Delegate, or Senator, or in case of a tie between two or more such qualified persons, a warrant of election shall be issued by the Speaker of the House of Delegates, or President of the Senate, as the case may be, for the election of another person in his place, of which election, not less than ten days' notice shall be given, exclusive of the day of the publication of the notice, and of the day of election; and, if during the recess of the Legislature, and more than ten days before its termination, such death shall occur, or such resignation, refusal to act, or disqualification be communicated, in writing to the Governor by the person, so resigning, refusing, or disqualified, it shall be the duty of the Governor to issue a warrant of election to supply the vacancy thus created, in the same manner, the said Speaker, or President, might have done, during the session of the General Assembly; provided, however, that unless a meeting of the General Assembly may intervene, the election, thus ordered to fill such vacancy, shall be held on the day of the ensuing election for Delegates and Senators.

SEC. 14. The General Assembly shall meet on the first Wednesday of January, eighteen hundred and sixty-eight, and on the same day in every second year thereafter, and at no other time, unless convened by Proclamation of the Governor.

SEC. 15. The General Assembly may continue its Session so long as, in its judgment, the public interest may require, for a period not longer than ninety days; and each member thereof, shall receive a compensation of five dollars per diem for every day he shall attend the session; but not for such days as he may be absent, unless absent on account of sickness, or by leave of the House of which he is a member; and he shall also receive such mileage as may be allowed by Law, not exceeding twenty cents per mile; and the Presiding officer of each House shall receive an additional compensation of three dollars per day. When the General Assembly shall be convened by Proclamation of the Governor, the session shall not continue longer than thirty days; and in such case, the compensation shall be the same as herein prescribed.

SEC. 16. No book, or other printed matter, not appertaining to the business of the session, shall be purchased, or subscribed for, for the use of the members of the General Assembly, or be distributed among them, at the public expense.

SEC. 17. No Senator or Delegate, after qualifying as such, notwithstanding he may thereafter resign, shall during the whole period of time, for which he was elected, be eligible to any office, which shall have been created, or the salary, or profits of which shall have been increased, during such term.

SEC. 18. No Senator or Delegate shall be liable in any civil action, or criminal prosecution, whatever, for words spoken in debate.

SEC. 19. Each House shall be judge of the qualifications and elections of its members, as prescribed by the Constitution and Laws of the State; shall appoint its own officers, determine the rules of its own proceedings, punish a member for disorderly or disrespectful behaviour, and with the consent of two-thirds of its whole number of members elected, expel a member; but no member shall be expelled a second time for the same offence.

SEC. 20. A majority of the whole number of members elected to each House shall constitute a quorum for the transaction of business; but a smaller number may adjourn from day to day, and compel the attendance of absent members, in such manner, and under such penalties, as each House may prescribe.

SEC. 21. The doors of each House, and of the Committee of the Whole, shall be open, except when the business is such as ought to be kept secret.

SEC. 22. Each House shall keep a Journal of its proceedings, and cause the same to be published. The yeas and nays of members on any question, shall at the call of any five of them in the House of Delegates, or one in the Senate, be entered on the Journal.

SEC. 23. Each House may punish by imprisonment, during the session of the General Assembly, any person, not a member, for disrespectful, or disorderly behaviour in its presence, or for obstructing any of its proceedings, or any of its officers in the execution of their duties; provided, such imprisonment shall not, at any one time, exceed ten days.

SEC. 24. The House of Delegates may inquire, on the oath of witnesses, into all complaints, grievances and offences, as the Grand Inquest of the State, and may commit any person, for any crime, to the public jail, there to remain, until discharged by due course of Law. They may examine and pass all accounts of the State, relating either to the collection or expenditure of the revenue, and appoint Auditors to state and adjust the same. They may call for all public, or official papers and records, and send for persons, whom they may judge necessary, in the course of their inquiries, concerning affairs relating to the public interest, and may direct all office bonds which shall be made payable to the State, to be sued for any breach thereof; and with the view to the more certain prevention, or correction of the abuses in the expenditures of the money of the State, the General Assembly shall create, at every session thereof, a joint Standing Committee of the Senate and House of Delegates, who shall have power to send for persons, and examine them on oath, and call for Public, or Official Papers and Records, and whose duty it shall be to examine and report upon all contracts made for printing stationery, and purchases for the Public offices, and the Library, and all expenditures therein, and upon all matters of alleged abuse in expenditures, to which their attention may be called by Resolution of either House of the General Assembly.

SEC. 25. Neither House shall, without the consent of the other, adjourn for more than three days, at any one time, nor adjourn to any other place, than that in which the House shall be sitting, without the concurrent vote of two-thirds of the members present.

SEC. 26. The House of Delegates shall have the sole power of impeachment in all cases; but a majority of all the members elected must concur in the impeachment. All impeachments shall be tried by the Senate, and when sitting for that purpose, the Senators shall be on oath, or affirmation, to do justice according to the law and the evidence; but no person shall be convicted without the concurrence of two-thirds of all the Senators elected.

SEC. 27. Any bill may originate in either House of the General Assembly, and be altered, amended, or rejected by the other; but no bill shall originate in either House during the last ten days of the session, unless two-thirds of the members elected thereto shall so determine by yeas and nays; nor shall any bill become a Law, until it be read on three different days of the session in each House, unless two-thirds of the members elected to the House, where such bill is pending, shall so determine by yeas and nays; and no bill shall be read a third time until it shall have been actually engrossed for a third reading.

SEC. 28. No bill shall become a Law unless it be passed

in each House by a majority of the whole number of members elected, and on its final passage, the yeas and nays be recorded; nor shall any Resolution, requiring the action of both Houses, be passed except in the same manner.

SEC. 29. The style of all Laws of this State shall be, "Be it enacted by the General Assembly of Maryland:" and all Laws shall be passed by original bill; and every Law enacted by the General Assembly shall embrace but one subject, and that shall be described in its title; and no Law, nor section of Law, shall be revived, or amended by reference to its title, or section only; nor shall any Law be construed by reason of its title, to grant powers, or confer rights which are not expressly contained in the body of the Act; and it shall be the duty of the General Assembly, in amending any article, or section of the Code of Laws of this State, to enact the same, as the said article, or section would read when amended. And whenever the General Assembly shall enact any Public General Law, not amendatory of any section, or article in the said Code, it shall be the duty of the General Assembly to enact the same, in articles and sections, in the same manner, as tho Code is arranged, and to provide for the publication of all additions and alterations, which may be made to the said Code.

SEC. 30. Every bill, when passed by the General Assembly, and sealed with the Great Seal, shall be presented to the Governor, who, if he approves it, shall sign the same in the presence of the presiding officers and Chief Clerks of the Senate and House of Delegates. Every Law shall be recorded in the office of the Court of Appeals, and in due time, be printed, published and certified under the Great Seal, to the several Courts, in the same manner as has been heretofore usual in this State.

SEC. 31. No Law passed by the General Assembly shall take effect, until the first day of June, next after the Session, at which it may be passed, unless it be otherwise expressly declared therein.

SEC. 32. No money shall be drawn from the Treasury of the State, by any order or resolution, nor except in accordance with an appropriation by Law, and every such Law shall distinctly specify the sum appropriated, and the object, to which it shall be applied; provided, that nothing herein contained shall prevent the General Assembly from placing a contingent fund at the disposal of the Executive, who shall report to the General Assembly, at each Session, the amount expended, and the purposes to which it was applied. An accurate statement of the receipts and expenditures of the public money, shall be attached to, and published with the Laws, after each regular Session of the General Assembly.

SEC. 33. The General Assembly shall not pass local, or special Laws, in any of the following enumerated cases, viz.: For extending the time for the collection of taxes; granting divorces; changing the name of any person; providing for the sale of real estate, belonging to minors, or other persons laboring under legal disabilities, by executors, administrators, guardians or trustees; giving effect to informal, or invalid deeds or wills; refunding money paid into the State Treasury, or releasing persons from their debts, or obligations to the State, unless recommended by the Governor, or officers of the Treasury Department. And the General Assembly shall pass no special Law, for any case, for which provision has been made, by an existing General Law. The General Assembly, at its first session after the adoption of this Constitution, shall pass General Laws, providing for the cases enumerated in this section, which are not already adequately provided for, and for all other cases, where a General Law can be made applicable.

SEC. 34. No debt shall be hereafter contracted by the General Assembly, unless such debt shall be authorized by a Law, providing for the collection of an annual tax, or taxes, sufficient to pay the interest on such debt, as it falls due; and also, to discharge the principal thereof, within fifteen years from the time of contracting the same; and the taxes, laid for this purpose, shall not be repealed, or applied to any other object, until the said debt, and interest thereon, shall be fully discharged. The credit of the State shall not in any manner be given, or loaned to, or in aid of any individual, association, or corporation; nor shall the General Assembly have the power, in any mode, to involve the State in the construction of Works of Internal Improvement, nor in granting any aid thereto, which shall involve the faith, or credit of the State; nor make any appropriation therefor, except in aid of the construction of Works of Internal Improvement, in the counties of Saint Mary's, Charles and Calvert, which have had no direct advantage, from such Works, as have been heretofore aided by the State; and provided, that such aid, advances, or appropriations shall not exceed in the aggregate the sum of five hundred thousand dollars. And they shall not use, or appropriate the proceeds of the Internal Improvement Companies, or of the State tax, now levied, or which may hereafter be levied, to pay off the public debt, to any other purpose until the interest and debt are fully paid, or the sinking fund shall be equal to the amount of the outstanding debt; but the General Assembly may, without laying a tax, borrow an amount never to exceed fifty thousand dollars, to meet temporary deficiencies in the Treasury, and may contract debts to any amount that may be necessary for the defence of the State.

SEC. 35. No extra compensation shall be granted, or allowed, by the General Assembly, to any Public Officer, Agent, Servant or Contractor, after the service shall have been rendered, or the contract entered into; nor shall the salary, or compensation of any public officer be increased, or diminished during his term of office.

SEC. 36. No Lottery grant shall ever hereafter be authorized by the General Assembly.

SEC. 37. The General Assembly shall pass no Law providing for payment, by this State, for Slaves emancipated from servitude in this State; but they shall adopt such measures, as they may deem expedient, to obtain from the United States, compensation for such Slaves, and to receive, and distribute the same, equitably, to the persons entitled.

SEC. 38. No person shall be imprisoned for debt.

SEC. 39. The General Assembly shall grant no charter for Banking purposes, nor renew any Banking Corporation, now in existence, except upon the condition that the Stockholders shall be liable to the amount of their respective Share, or Shares of Stock in such Banking Institution, for all its debts and liabilities, upon note, bill, or otherwise; the Books, papers, and accounts of all Banks shall be open to inspection, under such regulations as may be prescribed by Law.

SEC. 40. The General Assembly shall enact no Law authorizing private property, to be taken for public use, without just compensation, as agreed upon between the parties, or awarded by a jury, being first paid, or tendered to the party, entitled to such compensation.

SEC. 41. Any citizen of this State, who shall after the adoption of this Constitution, either in, or out of this State, fight a duel with deadly weapons, or send, or accept a challenge so to do, or who shall act as a second, or knowingly aid or assist in any manner, those offending, shall, ever thereafter, be incapable of holding any office of profit or trust, under this State, unless relieved from the disability by an act of the Legislature.

SEC. 42. The General Assembly shall pass Laws necessary for the preservation of the purity of Elections.

SEC. 43. The property of the wife shall be protected from the debts of her husband.

SEC. 44. Laws shall be passed by the General Assembly, to protect from execution a reasonable amount of the property of the debtor, not exceeding in value, the sum of five hundred dollars.

SEC. 45. The General Assembly shall provide a simple and uniform system of charges in the offices of Clerks of Courts, and Registers of Wills, in the Counties of this State, and the City of Baltimore, and for the collection thereof; provided, the amount of compensation to any of the said officers, in the various Counties, shall not exceed the sum of three thousand dollars a year, and in the City of Baltimore thirty-five hundred dollars a year, over and above office expenses, and compensation to assistants; and provided further, that such compensation, of Clerks, Registers, assistants and office expenses shall always be paid out of the fees, or receipts of the offices, respectively.

SEC. 46. The General Assembly shall have power to receive from the United States, any grant, or donation of land, money, or securities for any purpose designated by the United States, and shall administer, or distribute the same according to the conditions of the said grant.

SEC. 47. The General Assembly shall make provisions for all cases of contested elections of any of the officers, not herein provided for.

SEC. 48. Corporations may be formed under general Laws; but shall not be created by special act, except for municipal purposes, and except in cases, where no general Laws exist, providing for the creation of corporations of the same general character, as the corporation proposed to be created; and any act of incorporation, passed in violation of this section, shall be void. And as soon as practicable, after the adoption of this Constitution, it shall be the duty of the Governor, to appoint three persons learned in the Law, whose duty it shall be, to prepare drafts of general Laws, providing for the creation of corporations, in such cases as may be proper, and for all other cases, where a general Law can be made; and for revising and amending, so far as may be necessary, or expedient, the general Laws which may be in existence on the first day of June, eighteen hundred and sixty-seven, providing for the creation of corporations, and for other purposes; and such drafts of Laws shall by said commissioners, be submitted to the General Assembly, at its first meeting, for its action thereon; and each of said commissioners shall receive a compensation of five hundred dollars for his services, as such commissioner.

All Charters granted, or adopted, in pursuance of this section, and all Charters heretofore granted and created, subject to repeal or modification, may be altered, from time to time, or be repealed; provided, nothing herein contained shall be construed to extend to Banks, or the incorporation thereof.

SEC. 49. The General Assembly shall have power to regulate by Law, not inconsistent with this Constitution, all matters which relate to the Judges of election, time, place and manner of holding elections in this State, and of making returns thereof.

SEC. 50. It shall be the duty of the General Assembly, at its first session, held after the adoption of this Constitution, to provide by Law for the punishment, by fine, or imprisonment in the Penitentiary, or both, in the discretion of the Court, of any person, who shall bribe, or attempt to bribe, any Executive, or Judicial officer of the State of Maryland, or any member, or officer of the General Assembly of the State of Maryland, or of any Municipal Corporation in the State of Maryland, or any Executive officer of such corporation, in order to influence him in the performance of any of his official duties; and, also, to provide by Law for the punishment by fine, or imprisonment in the Penitentiary, or both, in the discretion of the Court, of any of said officers, or members, who shall demand, or receive any bribe, fee, reward, or testimonial, for the performance of his official duties, or for neglecting, or failing to perform the same; and, also, to provide by Law for compelling any person, so bribing, or attempting to bribe, or so demanding, or receiving a bribe, fee, reward, or testimonial, to testify against any person, or persons, who may have committed any of said offences; provided, that any person, so compelled to testify, shall be exempted from trial and punishment for the offence, of which he may have been guilty; and any person, convicted of such offence, shall, as part of the punishment thereof, be forever disfranchised and disqualified from holding any office of trust, or profit, in this State.

SEC. 51. The personal property of residents of this State, shall be subject to taxation in the county, or city, where the resident *bona fide* resides for the greater part of the year, for which the tax may, or shall be levied, and not elsewhere, except goods and chattels permanently located, which shall be taxed in the City, or County where they are so located.

SEC. 52. The General Assembly shall appropriate no money out of the Treasury for payment of any private claim against the State exceeding three hundred dollars, unless said claim shall have been first presented to the Comptroller of the Treasury, together with the proofs upon which the same is founded, and reported upon by him.

SEC. 53. No person shall be incompetent, as a witness, on account of race or color, unless hereafter so declared by Act of the General Assembly.

SEC. 54. No County of this State shall contract any debt, or obligation, in the construction of any Railroad, Canal, or other Work of Internal Improvement, nor give, or loan its credit to, or in aid of any association, or corporation, unless authorized by an Act of the General Assembly, which shall be published for two months before the next election for members of the House of Delegates in the newspapers published in such County, and shall also be approved by a majority of all the members elected to each House of the General Assembly at its next Session after said election.

SEC. 55. The General Assembly shall pass no Law suspending the privilege of the Writ of *Habeas Corpus.*

SEC. 56. The General Assembly shall have power to pass all such Laws as may be necessary and proper for carrying into execution the powers vested, by this Constitution, in any Department, or office of the Government, and the duties imposed upon them thereby.

SEC. 57. The Legal Rate of Interest shall be *six per cent. per annum;* unless otherwise provided by the General Assembly.

SEC. 58. The Legislature at its first session after the ratification of this Constitution shall provide by Law for State and municipal taxation upon the revenues accruing from business done in the State by all foreign corporations.

SEC. 59. The office of "State Pension Commissioner" is hereby abolished; and the Legislature shall pass no law creating such office, or establishing any general pension system within this State.

ARTICLE IV.

JUDICIARY DEPARTMENT.

PART I.—GENERAL PROVISIONS.

SECTION 1. The Judicial power of this State shall be vested in a Court of Appeals, Circuit Courts, Orphans' Courts, such Courts for the City of Baltimore as are hereinafter provided for, and Justices of the Peace; all said Courts shall be Courts of Record, and each shall have a seal to be used in the authentication of all process issuing therefrom. The process and official character of Justices of the Peace shall be authenticated as hath heretofore been practiced in this State, or may hereafter be prescribed by Law.

SEC. 2. The Judges of all of the said Courts shall be citizens of the State of Maryland, and qualified voters under this Constitution, and shall have resided therein not less than five years, and not less than six months next preceding their election, or appointment, in the Judicial Circuit, as the case may be, for which they may be, respectively, elected, or appointed. They shall be not less than thirty years of age at the time of their election, or appointment, and shall be selected from those who have been admitted to practice Law in this State, and who are most distinguished for integrity, wisdom and sound legal knowledge.

SEC. 3. The Judges of the said several Courts shall be elected in the Counties by the qualified voters in their respective Judicial Circuits, as hereinafter provided, at the general election to be held on the Tuesday after the first Monday in November next, and in the City of Baltimore, on the fourth Wednesday of October next. Each of the said Judges shall hold his office for the term of fifteen years from the time of his election, and until his successor is elected and qualified, or until he shall have attained the age of seventy years, whichever may first happen, and be re-eligible thereto until he shall have attained the age of seventy years, and not after; but in case of any Judge, who shall attain the age of seventy years whilst in office, such Judge may be continued in office by the General Assembly for such further time as they may think fit, not to exceed the term for which he was elected, by a Resolution to be passed at the session next preceding his attaining said age. In case of the inability of any of said Judges to discharge his duties with efficiency, by reason of continued sickness, or of physical or mental infirmity, it shall be in the power of the General Assembly, two-thirds of the members of each House concurring, with the approval of the Governor, to retire said Judge from office.

SEC. 4. Any Judge shall be removed from office by the Governor, on conviction in a Court of Law, of incompetency, of wilful neglect of duty, misbehaviour in office, or any other crime, or on impeachment, according to this Constitution, or the Laws of the State; or on the address of the General Assembly, two-thirds of each House concurring in such address, and the accused having been notified of the charges against him, and having had opportunity of making his defence.

SEC. 5. After the election for Judges, to be held as above mentioned, upon the expiration of the term, or in case of the death, resignation, removal, or other disqualification, of any Judge, the Governor shall appoint a person duly qualified to fill said office, who shall hold the same until the next general election for members of the General Assembly, when a successor shall be elected, whose tenure of office shall be the same, as hereinbefore provided; but if the vacancy shall occur in the City of Baltimore, the time of election shall be the fourth Wednesday in October following.

SEC. 6. All Judges shall, by virtue of their offices, be Conservators of the Peace throughout the State; and no fees, or perquisites, commission, or reward of any kind, shall be allowed to any Judge in this State, besides his annual salary, for the discharge of any Judicial duty.

SEC. 7. No Judge shall sit in any case wherein he may be interested, or where either of the parties may be connected with him, by affinity or consanguinity, within such degrees as now are, or may hereafter be prescribed by Law, or where he shall have been of counsel in the case.

SEC. 8. The parties to any cause may submit the same to the Court for determination, without the aid of a jury; and the Judge, or Judges of any Court of this State, except the Court of Appeals, shall order and direct the Record of proceedings in any suit, or action, issue, or petition, presentment, or indictment, pending in such Court, to be transmitted to some other Court, (and of a different Circuit, if the party applying shall so elect,) having jurisdiction in such cases, whenever any party to such cause, or the counsel of any party, shall make a suggestion, in writing, supported by the affidavit of such party, or his counsel, or other proper evidence, that the party cannot have a fair or impartial trial in the Court, in which such suit, or action, issue, or petition, presentment, or indictment is pending, or when the Judges of said Court shall be disqualified, under the provisions of this Constitution, to sit in any such suit, action, issue, or petition, presentment, or indictment; and the General Assembly shall make such modifications of existing Law as may be necessary to regulate and give force to this provision.

SEC. 9. The Judge, or Judges of any Court, may appoint such officers for their respective Courts as may be found necessary; and such officers of the Courts in the City of Baltimore shall be appointed by the Judges of the Supreme Bench of Baltimore City. It shall be the duty of the General Assembly to prescribe, by Law, a fixed compensation for all such officers; and said Judge, or Judges shall, from time to time, investigate the expenses, costs and charges of their respective Courts, with a view to a change or reduction thereof, and report the result of such investigation to the General Assembly for its action.

EC. 10. The Clerks of the several Courts, created, or continued by this Constitution, shall have charge and custody of the records and other papers, shall perform all the duties, and be allowed the fees, which appertain to their several offices, as the same now are, or may hereafter be regulated by Law. And the office and business of said Clerks, in all their departments, shall be subject to the visitorial power of the Judges of their respective Courts, who shall exercise the same, from time to time, so as to insure the faithful performance of the duties of said offices; and it shall be the duty of the Judges of said Courts respectively, to make, from time to time, such rules and regulations as may be necessary and proper for the government of said Clerks, and for the performance of the duties of their offices, which shall have the force of Law until repealed, or modified by the General Assembly.

SEC. 11. The election for Judges, hereinbefore provided, and all elections for Clerks, Registers of Wills, and other officers, provided in this Constitution, except State's Attorneys, shall be certified, and the returns made, by the Clerks of the Circuit Courts of the Counties, and the Clerk of the Superior Court of Baltimore city, respectively, to the Governor, who shall issue commissions to the different persons for the offices to which they shall have been, respectively, elected; and in all such elections, the person having the greatest number of votes, shall be declared to be elected.

SEC. 12. If in any case of election for Judges, Clerks of the Courts of Law, and Registers of Wills, the opposing candidates shall have an equal number of votes, it shall be the duty of the Governor to order a new election; and in case of any contested election, the Governor shall send the returns to the House of Delegates, which shall judge of the election and qualification of the candidates at such election; and if the judgment shall be against the one who has been returned elected, or the one who has been commissioned by the Governor, the House of Delegates shall order a new election within thirty days.

SEC. 13. All Public Commissions and Grants shall run thus: "The State of Maryland, &c.," and shall be signed by the Governor, with the Seal of the State annexed; all writs and process shall run in the same style, and be tested, sealed and signed, as heretofore, or as may hereafter be, provided by Law; and all indictments shall conclude, "against the peace, government and dignity of the State."

PART II.—COURT OF APPEALS.

SEC. 14. The Court of Appeals shall be composed of the Chief Judges of the first seven of the several Judicial Circuits of the State, and a Judge from the City of Baltimore specially elected thereto, one of whom shall be designated by the Governor, by and with the advice and consent of the Senate, as the Chief Judge: and in all cases, until action by the Senate can be had, the Judge so designated by the Governor, shall act as Chief Judge. The Judge of the Court of Appeals from the City of Baltimore shall be elected by the qualified voters of said City, at the election of Judges to be held therein, as hereinbefore provided; and in addition to his duties, as Judge of the Court of Appeals, shall perform such other duties as the General Assembly shall prescribe. The jurisdiction of said Court of Appeals shall be co-extensive with the limits of the State, and such as now is, or may hereafter be prescribed by Law. It shall hold its sessions in the city of Annapolis, on the first Monday in April, and the first Monday in October, of each and every year, or at such other times as the General Assembly may, by Law, direct. Its sessions shall continue not less than ten months in the year, if the business before it shall so require; and it shall be competent for the Judges, temporarily, to transfer their sittings elsewhere, upon sufficient cause.

SEC. 15. Four of said Judges shall constitute a quorum; no cause shall be decided without the concurrence of at least three; but the Judge who heard the cause below, shall not participate in the decision; in every case an opinion, in writing, shall be filed within three months after the argument, or submission of the cause; and the judgment of the Court shall be final and conclusive; and all cases shall stand for hearing at the first term after the transmission of the Record.

SEC. 16. Provision shall be made by Law for publishing Reports of all causes, argued and determined in the Court of Appeals, which the Judges shall designate as proper for publication.

SEC. 17. There shall be a Clerk of the Court of Appeals, who shall be elected by the legal and qualified voters of the State, who shall hold his office for six years, and until his successor is duly qualified; he shall be subject to removal by the said Court for incompetency, neglect of duty, misdemeanor in office, or such other cause, or causes, as may be prescribed by Law; and in case of a vacancy in the office of said Clerk, the Court of Appeals shall appoint a Clerk of said Court, who shall hold his office until the election and qualification of his successor, who shall be elected at the next general election for members of the General Assembly; and the person, so elected, shall hold his office for the term of six years from the time of election.

SEC. 18. It shall be the duty of the Judges of the Court of Appeals, as soon after their election, under this Constitution, as practicable, to make and publish rules and regulations for the prosecution of appeals to said appellate court, whereby they shall prescribe the periods within which appeals may be taken, what part or parts of the proceedings in the Court below shall constitute the record on appeal, and the manner in which such appeals shall be brought to hearing or determination, and shall regulate, generally, the practice of said Court of Appeals, so as to prevent delays, and promote brevity in all records and proceedings brought into said Court, and to abolish and avoid all unnecessary costs and expenses in the prosecution of appeals therein; and the said Judges shall make such reductions in the fees and expenses of the said Court, as they may deem advisable. It shall also be the duty of said Judges of the Court of Appeals, as soon after their election as practicable, to devise, and promulgate by rules or orders, forms and modes of framing and filing bills, answers, and other proceedings and pleadings in Equity; and also forms and modes of taking and obtaining evidence, to be used in Equity cases; and to revise and regulate, generally, the practice in the Courts of Equity of this State, so as to prevent delays, and to promote brevity and conciseness in all pleadings and proceedings therein, and to abolish all unnecessary costs and expenses attending the same. And all rules and regulations hereby directed to be made, shall, when made, have the force of Law, until rescinded, changed, or modified by the said Judges, or the General Assembly.

PART III.—CIRCUIT COURTS.

SEC. 19. The State shall be divided into eight Judicial Circuits, in manner following, viz.: the Counties of Worcester, Somerset and Dorchester, shall constitute the First Circuit; the Counties of Caroline, Talbot, Queen Anne's, Kent and Cecil, the Second; the Counties of Baltimore and Harford, the Third; the Counties of Alleghany and Washington, the Fourth; the Counties of Carroll, Howard and Anne Arundel, the Fifth; the Counties of Montgomery and Frederick, the Sixth; the Counties of Prince George's, Charles, Calvert and St. Mary's, the Seventh; and Baltimore City, the Eighth.

SEC. 20. A Court shall be held in each County of the State, to be styled the Circuit Court for the County, in which it may be held. The said Circuit Courts shall have and exercise, in the respective Counties, all the power, authority and jurisdiction, original and appellate, which the present Circuit Courts of this State now have and exercise, or which may hereafter be prescribed by Law.

SEC. 21. For each of the said Circuits (excepting the

Eighth,) there shall be a Chief Judge, and two Associate Judges, to be styled Judges of the Circuit Court, to be elected or appointed, as herein provided. And no two of said Associate Judges shall, at the time of their election, or appointment, or during the term, for which they may have been elected, or appointed, reside in the same County. If two or more persons shall be candidates for Associate Judge, in the same County, that one only in said County shall be declared elected, who has the highest number of votes in the Circuit. In case any two candidates for Associate Judge, residing in the same County, shall have an equal number of votes, greater than any other candidate for Associate Judge, in the Circuit, it shall be the duty of the Governor to order a new election for one Associate Judge; but the person, residing in any other County of the Circuit, and who has the next highest number of votes, shall be declared elected. The said Judges shall hold not less than two Terms of the Circuit Court in each of the Counties, composing their respective Circuits, at such times as are now, or may hereafter be prescribed, to which Jurors shall be summoned; and in those Counties, where only two such Terms are held, two other and intermediate Terms, to which Jurors shall not be summoned; they may alter or fix the times for holding any, or all Terms until otherwise prescribed, and shall adopt Rules to the end that all business not requiring the interposition of a Jury shall be, as far as practicable, disposed of at said intermediate Terms. One Judge, in each of the above Circuits, shall constitute a quorum for the transaction of any business; and the said Judges, or any of them, may hold Special Terms of their Courts, whenever, in their discretion, the business of the several Counties renders such Terms necessary.

SEC. 22. Where any Term is held, or trial conducted by less than the whole number of said Circuit Judges, upon the decision, or determination of any point, or question, by the Court, it shall be competent to the party, against whom the ruling or decision is made, upon motion, to have the point, or question reserved for the consideration of the three Judges of the Circuit, who shall constitute a Court in *banc* for such purposes; and the motion for such reservation shall be entered of record, during the sitting, at which such decision may be made; and the several Circuit Courts shall regulate, by rules, the mode and manner of presenting such points, or questions to the Court in *banc*, and the decision of the said Court in *banc* shall be the effective decision in the premises, and conclusive, as against the party, at whose motion said points, or questions were reserved; but such decision in *banc* shall not preclude the right of Appeal, or writ of error to the adverse party, in those cases, civil or criminal, in which appeal, or writ of error to the Court of Appeals may be allowed by Law. The right of having questions reserved shall not, however, apply to trials of Appeals from judgments of Justices of the Peace, nor to criminal cases below the grade of felony, except when the punishment is confinement in the Penitentiary; and this Section shall be subject to such provisions as may hereafter be made by Law.

SEC. 23. The Judges of the respective Circuit Courts of this State, and of the Courts of Baltimore City, shall render their decisions, in all cases argued before them, or submitted for their judgment, within two months after the same shall have been so argued or submitted.

SEC. 24. The salary of each Chief Judge, and of the Judge of the Court of Appeals from the City of Baltimore shall be three thousand five hundred dollars, and of each Associate Judge of the Circuit Court, shall be two thousand eight hundred dollars per annum, payable quarterly, and shall not be diminished during his continuance in office.

SEC. 25. There shall be a Clerk of the Circuit Court

for each County, who shall be elected by a plurality of the qualified voters of said County, and shall hold his office for six years from the time of his election, and until his successor is elected and qualified, and be re-eligible, subject to be removed for wilful neglect of duty, or other misdemeanor in office, on conviction in a Court of Law. In case of a vacancy in the office of Clerk of a Circuit Court, the Judges of said Court shall have power to fill such vacancy until the general election for Delegates to the General Assembly, to be held next thereafter, when a successor shall be elected for the term of six years.

SEC. 26. The said Clerks shall appoint, subject to the confirmation of the Judges of their respective Courts, as many deputies under them, as the said Judges shall deem necessary, to perform, together with themselves, the duties of the said office, who shall be removable by the said Judges for incompetency, or neglect of duty, and whose compensation shall be according to existing, or future provisions of the General Assembly.

PART IV.—COURTS OF BALTIMORE CITY.

SEC. 27. There shall be in the Eighth Judicial Circuit, six Courts, to be styled the Supreme Bench of Baltimore City, the Superior Court of Baltimore City, the Court of Common Pleas, the Baltimore City Court, the Circuit Court of Baltimore City, and the Criminal Court of Baltimore.

SEC. 28. The Superior Court of Baltimore City, the Court of Common Pleas, and the Baltimore City Court shall, each, have concurrent jurisdiction in all civil common Law cases, and, concurrently, all the jurisdiction which the Superior Court of Baltimore City and the Court of Common Pleas now have, except jurisdiction in Equity, and except in applications for the benefit of the Insolvent Laws of Maryland, and in cases of Appeal from judgments of Justices of the Peace in said City, whether civil or criminal, or arising under the ordinances of the Mayor and City Council of Baltimore, of all of which appeal cases the Baltimore City Court shall have exclusive jurisdiction; and the said Court of Common Pleas shall have exclusive jurisdiction in all applications for the benefit of the Insolvent Laws of Maryland, and the supervision and control of the Trustees thereof.

SEC. 29. The Circuit Court of Baltimore City shall have exclusive jurisdiction in Equity within the limits of said city, and all such jurisdiction as the present Circuit Court of Baltimore City has; provided, the said Court shall not have jurisdiction in applications for the writ of *habeas corpus* in cases of persons charged with criminal offences.

SEC. 30. The Criminal Court of Baltimore shall have and exercise all the jurisdiction, now held and exercised by the Criminal Court of Baltimore, except in such Appeal Cases as are herein assigned to the Baltimore City Court.

SEC. 31. There shall be elected by the legal and qualified voters of said City, at the election, hereinbefore provided for, one Chief Judge, and four Associate Judges, who, together, shall constitute the Supreme Bench of Baltimore City, and shall hold their offices for the term of fifteen years, subject to the provisions of this Constitution with regard to the election and qualifications of Judges, and their removal from office, and shall exercise the jurisdiction, hereinafter specified, and shall each receive an annual salary of three thousand five hundred dollars, payable quarterly, which shall not be diminished during their term of office; but authority is hereby given to the Mayor and City Council of Baltimore to pay to each of the said Judges an annual addition of five hundred dollars to their respective salaries; provided, that the same, being once granted, shall not be diminished, nor increased, during the continuance of said Judges in office.

SEC. 32. It shall be the duty of the said Supreme Bench

of Baltimore City, as soon as the Judges thereof shall be elected and duly qualified, and from time to time, to provide for the holding of each of the aforesaid Courts, by the assignment of one, or more of their number to each of the said Courts, who may sit, either separately, or together, in the trial of cases; and the said Supreme Bench of Baltimore City may, from time to time, change the said assignment, as circumstances may require, and the public interest may demand; and the Judge, or Judges, so assigned to the said several Courts, shall, when holding the same, have all the powers and exercise all the jurisdiction, which may belong to the Court so being held; and it shall also be the duty of the said Supreme Bench of Baltimore City, in case of the sickness, absence, or disability of any Judge or Judges, assigned as aforesaid, to provide for the hearing of the cases, or transaction of the business assigned to said Judge, or Judges, as aforesaid, before some one, or more of the Judges of said Court.

SEC. 33. The said Supreme Bench of Baltimore City shall have power, and it shall be its duty, to provide for the holding of as many general Terms as the performance of its duties may require, such general Terms to be held by not less than three Judges; to make all needful rules and regulations for the conduct of business in each of the said Courts, during the session thereof, and in vacation, or in Chambers, before any of said Judges; and shall also have jurisdiction to hear and determine all motions for a new trial in cases tried in any of said Courts, where such motions arise, either on questions of fact, or for misdirection upon any matters of Law, and all motions in arrest of judgment, or upon any matters of Law determined by the said Judge, or Judges, while holding said several Courts; and the said Supreme Bench of Baltimore City shall make all needful rules and regulations for the hearing before it of all of said matters; and the same right of appeal to the Court of Appeals shall be allowed from the determination of the said Court on such matters, as would have been the right of the parties if said matters had been decided by the Court in which said cases were tried.

SEC. 34. No appeal shall lie to the Supreme Bench of Baltimore City from the decision of the Judge, or Judges, holding the Baltimore City Court, in case of appeal from a Justice of the Peace; but the decision by said Judge, or Judges, shall be final; and all writs and other process issued out of either of said Courts, requiring attestation, shall be attested in the name of the Chief Judge of the said Supreme Bench of Baltimore City.

SEC. 35. Three of the Judges of said Supreme Bench of Baltimore City, shall constitute a quorum of said Court.

SEC. 36. All causes depending, at the adoption of this Constitution, in the Superior Court of Baltimore City, the Court of Common Pleas, the Criminal Court of Baltimore, and the Circuit Court of Baltimore City, shall be proceeded in, and prosecuted to final judgment, or decree, in the Courts, respectively, of the same name established by this Constitution, except cases belonging to that class, jurisdiction over which is by this Constitution transferred to the Baltimore City Court, all of which shall, together with all cases now pending in the City Court of Baltimore, be proceeded in, and prosecuted to final judgment in said Baltimore City Court.

SEC. 37. There shall be a Clerk of each of the said Courts of Baltimore City, except the Supreme Bench, who shall be elected by the legal and qualified voters of said City, at the election to be held in said city on the Tuesday next after the First Monday of November, in the year eighteen hundred and sixty-seven, and shall hold his office for six years from the time of his election, and until his successor is elected and qualified, and be re-eligible thereto, subject to be removed for wilful neglect of duty, or other misdemeanor in office, on conviction in a Court of Law. The salary of each of the said Clerks shall be thirty-five hundred dollars a year, payable only out of the fees and receipts collected by the Clerks of said City, and they shall be entitled to no other perquisites, or compensation. In case of a vacancy in the office of Clerk of any of said Courts, the Judges of said Supreme Bench of Baltimore City shall have power to fill such vacancy until the general election of Delegates to the General Assembly, to be held next thereafter, when a Clerk of said Court shall be elected to serve for six years thereafter; and the provisions of this Article in relation to the appointment of Deputies by the Clerks of the Circuit Courts in the Counties shall apply to the Clerks of the Courts in Baltimore City.

SEC. 38. The Clerk of the Court of Common Pleas shall have authority to issue within said City, all marriage and other licenses required by Law, subject to such provisions as are now, or may be prescribed by Law. The Clerk of the Superior Court of said City shall receive and record all Deeds, Conveyances, and other papers, which are, or may be required by Law, to be recorded in said City. He shall also have custody of all papers connected with the proceedings on the Law, or Equity side of Baltimore County Court, and of the Dockets thereof, so far as the same have relation to the City of Baltimore, and shall also discharge the duties of Clerk to the Supreme Bench of Baltimore City, unless otherwise provided by Law.

SEC. 39. The General Assembly shall, whenever it may think the same proper and expedient, provide, by Law, another Court for the City of Baltimore, and prescribe its jurisdiction and powers; in which case there shall be elected by the voters of said City, qualified under this Constitution, another Judge of the Supreme Bench of Baltimore City, who shall be subject to the same constitutional provisions, hold his office for the same term of years, receive the same compensation, and have the same powers, as are herein provided for the Judges of said

Supreme Bench of Baltimore City; and all of the provisions of this Constitution relating to the assignment of Judges to the Courts, now existing in said City, and for the dispatch of business therein, shall apply to the Court, for whose creation provision is made by this Section. And the General Assembly may reapportion, change, or enlarge the jurisdiction of the several Courts in Baltimore City. Until otherwise provided by Law, the Clerk of the Superior Court of Baltimore City, of the Court of Common Pleas, of the Circuit Court of Baltimore City, of the Baltimore City Court, and of the Criminal Court of Baltimore, shall each give Bond in such penalty as is now prescribed, by Law, to be given by the Clerks of the Courts, bearing the same names, under the present Constitution.

PART V.—ORPHANS' COURTS.

SEC. 40. The qualified voters of the City of Baltimore, and of the several Counties, shall on the Tuesday next after the first Monday in November next, and on the same day in every fourth year thereafter, elect three men to be Judges of the Orphans' Courts of said City and Counties, respectively, who shall be citizens of the State, and residents for the twelve months preceding, in the City, or County, for which they may be elected. They shall have all the powers now vested in the Orphans' Courts of the State, subject to such changes as the Legislature may prescribe. Each of said Judges shall be paid a per diem for the time they are actually in session, to be regulated by Law, and to be paid by the said City, or Counties respectively. In case of a vacancy in the office of Judge of the Orphans' Court, the Governor shall appoint, subject to confirmation, or rejection by the Senate, some suitable person to fill the same for the residue of the term.

SEC. 41. There shall be a Register of Wills in each county of the State, and the city of Baltimore, to be elected by the legal and qualified voters of said counties and city, respectively, who shall hold his office for six years from the time of his election, and until his successor is elected and qualified; he shall be re-eligible, and subject at all times to removal for wilful neglect of duty, or misdemeanor in office in the same manner that the Clerks of the Courts are removable. In the event of any vacancy in the office of Register of Wills, said vacancy shall be filled by the Judges of the Orphans' Court, in which such vacancy occurs, until the next general election for Delegates to the General Assembly, when a Register shall be elected to serve for six years thereafter.

PART VI.—JUSTICES OF THE PEACE.

SEC. 42. The Governor, by and with the advice and consent of the Senate, shall appoint such number of Justices of the Peace, and the County Commissioners of the several counties, and the Mayor and City Council of Baltimore, respectively, shall appoint such number of Constables, for the several Election Districts of the Counties, and Wards of the City of Baltimore, as are now, or may hereafter be prescribed by Law; and Justices of the Peace and Constables, so appointed, shall be subject to removal by the Judge, or Judges, having criminal jurisdiction in the county, or city, for incompetency, wilful neglect of duty, or misdemeanor in office, on conviction in a Court of Law. The Justices of the Peace and Constables, so appointed, and commissioned, shall be Conservators of the Peace, shall hold their office for two years, and shall have such jurisdiction, duties and compensation, subject to such right of appeal, in all cases, from the judgment of Justices of the Peace, as hath been heretofore exercised, or shall be hereafter prescribed by Law.

SEC. 43. In the event of a vacancy in the office of a Justice of the Peace, the Governor shall appoint a person to serve, as Justice of the Peace, for the residue of the term; and in case of a vacancy in the office of Constable, the County Commissioners of the county in which the vacancy occurs, or the Mayor and City Council of Baltimore, as the case may be, shall appoint a person to serve as Constable for the residue of the term.

PART VII. — SHERIFFS.

SEC. 44. There shall be elected in each county, and in the City of Baltimore, in every second year, one person, resident in said county or city, above the age of twenty-five years, and at least five years preceding his election, a citizen of this State, to the office of Sheriff. He shall hold his office for two years, and until his successor is duly elected and qualified; shall be ineligible for two years thereafter, shall give such bond, exercise such powers, and perform such duties as now are, or may hereafter be fixed by Law. In case of a vacancy by death, resignation, refusal to serve, or neglect to qualify, or give bond, or by disqualification, or removal from the county, or city, the Governor shall appoint a person to be Sheriff for the remainder of the official term.

SEC. 45. Coroners, Elisors, and Notaries Public may be appointed for each county, and the city of Baltimore, in the manner, for the purpose, and with the powers now fixed, or which may hereafter be prescribed by Law.

ARTICLE V.

ATTORNEY GENERAL AND STATE'S ATTORNEYS.

ATTORNEY GENERAL.

SECTION 1. There shall be an Attorney General elected by the qualified voters of the State, on general ticket, on the Tuesday next after the first Monday in the month of

November, eighteen hundred and sixty-seven, and on the same day, in every fourth year thereafter, who shall hold his office for four years from the time of his election and qualification, and until his successor is elected and qualified, and shall be re-eligible thereto, and shall be subject to removal for incompetency, wilful neglect of duty, or misdemeanor in office, on conviction in a Court of Law.

SEC. 2. All elections for Attorney General shall be certified to, and returns made thereof by the Clerks of the Circuit Courts of the several counties, and the Clerk of the Superior Court of Baltimore City, to the Governor of the State, whose duty it shall be to decide on the election and qualification of the person returned; and in case of a tie between two or more persons, to designate which of said persons shall qualify as Attorney General, and to administer the oath of office to the person elected.

SEC. 3. It shall be the duty of the Attorney General to prosecute and defend on the part of the State, all cases, which at the time of his appointment and qualification, and which thereafter may be depending in the Court of Appeals, or in the Supreme Court of the United States, by or against the State, or wherein the State may be interested; and he shall give his opinion in writing whenever required by the General Assembly, or either Branch thereof, the Governor, the Comptroller, the Treasurer, or any State's Attorney, on any legal matter, or subject depending before them, or either of them; and when required by the Governor, or the General Assembly, he shall aid any State's Attorney in prosecuting any suit or action brought by the State in any Court of this State; and he shall commence and prosecute, or defend, any suit or action in any of said Courts, on the part of the State, which the General Assembly, or the Governor, acting according to Law, shall direct to be commenced, prosecuted or defended; and he shall receive for his services an annual salary of Three Thousand dollars; but he shall not be entitled to receive any fees, perquisites, or rewards, whatever, in addition to the salary aforesaid, for the performance of any official duty; nor have power to appoint any agent, representative, or deputy, under any circumstances, whatever; nor shall the Governor employ any additional counsel in any case, whatever, unless authorized by the General Assembly.

SEC. 4. No person shall be eligible to the office of Attorney General, who is not a citizen of this State, and a qualified voter therein, and has not resided and practised Law in this State for at least ten years.

SEC. 5. In case of vacancy in the office of Attorney General, occasioned by death, resignation, removal from the State, or from office, or other disqualification, the said vacancy shall be filled by the Governor, for the residue of the term thus made vacant.

SEC. 6. It shall be the duty of the Clerk of the Court of Appeals and of the Commissioner of the Land Office, respectively, whenever a case shall be brought into said Court, or office, in which the State is a party, or has interest, immediately to notify the Attorney General thereof.

THE STATE'S ATTORNEYS.

SEC. 7. There shall be an Attorney for the State in each county, and the city of Baltimore, to be styled "The State's Attorney," who shall be elected by the voters thereof, respectively, on the Tuesday next after the first Monday in November in the year eighteen hundred and sixty-seven, and on the same day every fourth year thereafter; and shall hold his office for four years from the first Monday in January next ensuing his election, and until his successor shall be elected and qualified; and shall be re-eligible thereto, and be subject to removal therefrom, for incompetency, wilful neglect of duty, or misdemeanor in office, on conviction in a Court of Law, or by a vote of two-thirds of the Senate, on the recommendation of the Attorney General.

SEC. 8. All elections for the State's Attorney shall be certified to, and Returns made thereof, by the Clerks of the said counties and city, to the Judges thereof, having criminal jurisdiction, respectively, whose duty it shall be to decide upon the elections and qualifications of the Persons returned; and, in case of a tie between two or more Persons, to designate which of said Persons shall qualify as State's Attorney, and to administer the oaths of office to the Person elected.

SEC. 9. The State's Attorney shall perform such duties and receive such fees and commissions as are now, or may hereafter be, prescribed by law, and if any State's Attorney shall receive any other fee or reward, than such as is, or may be allowed by Law, he shall, on conviction thereof, be removed from office; *provided*, that the State's Attorney for Baltimore City shall have power to appoint one Deputy, at a salary of not more than Fifteen Hundred dollars per annum, to be paid by the State's Attorney out of the fees of his office, as has heretofore been practiced.

SEC. 10. No person shall be eligible to the office of State's Attorney, who has not been admitted to practice Law in this State, and who has not resided, for at least two years, in the county, or city, in which he may be elected.

SEC. 11. In case of vacancy in the office of State's Attorney, or, of his removal from the county, or city, in which he shall have been elected, or, on his conviction, as herein specified, the said vacancy shall be filled by the Judge of the county, or city, respectively, having criminal jurisdiction, in which said vacancy shall occur, for the residue of the term thus made vacant.

SEC. 12. The State's Attorney, in each county, and the city of Baltimore, shall have authority to collect, and give receipt, in the name of the State, for such sums of money as may be collected by him, and forthwith make return of, and pay over the same, to the proper accounting officer. And the State's Attorney of each county, and the city of

Baltimore, before he shall enter on the discharge of his duties, shall execute a Bond to the State of Maryland, for the faithful performance of his duties, in the penalty of ten thousand dollars, with two or more sureties, to be approved by the Judge of the Court, having criminal jurisdiction, in said counties or city.

ARTICLE VI.

TREASURY DEPARTMENT.

SECTION 1. There shall be a Treasury Department, consisting of a Comptroller, chosen by the qualified electors of the State, at each regular election of members of the House of Delegates, who shall receive an annual salary of Two Thousand Five Hundred dollars; and a Treasurer to be appointed by the two Houses of the Legislature, at each regular session thereof, on joint ballot, who shall receive an annual salary of Two Thousand Five Hundred dollars; and the terms of office of the said Comptroller and Treasurer shall be for two years, and until their successors shall qualify; and neither of the said officers shall be allowed, or receive any fees, commissions or perquisites of any kind, in addition to his salary, for the performance of any duty or services whatsoever. In case of a vacancy in either of the offices, by death, or otherwise, the Governor, by and with the advice and consent of the Senate, shall fill such vacancy, by appointment to continue until another election, or a choice by the Legislature, as the case may be, and until the qualification of the successor. The Comptroller and the Treasurer shall keep their offices at the seat of Government, and shall take such oath, and enter into such bonds for the faithful discharge of their duties as are now, or may hereafter be, prescribed by Law.

SEC. 2. The Comptroller shall have the general superintendence of the fiscal affairs of the State; he shall digest and prepare plans for the improvement and management of the Revenue, and for the support of the Public Credit; prepare and report estimates of the Revenue and Expenditures of the State; superintend and enforce the prompt collection of all Taxes and Revenue; adjust and settle, on terms, prescribed by Law, with delinquent Collectors and Receivers of taxes and State revenue; preserve all Public Accounts; decide on the forms of keeping and stating Accounts; grant, under regulations, prescribed by Law, all warrants for money to be paid out of the Treasury, in pursuance of appropriations by Law; and countersign all checks drawn by the Treasurer upon any Bank or Banks, in which the moneys of the State may, from time to time, be deposited; prescribe the formalities of the transfer of stock, or other evidence of the State Debt, and countersign the same, without which, such Evidence shall not be valid; he shall make to the General Assembly full Reports of all his proceedings, and of the state of the Treasury Department, within ten days after the commencement of each Session; and perform such other duties as shall be prescribed by Law.

SEC. 3. The Treasurer shall receive the moneys of the State, and, until otherwise prescribed by Law, deposit them, as soon as received, to the credit of the State, in such Bank, or Banks, as he may, from time to time, with the approval of the Governor, select, (the said Bank or Banks giving security, satisfactory to the Governor, for the safe keeping and forthcoming, when required, of said Deposits,) and shall disburse the same for the purposes of the State, according to Law, upon warrants drawn by the Comptroller, and on checks, countersigned by him, and not otherwise; he shall take receipts for all moneys paid by him; and receipts for moneys received by him shall be endorsed upon warrants, signed by the Comptroller; without which warrants, so signed, no acknowledgment of money received into the Treasury shall be valid; and upon warrants, issued by the Comptroller, he shall make arrangements for the payment of the interest of the Public Debt, and for the purchase thereof on account of the Sinking Fund. Every Bond, Certificate, or other Evidence of the debt of the State, shall be signed by the Treasurer, and countersigned by the Comptroller; and no new Certificate, or other Evidence intended to replace another, shall be issued until the old one shall be delivered to the Treasurer, and authority executed in due form for the transfer of the same filed in his office, and the transfer accordingly made on the books thereof, and the certificate or other evidence cancelled; but the Legislature may make provisions for the loss of certificates, or other evidences of the debt; and may prescribe by Law, the manner in which the Treasurer shall receive and keep the moneys of the State.

SEC. 4. The Treasurer shall render his Accounts, quarterly, to the Comptroller; and shall publish, monthly, in such newspapers as the Governor may direct, an abstract thereof, showing the amount of cash on hand, and the place, or places of deposit thereof; and on the third day of each regular session of the Legislature, he shall submit to the Senate and House of Delegates fair and accurate copies of all Accounts by him, from time to time, rendered and settled with the Comptroller. He shall, at all times, submit to the Comptroller the inspection of the money in his hands, and perform all other duties that shall be prescribed by Law.

SEC. 5. The Comptroller shall qualify, and enter on the duties of his office, on the third Monday of January next succeeding the time of his election, or as soon thereafter as practicable. And the Treasurer shall qualify within one month after his appointment by the Legislature.

SEC. 6. Whenever during the recess of the Legislature charges shall be preferred to the Governor against the

Comptroller or Treasurer, for incompetency, malfeasance in office, wilful neglect of duty, or misappropriation of the funds of the State, it shall be the duty of the Governor forthwith to notify the party so charged, and fix a day for a hearing of said charges; and if, from the evidence taken, under oath, on said hearing before the Governor, the said allegations shall be sustained, it shall be the duty of the Governor to remove said offending officer, and appoint another in his place, who shall hold the office for the unexpired term of the officer so removed.

ARTICLE VII.

SUNDRY OFFICERS.

SECTION 1. County Commissioners shall be elected on general ticket of each County, by the qualified voters of the several Counties of this State, on the Tuesday next after the first Monday in the month of November, eighteen hundred and sixty-seven, and on the same day in every second year thereafter. Their number in each County, their compensation, powers and duties, shall be such as are now, or may be hereafter prescribed by Law.

SEC. 2. The qualified voters of each County, and of the City of Baltimore, shall, on the Tuesday next after the first Monday in the month of November, in the year eighteen hundred and sixty-seven, and on the same day in every second year thereafter, elect a Surveyor for each County and the City of Baltimore, respectively, whose term of office shall commence on the first Monday of January next ensuing their election; and whose duties and compensation shall be the same as are now, or may hereafter be prescribed by Law. And any vacancy in the office of Surveyor, shall be filled by the Commissioners of the Counties, or by the Mayor and City Council of Baltimore, respectively, for the residue of the term.

SEC. 3. The State Librarian shall be appointed by the Governor, by and with the advice and consent of the Senate, and shall hold his office during the term of the Governor, by whom he shall have been appointed, and until his successor shall be appointed and qualified. His salary shall be Fifteen Hundred dollars a year; and he shall perform such duties as are now, or may hereafter be prescribed by Law; and no appropriation shall be made by Law, to pay for any Clerk, or assistant to the Librarian: And it shall be the duty of the Legislature, at its first Session after the adoption of this Constitution, to pass a Law regulating the mode and manner in which the Books in the Library shall be kept and accounted for by the Librarian, and requiring the Librarian to give a Bond, in such penalty as the Legislature may prescribe, for the proper discharge of his duties.

SEC. 4. There shall be a Commissioner of the Land Office, who shall be appointed by the Governor, by and with the advice and consent of the Senate, who shall hold his office during the term of the Governor, by whom he shall have been appointed, and until his successor shall be appointed and qualified. He shall perform such duties as are now required of the Commissioner of the Land Office, or such as may hereafter be prescribed by Law, and shall also be the Keeper of the Chancery Records. He shall receive a salary of One Thousand Five Hundred dollars per annum, to be paid out of the Treasury, and shall charge such fees as are now, or may be hereafter fixed by Law. He shall make a semi-annual report of all the fees of his office, both as Commissioner of the Land Office, and as Keeper of the Chancery Records, to the Comptroller of the Treasury, and shall pay the same semi-annually into the Treasury.

SEC. 5. The Commissioner of the Land Office shall also, without additional compensation, collect, arrange, classify, have charge of, and safely keep all Papers, Records,

Relics, and other Memorials connected with the Early History of Maryland, not belonging to any other office.

SEC. 6. The qualified voters of Worcester County shall, on the Tuesday next after the first Monday in the month of November in the year Eighteen Hundred and Sixty-seven, and every two years thereafter, elect a Wreck Master for said County, whose duties and compensation shall be the same as are now, or may be hereafter, prescribed by Law; the term of office of said Wreck Master shall commence on the first Monday of January, next succeeding his election, and a vacancy in said office shall be filled by the County Commissioners of said County for the residue of the term.

ARTICLE VIII.

EDUCATION.

SECTION 1. The General Assembly, at its First Session after the adoption of this Constitution, shall by Law establish throughout the State a thorough and efficient system of Free Public Schools; and shall provide by taxation, or otherwise, for their maintenance.

SEC. 2. The System of Public Schools, as now constituted, shall remain in force until the end of the said First Session of the General Assembly, and shall then expire; except so far as adopted, or continued, by the General Assembly.

SEC. 3. The School Fund of the State shall be kept inviolate, and appropriated only to the purposes of Education.

ARTICLE IX.

MILITIA AND MILITARY AFFAIRS.

SECTION 1. The General Assembly shall make, from time to time, such provision for organizing, equipping and disciplining the Militia, as the exigency may require, and pass such Laws to promote Volunteer Militia Organizations as may afford them effectual encouragement.

SEC. 2. There shall be an Adjutant General, appointed by the Governor, by and with the advice and consent of the Senate. He shall hold his office until the appointment and qualification of his successor, or until removed in pursuance of the sentence of a Court Martial. He shall perform such duties, and receive such compensation, or emoluments, as are now, or may be prescribed by Law. He shall discharge the duties of his office at the seat of Government, unless absent, under orders, on duty; and no other officer of the General Staff of the Militia shall receive salary or pay, except when on service, and mustered in with troops.

SEC. 3. The existing Militia Law of the State shall expire at the end of the next Session of the General Assembly, except so far as it may be re-enacted, subject to the provisions of this Article.

ARTICLE X.

LABOR AND AGRICULTURE.

SECTION 1. There shall be a Superintendent of Labor and Agriculture, elected by the qualified voters of this State at the first general election for Delegates to the General Assembly after the adoption of this Constitution, who shall hold his office for the term of four years, and until the election and qualification of his successor.

SEC. 2. His qualifications shall be the same as those prescribed for the Comptroller; he shall qualify and enter upon the duties of his office on the second Monday of January next, succeeding the time of his election; and a vacancy in the office shall be filled by the Governor for the residue of the term.

SEC. 3. He shall perform such of the duties now devolved by Law upon the Commissioner of Immigration, and the Immigration Agent, as will promote the object, for which those officers were appointed, and such other duties as may be assigned to him by the General Assembly, and shall receive a salary of Twenty-five Hundred dollars a year; and after his election and qualification, the offices before mentioned shall cease.

SEC. 4. He shall supervise all the State Inspectors of agricultural products and fertilizers; and from time to time, shall carefully examine and audit their accounts, and prescribe regulations, not inconsistent with Law, tending to secure economy and efficiency in the business of their offices. He shall have the supervision of the Tobacco Warehouses, and all other buildings used for inspection and storage purposes by the State; and may, at the discretion of the Legislature, have the supervision of all public buildings, now belonging to, or which may hereafter be erected by the State. He shall frequently inspect such buildings as are committed to his charge, and examine all accounts for labor and materials required for their construction, or repairs.

SEC. 5. He shall inquire into the undeveloped resources of wealth of the State of Maryland more especially concerning those within the limits of the Chesapeake Bay and its tributaries, which belong to the State, and suggest such plans as may be calculated to render them available as sources of revenue.

SEC. 6. He shall make detailed reports to every General Assembly within the first week of its session, in reference to each of the subjects committed to his charge, and he shall also report to the Governor, in the recess of the Legislature, all abuses, or irregularities, which he may find to exist in any Department of public affairs, with which his office is connected.

SEC. 7. The office hereby established shall continue for

four years from the date of the qualification of the first incumbent thereof; and shall then expire, unless continued by the General Assembly.

ARTICLE XI.

CITY OF BALTIMORE.

SECTION 1. The Inhabitants of the City of Baltimore, qualified by Law to vote in said city for members of the House of Delegates, shall on the fourth Wednesday of October, eighteen hundred and sixty-seven, and on the same day in every fourth year thereafter, elect a person to be Mayor of the City of Baltimore, who shall have such qualifications, receive such compensation, discharge such duties, and have such powers as are now, or may hereafter be prescribed by Law; and the term of whose office shall commence on the first Monday of November succeeding his election, and shall continue for four years, and until his successor shall have qualified; and he shall be ineligible for the term next succeeding that for which he was elected.

SEC. 2. The City Council of Baltimore shall consist of Two Branches, one of which shall be called the First Branch, and the other the Second Branch; and each shall consist of such number of members, having such qualification, receiving such compensation, performing such duties, possessing such powers, holding such terms of office, and elected in such manner, as are now, or may hereafter be prescribed by Law.

SEC. 3. An election for members of the First and Second Branch of the City Council of Baltimore shall be held in the City of Baltimore on the fourth Wednesday of October, eighteen hundred and sixty-seven; and for members of the First Branch on the same day in every year thereafter; and for members of the Second Branch on the same day in every second year thereafter; and the qualification for electors of the members of the City Council shall be the same as those prescribed for the electors of Mayor.

SEC. 4. The regular sessions of the City Council of Baltimore, (which shall be annual,) shall commence on the third Monday of January of each year, and shall not continue more than ninety days, exclusive of Sundays; but the Mayor may convene the City Council in extra session whenever, and as often as it may appear to him that the public good may require; but no called, or extra session shall last longer than twenty days, exclusive of Sundays.

SEC. 5. No person, elected and qualified as Mayor, or as a member of the City Council, shall, during the term for which he was elected, hold any other office of profit or trust, created, or to be created, by the Mayor and City Council of Baltimore, or by any Law relating to the Corporation of Baltimore, or hold any employment, or position, the compensation of which shall be paid, directly or indirectly, out of the City Treasury; nor shall any such person be interested, directly or indirectly, in any contract, to which the City is a party; nor shall it be lawful for any person, holding any office, under the City, to be interested, while holding such office, in any contract, to which the City is a party.

SEC. 6. The Mayor shall, on conviction in a Court of Law, of wilful neglect of duty, or misbehavior in office, be removed from office by the Governor of the State, and a successor shall thereafter be elected, as in a case of vacancy.

SEC. 7. From and after the adoption of this Constitution, no debt (except as hereinafter excepted,) shall be created by the Mayor and City Council of Baltimore; nor shall the credit of the Mayor and City Council of Baltimore be given, or loaned to, or in aid of any individual, association, or corporation; nor shall the Mayor and City Council of Baltimore have the power to involve the City of Baltimore in the construction of Works of Internal Improvement, nor in granting any aid thereto, which shall involve the faith and credit of the City, nor make any appropriations therefor, unless such debt, or credit be authorized by an Act of the General Assembly of Maryland, and by an Ordinance of the Mayor and City Council of Baltimore, submitted to the legal voters of the City of Baltimore at such time and place as may be fixed by said Ordinance, and approved by a majority of the votes cast at such time and place; but the Mayor and City Council may, temporarily, borrow any amount of money to meet any deficiency in the City Treasury, or to provide for any emergency arising from the necessity of maintaining the Police, or preserving the safety and sanitary condition of the City, and may make due and proper arrangements and agreements for the removal and extension, in whole or in part, of any and all debts and obligations, created according to Law before the adoption of this Constitution.

SEC. 8. All Laws and Ordinances, now in force, applicable to the City of Baltimore, not inconsistent with this Article, shall be, and they are hereby continued until changed in due course of Law.

SEC. 9. The General Assembly may make such changes in this Article, except in Section seventh thereof, as it may deem best; and this Article shall not be so construed, or taken as to make the political Corporation of Baltimore independent, of, or free from the control, which the General Assembly of Maryland has over all such corporations in this State.

ARTICLE XII.

PUBLIC WORKS.

SECTION 1. The Governor, the Comptroller of the Treasury, and the Treasurer, shall constitute the Board of Public Works in this State. They shall keep a journal of their proceedings, and shall hold regular sessions in the City of Annapolis, on the first Wednesday in January, April, July, and October, in each year, and oftener, if necessary; at which sessions they shall hear and determine such matters as affect the Public Works of the State, and as the General Assembly may confer upon them the power to decide.

SEC. 2. They shall exercise a diligent and faithful supervision of all Public Works in which the State may be interested as Stockholder or Creditor, and shall represent, and vote the stock of the State of Maryland, in all meetings of the stockholders of the Chesapeake and Ohio Canal; and shall appoint the Directors in every Railroad and Canal Company, in which the State has the legal power to appoint Directors, which said Directors shall represent the State in all meetings of the Stockholders of the respective Companies, for which they are appointed or elected. And the President and Directors of the said Chesapeake and Ohio Canal Company shall so regulate the tolls of said Company, from time to time, as to produce the largest amount of revenue, and to avoid the injurious effects to said Company of rival competition by other Internal Improvement Companies. They shall require the Directors of all said Public Works to guard the public interest, and prevent the establishment of tolls which shall discriminate against the interest of the citizens or products of this State, and from time to time, and as often as there shall be any change in the rates of toll on any of the said Works, to furnish the said Board of Public Works a schedule of such modified rates of toll, and so adjust them as to promote the agricultural interests of the State; they shall report to the General Assembly at each regular session, and recommend such legislation as they may deem necessary and requisite to promote or protect the interests of the State in the said Public Works; they shall perform such other duties as may be hereafter prescribed by Law; and a majority of them shall be competent to act. The Governor, Comptroller and Treasurer shall receive no additional salary for services rendered by them as members of the Board of Public Works. The provisions of the Act of the General Assembly of Maryland of the year 1867, chapter 359, are hereby declared null and void.

SEC. 3. The Board of Public Works is hereby authorized to exchange the State's interest as Stockholder and Creditor in the Baltimore and Ohio Rail-road Company for an equal amount of the bonds or registered debt now owing by the State, to the extent only of all the preferred stock of the State on which the State is entitled to only six per cent. interest, provided such exchange shall not be made at less than par, nor less than the market value of said stock, and the said Board is authorized subject to such regulations and conditions as the General Assembly may from time to time prescribe, to sell the State's interest in the other Works of Internal Improvement, whether as a Stockholder or a Creditor, and also the State's interest in any banking corporation, receiving in payment the bonds and registered debt now owing by the State, equal in amonnt to the price obtained for the State's said interest; provided, that the interest of the State in the Washington Branch of the Baltimore and Ohio Rail Road be reserved and excepted from sale; and provided further, that no sale or contract of sale of the State's interest in the Chesapeake and Ohio Canal, the Chesapeake and Delaware Canal, and the Susquehanna and Tide-water Canal Companies shall go into effect until the same shall be ratified by the ensuing General Assembly.

ARTICLE XIII.

NEW COUNTIES.

SECTION 1. The General Assembly may provide, by Law, for organizing new Counties, locating and removing county seats, and changing county lines; but no new county shall be organized without the consent of the majority of the legal voters residing within the limits proposed to be formed into said new county; and whenever a new county shall be proposed to be formed out of portions of two or more Counties, the consent of a majority of the legal voters of such part of each of said counties, respectively, shall be required; nor shall the lines of any county be changed without the consent of a majority of the legal voters, residing within the district, which, under said proposed change, would form a part of a county different from that to which it belonged prior to said change; and no new county shall contain less than four hundred square miles, nor less than ten thousand white Inhabitants; nor shall any change be made in the limits of any county, whereby the population of said county would be reduced to less than ten thousand white Inhabitants, or its territory reduced to less than four hundred square miles.

SEC. 2. At the election to be held for the adoption, or rejection of this Constitution, in each election district, in those parts of Worcester and Somerset Counties, comprised within the following limits, viz.: Beginning at the point, where Mason and Dixon's line crosses the channel of Pocomoke River, thence following said line to the channel of the Nanticoke River, thence with the channel of said River to Tangier Sound, or the intersection of Nanticoke and Wicomico Rivers, thence up the channel of the Wicomico River to the mouth of Wicomico Creek, thence with the Channel of said creek and Passerdyke Creek to Dashield's, or Disharoon's Mills, thence with the millpond of said mills and Branch following the middle prong of said Branch, to Meadow Bridge, on the road, dividing the Counties of Somerset and Worcester, near the southwest corner of the farm of William P. Morris, thence due east to the Pocomoke River, thence with the channel of said river to the beginning, the Judges of election, in each of said Districts, shall receive the ballots of each elector, voting at said election, who has resided for six months, preceding said election within said limits, for or against a new County; and the Return Judges of said Election Districts shall certify the result of such voting, in the manner, now prescribed by Law, to the Governor, who shall by Proclamation make known the same; and if a majority of the legal votes, cast within that part of Worcester County, contained within said lines, and also a majority of the legal votes cast within that part of Somerset County, contained within said lines, shall be in favor of a new County, then said parts of Worcester and Somerset Counties shall become and constitute a new County, to be called Wicomico County; and Salisbury shall be the County Seat. And the Inhabitants thereof shall thenceforth have and enjoy all such rights and privileges as are held and enjoyed by the Inhabitants of the other Counties of this State.

SEC. 3. When said new County shall have been so created, the Inhabitants thereof shall cease to have any claim to, or interest in the county buildings, and other public property of every description, belonging to said Counties of Somerset and Worcester, respectively, and shall be liable for their proportionate shares of the then existing debts and obligations of the said Counties, according to the last assessment in said Counties, to be ascertained and apportioned by the Circuit Court of Somerset County, as to the debts and obligations of said County, and by the Circuit Court of Worcester County, as to the debts and obligations of Worcester County, on the petition of the County Commissioners of the said Counties, respectively; and the property in each part of the said Counties, included in said new County, shall be bound only for the share of the debts and obligations of the county from which it shall be separated; and the Inhabitants of said new County shall also pay the County taxes, levied upon them at the time of the creation of such new County, as if such new County had not been created; and on the application of twelve citizens of the proposed county of Wicomico, the Surveyor of Worcester County shall run and locate the line from Meadow Bridge to the Pocomoke River, previous to the adoption, or rejection of this Constitution, and at the expense of said petitioners.

SEC. 4. At the first general election, held under this Constitution, the qualified voters of said new County shall be entitled to elect a Senator, and two Delegates to the General Assembly, and all such County, or other officers as this Constitution may authorize, or require to be elected by other Counties of the State; a notice of such election shall be given by the Sheriffs of Worcester and Somerset Counties in the manner now prescribed by Law; and in case said new County shall be established, as aforesaid, then the Counties of Somerset and Worcester shall be entitled to elect but two Delegates each to the General Assembly.

SEC. 5. The County of Wicomico, if formed according to the provisions of this Constitution, shall be embraced in the First Judicial Circuit; and the times for holding the Courts therein shall be fixed and determined by the General Assembly.

SEC. 6. The General Assembly shall pass all such Laws as may be necessary more fully to carry into effect the provisions of this Article.

ARTICLE XIV.

AMENDMENTS TO THE CONSTITUTION.

SECTION 1. The General Assembly may propose Amendments to this Constitution; provided, that each Amendment shall be embraced in a separate Bill, embodying the Article or Section, as the same will stand when amended and passed by three-fifths of all the members elected to each of the two Houses, by yeas and nays, to be entered on the Journals with the proposed Amendment. The Bill, or Bills, proposing amendment, or amendments, shall be published by order of the Governor, in at least two newspapers in each county, where so many may be published, and where not more than one may be published, then in that newspaper, and in three newspapers published in the City of Baltimore, one of which shall be in the German language, once a week, for at least three months preceding the next ensuing general election, at which the said proposed amendment, or amendments shall be submitted, in a form to be prescribed by the General Assembly, to the qualified voters of the State for adoption or rejection. The votes cast for and against said proposed amendment, or amendments, severally, shall be returned to the Governor, in the manner prescribed in other cases, and if it shall appear to the Governor that a majority of the votes cast at said election on said amendment, or amendments, severally, were cast in favor thereof, the Governor shall, by his Proclamation, declare the said amendment, or amendments, having received said majority of votes, to have been adopted by the people of Maryland as part of the Constitution thereof, and thenceforth said amendment, or amendments shall be part of the said Constitution. When two or more amendments shall be submitted, in manner aforesaid, to the voters of this State at the same election, they shall be so submitted as that each amendment shall be voted on separately.

SEC. 2. It shall be the duty of the General Assembly to provide by Law for taking, at the general election to be held in the year eighteen hundred and eighty-seven, and every twenty years thereafter, the sense of the People in regard to calling a Convention for altering this Constitution; and if a majority of voters at such election or elections shall vote for a Convention, the General Assembly, at its next session, shall provide by Law for the assembling of such Convention, and for the election of Delegates thereto. Each County, and Legislative District of the City of Baltimore, shall have in such Convention a number of

Delegates equal to its representation in both Houses at the time at which the Convention is called. But any Constitution, or change, or amendment of the existing Constitution, which may be adopted by such Convention, shall be submitted to the voters of this State, and shall have no effect unless the same shall have been adopted by a majority of the voters voting thereon.

ARTICLE XV.

MISCELLANEOUS.

SECTION 1. Every person holding any office created by, or existing under the Constitution, or Laws of the State, (except Justices of the Peace, Constables and Coroners,) or holding any appointment under any Court of this State, whose pay, or compensation is derived from fees, or moneys coming into his hands for the discharge of his official duties, or, in any way, growing out of, or connected with his office, shall keep a book in which shall be entered every sum, or sums of money, received by him, or on his account, as a payment or compensation for his performance of official duties, a copy of which entries in said book, verified by the oath of the officer, by whom it is directed to be kept, shall be returned yearly to the Comptroller of the State for his inspection, and that of the General Assembly of the State, to which the Comptroller shall, at each regular session thereof, make a report showing what officers have complied with this Section; and each of the said officers, when the amount received by him for the year shall exceed the sum which he is by Law entitled to retain, as his salary, or compensation for the discharge of his duties, and for the expenses of his office, shall yearly pay over to the Treasurer of the State the amount of such excess, subject to such disposition thereof as the General Assembly may direct; if any of such officers shall fail to comply with the requisitions of this Section for the period of thirty days after the expiration of each and every year of his office, such officer shall be deemed to have vacated his office, and the Governor shall declare the same vacant, and the vacancy therein shall be filled as in case of vacancy for any other cause, and such officer shall be subject to suit by the State for the amount that ought to be paid into the treasury; and no person holding any office created by, or existing under this Constitution, or Laws of the State, or holding any appointment, under any Court in this State, shall receive more than three thousand dollars a year as a compensation for the discharge of his official duties, except in cases specially provided in this Constitution.

SEC. 2. The several Courts existing in this State at the time of the adoption of this Constitution, shall, until superseded under its provisions, continue with like powers and jurisdiction, and in the exercise thereof, both at Law and in Equity, in all respects, as if this Constitution had not been adopted; and when said Courts shall be so superseded, all causes, then depending in said Courts, shall pass into the jurisdiction of the several Courts, by which they may, [*be*] respectively, superseded.

SEC. 3. The Governor, and all officers, civil and military, now holding office under this State, whether by election or appointment, shall continue to hold, exercise and discharge the duties of their offices (unless inconsistent with, or otherwise provided in this Constitution) until they shall be superseded, under its provisions, and until their successors shall be duly qualified.

SEC. 4. If at any election directed by this Constitution, any two or more candidates shall have the highest and an equal number of votes, a new election shall be ordered by the Governor, except in cases specially provided for by this Constitution.

SEC. 5. In the trial of all criminal cases, the Jury shall be the Judges of Law, as well as of fact.

SEC. 6. The right of trial by Jury of all issues of fact in civil proceedings in the several Courts of Law in this State, where the amount in controversy exceeds the sum of five dollars, shall be inviolably preserved.

SEC. 7. All general elections in this State shall be held on the Tuesday next after the first Monday in the month of November, in the year in which they shall occur; and the first election of all officers, who, under this Constitution, are required to be elected by the People, shall, except in cases herein specially provided for, be held on the Tuesday next after the first Monday of November, in the year eighteen hundred and sixty-seven.

SEC. 8. The Sheriffs of the several Counties of this State, and of the City of Baltimore, shall give notice of the several elections authorized by this Constitution, in the manner prescribed by existing Laws for elections to be held in this State, until said Laws shall be changed.

SEC. 9. The term of office of all Judges and other officers, for whose election provision is made by this Constitution, shall except in cases otherwise expressly provided herein, commence from the time of their election; and all such officers shall qualify as soon after their election as practicable, and shall enter upon the duties of their respective offices immediately upon their qualification; and the Term of office of the State Librarian and of the Commissioner of the Land Office shall commence from the time of their appointment.

SEC. 10. Any officer elected or appointed in pursuance of the provisions of this Constitution, may qualify, either according to the existing provisions of Law, in relation to officers under the present Constitution, or before the Governor of the State, or before any Clerk of any Court of Record in any part of the State; but in case an officer shall qualify out of the County in which he resides, an official copy of his oath shall be filed and recorded in the Clerk's office of the Circuit Court of the County in which he may reside, or in the Clerk's office of the Superior Court of the City of Baltimore, if he shall reside therein.

END OF THE CONSTITUTION.

CPSIA information can be obtained
at www.ICGtesting.com
Printed in the USA
LVHW030733230323
742065LV00026B/151

9 783382 128890